THE DEPARTMENT OF EXTRAORDINARY EMIGRATION AND DELIVERY

DEED

Jim Doran

ISBN-13 eBook: 978-0-9601017-9-5
ISBN-13 Paperback: 978-0-9601017-8-8

Cover design by: Maria Spada
Printed in the United States of America

For T. M. Doran, whose novels continue to inspire

"Eyes hast thou, but thy deeds thou canst not see."

"OEDIPUS REX" - SOPHOCLES

CONTENTS

NOTHING IN
THE ATTIC

February - Amherst, Nova Scotia, Canada

***N**obody knows what I am, and I must keep it that way.*
Rebecca Eidelweiss whistled Irving Berlin's century-old tune "Always" while she waited at the front entrance to a suburban home. Adjusting her shoulder bag over a business jacket, she looked the part she was playing. She had fooled the customs agent she'd met earlier this morning flying into Halifax. The agent had welcomed her back to Canada, remarking on the multiple pages of stamps in her passport. Rebecca was a world traveler, but only because she had to traverse the globe for her job. She never traveled for pleasure.

The cold air bit at Rebecca's exposed ears, and she squinted in the brilliant sunshine. The light reflected off the four-paned windows on the pastel-green door. The shade of green reminded her of the color of the bus she had taken from the airport to the car lot. The driver had tipped his hat and wished her a successful business trip. A business trip was a decent assumption, considering Rebecca had changed into a black blazer, all-cotton dress shirt, and tailored suit pants at the airport.

After exiting the bus, Rebecca had proceeded to her customized VW Passat in the parking lot. She worked hard for a living, though not for any typical company. Some people—such as a woman in Switzerland who had nearly killed her on the roof of a ski resort—would swear she was in a shady business. The shady business of kidnapping, that was. The woman believed Rebecca was a bounty hunter. But no, not a kidnapper, nor a bounty hunter.

For Chiron's sake, the temperature was frigid out here, and nobody had answered the door. Rebecca knocked again, the equipment in her bag rattling. She had filled the bag from a locker en route to the house. Yes, if people knew she carried a bola, a Glock, a taser, earpieces, a syringe, and a ragged pocketknife, they might guess she was a hired assassin. And they'd still be wrong. They didn't account for the skirt folded at the bottom. She always carried a skirt in case the transformation ruined her pants.

A man's head appeared in the four-square windows. With his two-day-old stubble and sagging jowls, the homeowner examined her through the panes of glass. To this man, Rebecca Eidelweiss wasn't anyone of consequence. He unlocked and cracked open the door.

"You from Child Protective Services?"

"I am Rebecca Eidelweiss." She used the accent she had been practicing all morning—the eastern coast of North America. "Protective Services."

She had said "protective" as "proe-tec-tive" instead of "prah-tec-tive," emphasizing the long "o." Ah, the ambrosial taste of nailing an accent.

The stubbled homeowner swung open the door. His guess at her occupation was, in many ways, the most accurate. Rebecca was a government worker, and she protected children. But she was careful not to say she was from Canada's Child Protective Services.

The man stepped aside, and Rebecca advanced into his house. The heat was welcome if a bit cloying as the frigid February air had chilled her this morning. Her nose wrinkled at the scent of cigarettes mixed with what smelled like yesterday's fish dinner. The furniture—a couch, rocking chair, recliner, and television on the ground leaning against a wall—was shabby but not dirty. Yet, she spied dust on a painting above a fireplace.

While the man shut the door behind her, she remained in place in the living room, eyeing a narrow staircase leading to the second floor.

To the naked eye, this residence was a typical house in Amherst. The small, two-bedroom dwelling might have been homey in the past, but no longer.

A death in the family.

Rebecca noted the layout of the house. Front entrance with a staircase up to two bedrooms at the entry, and on the first floor, a hallway leading to the kitchen and dining room in the back—with a door to the yard. Rebecca had studied the floor plans of the residence on her flight to Canada in case she encountered trouble. Now, she surveyed the actual house while running potential escape routes through her head.

The man rubbed a grizzled chin, mouth turned downward. Rebecca suppressed a scowl of her own. "My visit is most peculiar, Mr. Kralston. This is Nova Scotia, not some urban city filled with crime. The force majeure of your wife's death doesn't break the contract of fatherhood. In short, we don't give away our children here."

Kralston's voice was grating. "I don't wan' money. And I don't wan' *her*."

His response held a ghastly sentiment, but his attitude would make everything easier. Rebecca had taken children from parents who permitted it. She wasn't a kidnapper, but in circumstances where the children had wanted to stay, removing them felt like abduction. In this case, Kralston had called Canadian Child Protective Services. A mole from Rebecca's country, Elysium, had rerouted the phone call to her department, and one of her own had talked to Kralston on the phone and arranged this meeting.

Rebecca utilized her commanding, college-professor tone with this man. "I could do with a cup of tea before I see her. Would you indulge me and put one on?"

Her forwardness had taken him off guard. Kralston smacked his lips. "No tea. I'll bring you to her."

Sludge. Kralston didn't take the bait to serve some tea. Rebecca's assignment was going to be a little more complicated now, though not *overly* demanding. She was Rebecca Eidelweiss, after all. Kralston wouldn't be the problem, but the girl? The girl might be.

As they turned toward the stairs, Rebecca spied the red light of a baby monitor tucked under the couch. The pinpoint glow shone through the shadows with the intensity of a Cyclops' bloodshot eye. Young ears were listening.

Kralston ascended the steps of the wooden staircase. "I don't abuse her ifn that's wha' yer worried about. Taken care of Nothing since my wife died a month ago."

He did what? Was this a New England colloquialism? "You've taken care of nothing? The child has taken care of the arrangements?"

Kralston snorted. "Nah. The child's name is Nothing."

Rebecca halted. The cruelty of naming a child *Nothing* struck her speechless, a rarity. Chin set, she continued her trek up the stairs.

Kralston ran his hand along the wall as he moved upward. "The wife, she didn't like it. But I put my foot down when we found it on the doorstep. 'Ifn we bring that *thing* into this house, its name will be Nothing,' I had said."

Rebecca glared at the man's back. Slag-heads like Kralston thought all abuse was physical. They didn't realize the other type of damage they did. "I absolutely refuse to call her Nothing."

"Done care what yer call 'er."

Rebecca took another step. "I'll name her after my Aunt Aurora."

Rebecca never had an Aunt Aurora. She had been thinking earlier that she might catch the aurora borealis later tonight. She had always favored the word "aurora." The charming word belonged in ancient spells—too bad magic wasn't real.

Kralston grunted. "Named aftern the lights."

"The aurora borealis is a magical experience."

Kralston stopped at the landing. "Lot you know. Just weather." He sneered. "Not magic."

Rebecca joined him on the landing. She wasn't about to let this breviloquent lowlife lecture her. "The magic is in how it affects people, Mr. Kralston. The northern lights connect with us in a way science can't explain."

Kralston grimaced.

Rebecca pressed on. "Why do we love unusual phenomena? Because it's different and spectacular. We should also love people with unusual differences."

The homeowner shook off her lecture with an eye roll. Rebecca had experienced such reactions before with mansplainers who dismissed women's ideas. If he was on her bad side up to this point, he now put himself in her revenge column. She would enjoy the task ahead but play nice for the child's sake.

Kralston reached up to a ring on the ceiling. "Nothing lives in the attic."

Rebecca examined the two bedrooms on the second floor. One bedroom was open and stocked with fishing gear and trophies. The brute had stored his hobbies there rather than house the other occupant in a room on this floor. "The attic? I warn you, Mr. Kralston, the child had better be in sound condition."

"Or wha'?" the man rejoined.

Kralston pulled down a hatch door with built-in stairs. He placed his foot on the first step without offering to allow Rebecca to go first or even think to help her. She wasn't helpless—ha— but she also didn't care for his lack of manners. The homeowner wanted to rid himself of his wife's child. The quicker, the better.

Rebecca ascended to the attic and stepped into the small room. This level of the house was colder and darker, and her hair scraped the ceiling. Thankfully, the cigarette stench wasn't present here. Dust covered discarded boxes in half of the room like filthy snow. The other half was tidier, with an oblong carpet under a few pieces of furniture.

Rebecca hung back behind Kralston, eyes focusing on the third person in the room. A mattress lay in front of a window at the end of the attic. Next to it was a table without chairs. The table's legs were cut in half. A meter from the table, an unvarnished rocking chair held a small girl with an afghan over her lower body.

Rebecca had read the child's profile multiple times. She was eight years old with long, tangled, umber-colored hair. Her pale complexion offset her honey-brown pupils. She had a round chin and a drawn face. Her lips puckered inward while her small frame crouched down on itself.

Despite the lack of any normal grooming, the girl was beautiful. Rebecca wanted to pick her up and run, but she had to confirm what the blanket covered before she made her move.

Kralston nodded her way as if indicating discarded furniture. "Thar's she. Nothing, quit yer sooking."

Rebecca removed her shoulder bag while unzipping it. "You mentioned her legs were deformed? I'd like her to remove the blanket."

Kralston pinched his face as if reacting to a rotten cabbage a skunk had sprayed. "She can show you 'er disgusting legs in your car."

Rebecca stepped out of Kralston's sightline. She reached into her bag. "Not good enough, Mr. Kralston. I must verify no signs of abuse before I leave this house."

Grunting, Kralston waved at the attic dweller to indicate she should remove the blanket. The girl colored in shame as she lifted one side of the afghan. Attached to her hips was a spindly, crooked, hairy limb ending in a hoof, similar to a goat's front leg.

And verified! Rebecca examined the girl's head again, confirming the shape was round. What would Kralston have done when her skull started to change shape?

Quietly stepping backward again, Rebecca put on a warm smile while removing an object from her bag, a rod with cords and spheres on the end. "Your leg is lovely, young lady. I'm so sorry you must see this."

The girl blinked at her. Naturally, the child didn't understand what Rebecca meant, but she would in a few seconds. The taser would be quicker, but Kralston's gyrations would be horrible to witness. Binding him with the cords of her bola was more humane.

Rebecca rotated the bola in her hand—swish, swish, swish. Kralston turned and gaped at what he was witnessing. His hesitation gave her the time she needed. She aimed the weapon, released it, and their tight ropes wrapped around his arms and upper legs. Bound and unsteady, Kralston toppled over and crashed to the ground.

"Wha-!" A string of thersitical words poured from his lips like water from a fire hose.

Rebecca reached into her container and grabbed a tiny syringe. She removed the plastic tip from the sharp end and positioned it over Kralston's neck. His eyes widened. "Wha yer going to do with—?"

Kralston screamed, banging his head against the floor. The girl jumped to her hooves, revealing both goat legs. She clip-clopped to the window, her posterior against the glass. Her reaction wasn't a bright move, but a lucky one for Rebecca. She didn't want to chase and restrain the child.

Rebecca patted Kralston's cheek, the last one more of a slap. "Everything's ducky, Mr. Kralston."

Apoplectic, Kralston struggled against the fetters. "What'd you do to mah...?"

His words were starting to slur. Rebecca capped the needle and placed it in her bag. "The drug is fast-acting but temporary. I'm not going to hurt you. But before you sleep, I'll leave you with this warning. It would be best if you forget me and Aurora. As they say around here, I come *from away*, and that's where I'll take her. You'll never see either of us again."

The child whimpered from the corner of the room, and her eyes turned to the hatch. With a few strides, she could drop through the opening. Rebecca couldn't let her escape.

Rebecca moved closer to the hatch, cutting off the foundling's exit. "Easy, child. I've come to help you."

The girl discovered her voice. High, sweet, innocent, pure. "What are you going to do to me?"

"You do *not* have deformed legs." Rebecca gestured to the youth's lower limbs. "They're perfectly natural. Your birth mother and father had them, too."

Kralston's voice croaked, but the sound was weak. "Call... cops..."

Rebecca folded her arms. "Wait. He's almost asleep. He can't hear what I tell you."

The eight-year-old reached into her overalls and moved her hand around inside. "I'm calling for help."

As if this brutish giant would give his captive a phone! "May I call you Aurora? I know you were listening in to our conversation downstairs."

The girl's breath hitched. "They're on their way. You'd better leave."

"You didn't say I couldn't call you Aurora." Rebecca untangled her bola from Kralston and retrieved her shoulder bag. "So, I shall. Aurora, your poor excuse for a guardian is asleep now. He called Child Protective Services because of you. And though Canada has excellent services, we can't let them take you into their care. We know who you are, but more importantly, *what* you are. And we want to help you be *all* that you are."

Rebecca had her attention, but Aurora still sidestepped away. Clip clop. "Who is 'we'?"

"None of this is going to make sense at first. I'm from the Department of Extraordinary Emigration and Delivery, or DEED. An emigrant is a person who travels to a new country. We rescue people like you from horrible situations and provide them with loving homes."

Not convinced yet, the girl pushed herself back to the wall. "What do you mean like me?"

If only Kralston had offered tea, she would have slipped the drug into his cup, and he would have been asleep in seconds.

Aurora wouldn't be alarmed. Rebecca had to reveal the truth. Now!

"You're a faun, Aurora."

"I'm an animal. Like a deer?" The child shivered.

"Like the legend," corrected Rebecca. "And a person. You're a girl, but you're not human. We call ourselves mythicals."

Aurora's shoulders lowered. "Mythicals." She breathed the word.

"Fauns have lived alongside humans for centuries." Rebecca took a step forward. "Humans wrote about fauns and many other mythicals early in the ancient world, but we had to hide from non-mythicals. Now humans think that we aren't real. My department helps mythicals such as you move to a place where everyone will accept you for who you are. And what you are is a perfectly normal, lovely young faun."

Aurora opened her mouth and then closed it.

"A lot of words, sorry." Rebecca hung her head. "But I have to say it all. I know you heard the five most important words. Department, Extraordinary, Emigration, Delivery. DEED."

A step forward. Clip. Then backward again. Yet, Aurora's defenses were down. "Are you a faun, too?"

The moment had come. Rebecca would have to reveal her true nature before Kralston came around. Her eyes twinkled.

"Prepare yourself, Aurora."

Rebecca kicked off her shoes as her pants split apart along Velcro seams, turning into a skirt. Her legs grew thinner, covered in hair, and ending in hooves. At the same time, her body expanded backward, and two more horse limbs emerged and grew. Coarse hair also covered her back legs and hindquarters. When she finished stretching, she was half-woman and half-horse, but still in a black blazer.

"You're a...a..."

"Centaur, Aurora." Rebecca pointed at her. "A mythical like you, but of a different species. I couldn't change in front of your guardian. He mustn't know about us."

Aurora blinked, taking in Rebecca's new form. First-timers

scrutinizing her body never bothered Rebecca, but she was on the clock. "I want to take you to live with other fauns and centaurs. And many other species."

Aurora tilted her head. "But where are you from?"

Rebecca's hooves crossed the distance between them, and she offered her hand. "Someplace hidden and far away, Aurora. But *where* it is doesn't matter. All that matters is *what* it is."

Aurora reached and clasped Rebecca's hand. "What is it?"

"Home," answered Rebecca in her most comforting voice. "And I am your DEED."

PURSUIT

February - St. John, New Brunswick, Canada

Shepherding a willing refugee was the easiest part of Rebecca's job. She had spent too much time tracking mythicals who had run away, not wanting to return. She was content for once to rescue someone and inform them they had a place in this world.

Rebecca had warned Aurora that the drive would be more than four hours long. Still, Aurora had climbed into a stranger's car without hesitation—a potential sign of a desperate child. Showing the youth her proper form had earned her trust—Rebecca supposed—but she drove for two hours without a peep from Aurora in the back seat. The agent had traveled the world, but not this part of Canada. The roads and terrain were new, and she had to make it to the United States border before a set time. Rebecca had to concentrate and had asked Aurora to hold her inquiries. Seemingly overwhelmed, the child had complied.

Up to a point.

In her rearview mirror, Rebecca spied a crease in Aurora's forehead. The faun bit her lip. "Am I still a girl or am I a creature now?"

"You are a girl and also a faun, but you aren't human." Rebecca cleared her throat. "In ancient times, the words 'boy,' 'girl,' 'woman,' 'man,' and 'person' encompassed both humans and mythicals. After we hid, humans limited those words to mean only themselves."

Aurora replaced the crease in her forehead with lifted eyebrows.

"We mythicals are creatures, as are humans, but we don't prefer the word creature." Rebecca wrinkled her nose. "That sounds as though we're monsters, and we're not."

Now that Rebecca had answered her, Aurora started asking other questions. "Why didn't you come for me sooner?"

Rebecca blinked at the query. She had expected a question about the mythicals or their world. Or perhaps a practical question concerning rest stops and the need to use the facilities. Instead, the faun had broached a delicate topic that had arisen in the DEED home office.

Rebecca cleared her throat. "Some mythicals still live among humans but keep safeguards from being discovered. Your mother and father were from a colony of fauns in northern Canada. Your mother married someone your grandparents disapproved of. The leaders of the colony drove out your parents."

Hope rose in the faun's eyes. Rebecca hated this part. "They're both dead, Aurora. They caught a disease and didn't recover. Before perishing, your mother found a woman she trusted with her newborn baby."

"She left me on Mum's doorstep." Aurora lowered her head.

In the rearview mirror, Rebecca spied a gray Toyota Camry passing a large truck on the right. "DEED debated taking you as a newborn but decided to allow you to live with the Kralstons. Your human mother raised you with love. When she passed, we knew we had to step in."

As she approached the city of St. John in New Brunswick, Rebecca tapped the Passat's accelerator. Aurora pressed her hands on the window and her face against the glass of the back seat window. "A city!"

How easily distracted.

Aurora stared out the window. "But then you came."

Or maybe not.

The gray sedan had tinted windows. It had maintained the same speed for the last half hour, staying three car lengths behind. "Fortunately, your father made coming for you easier when he called Protective Services," finished Rebecca.

Aurora tapped the window glass. "Is that a real city?"

"St. John." *Many sedans have tinted windows, Rebecca. Stop being paranoid.* "New Brunswick."

"I've only seen cities on Mum's tablet."

Rebecca maintained the legal speed limit through the city, though she would have preferred to increase the speed of the DEED-supplied vehicle.

St. John resembled a European city with its angled rooftops and brick-to-steel ratio. Most European settlers brought their architectural styles to Canada, especially in this area.

After passing the sign for the exit to the Reversing Falls, Rebecca pulled off the expressway. The gray sedan behind them had also exited, and had stopped at the light, a Ford truck between them.

It's time to be paranoid!

As an enforcer agent, Rebecca had learned to watch traffic in her rearview mirror. When a break in the cross traffic occurred, she gunned the engine and raced through the intersection despite the red light. The pursuers would be back on the road, speeding after her in moments. Her little trick had now tipped them off.

The constant danger of Rebecca's life was one reason she often passed on child extraction cases. She preferred assignments with more grit to them. When Rebecca had expressed her boredom to her handler while waiting for her next task, the woman on the other end pulled the Amherst file.

Faux grin in place, Rebecca called over her shoulder. "You're buckled in, right?"

The spindly child nodded.

"Hold on."

Rebecca floored the accelerator and swerved around other

vehicles on the expressway as if she were a small rodent avoiding a flock of predatory birds. Hoping the police weren't in the area, she drove up the incline over the St. John River. The gray Camry, four car lengths behind her, went faster still. It weaved through the traffic between them.

Baelz Bells!

DEED had enemies around the world. To stay hidden, they had to discredit any human witnesses. Some had tried to retaliate. And a handful of the vengeful, with money and power at their disposal, hired experts.

Rebecca had to assume the driver was out to eliminate her, and Aurora would be collateral damage. She had given them a bridge to ram her Passat over the side. Would they try a maneuver so sensational? The incident would draw as much attention to her enemy as it would to DEED.

Rebecca gritted her teeth and pressed on her horn. The Canadian custom of politeness applied to its people and the road as the vehicles in front of her pulled over. She had an open path through traffic.

Two car lengths behind, the gray sedan kept pace with Rebecca as she crested the bridge. If the sedan's driver was going to make a drastic maneuver, he would try so now. DEED's primary rule was not to attract attention, but if she had to, she would pull out her Glock and aim for the tires.

Then, an SUV far ahead of Rebecca pulled out of her lane, and she had a straight shot down the bridge. She reached for the dashboard and pressed an inch square panel almost invisible to the eye. The panel slid aside to reveal a steel-blue button. Rebecca pressed it with her middle finger.

The automobile responded with a boost of fire out of a hidden exhaust. The acceleration thrust the agent and child against their seats. Aurora gasped while Rebecca prayed nobody would pull into her lane. She couldn't stop her car. The needle on her speed gauge flirted with one hundred eighty kilometers per hour. The gray sedan accelerated, but a pickup truck had pulled in between them—the break Rebecca needed.

Rebecca's four-door coupe slowed down off Route One into the St. John West area, and she surveyed the neighborhood. A small road between two red brick buildings would suffice. Her GPS indicated a parking lot behind the buildings. She gunned it toward the narrow street.

Rebecca pulled into the quarter-full, paved lot. Her coupe stood out among the other cars parked here. To shake her tail, Rebecca counted on it.

Parking, Rebecca figured she had about a minute until the sedan arrived. Before shutting off the coupe, she danced her fingers over the car's console. Four keystrokes later, the Passat jolted, and ten equidistant panels, about the size of a golf hole, slid aside around the car.

Aurora released a shaky breath. "What's going on?"

"Please, listen. Unbuckle, and duck down to the floor. Don't let them see you."

The faun didn't comply, gaping at the activity outside their automobile. Miniature hoses with nozzles snaked from the holes, and encircled their coupe, spraying colors all over the exterior. They covered the original powder blue paint with a golden yellow. A whirring in the front of the vehicle indicated that a different brand of headlight replaced the ones there before. The antenna was retracting at the same time. Yes, her coupe remained the same make and model, but the agent hoped the change in color and other minor modifications would leave their pursuers to imagine this was a different car.

"Down, Aurora!"

The girl ducked, and Rebecca grabbed her shoulder bag of weapons, unlatching it. She'd feel better with bolas in her hand, but a dart gun would be best. Rebecca had groused when assembling it the night before. But now, grateful to a past version of herself, she gripped the weapon's handle.

A NEW LIFE

February - St. John, New Brunswick, Canada

Another car motored down the street between the buildings. Rebecca eyed the console. A miniature camera gave her a view of the street leading to the parking lot. The Toyota Camry rolled past her coupe, never slowing. She pressed buttons on the console, manipulating the camera to follow the sedan as it turned down another road.

When she finished counting to three, Rebecca sprang up. "Buckle in, Aurora."

The agent didn't wait for the child to secure herself. She started the coupe and drove out of the parking lot. Hitting the speed limit on this street, she mapped out an indirect way back to Route One.

The child had questions about the narrow escape, and Rebecca felt compelled to answer them this time. Yes, this was a spy car. No, she didn't know who was in the other car. Yes, their vehicle was equipped with other defense mechanisms. No, it didn't come with an oil slick. Oil slicks were only in movies.

The questions changed from focusing less on their pursuer and more on Aurora's current situation when the faun asked, "Will I be home in two hours?"

"No, Aurora." Rebecca merged onto Route One again. "I'm taking you to what is called a safe house tonight. There, you'll meet a DEED education agent. She will teach you about your new home and help you acclimate before you arrive."

Aurora scratched her chin. "Is she a centaur like you?"

"No, she's something special. We call her a verdurian. She's part plant."

Aurora jounced her head. "Did you say plant?"

"Yes, she has a brain and muscles like you and me, but chlorophyll for blood and bendable bone structure. She disguises herself to appear human. Don't let her green complexion scare you. She's the nicest person I know."

Verdurian Sonya was milk and honey to my gin and tonic.

"Fauns, centaurs, and plant-people." Aurora counted on her fingers. "What else is there?"

Rebecca clicked the cruise control with her thumb. "The real question is 'What isn't there?' Aurora, you're about to enter a world full of amazing kinds of people, and we're living right under the noses of humans."

"Do mermaids exist?"

"One of my best friends is a mermaid. Her name is Josie-Ann."

Aurora brightened. "Does she have a good singing voice?"

"Mermaids have excellent vocal cords," Rebecca answered. "Just don't ask her to sing 'Under the Sea.' She's not fond of that song."

Aurora giggled. "What about giants?"

"Only tall ones. We leave short giants to the humans."

For a moment, Aurora blanched. "Do you mean certain mythicals aren't allowed in your homeland?"

She took my joke the wrong way. Kids! "No, Aurora. Everyone is welcome except humans. They're not allowed."

Aurora cupped her chin. "How about vampires and werewolves? Are they nice?"

"No vampires." Rebecca flipped on her turn signal to switch lanes. "Werewolves exist only in movies. We have something similar, but they're sweet-natured."

Aurora looked at the sky. "Do any of our kind fly?"

"Yup."

"And do you all get along?"

Rebecca considered her answer. "We disagree with each other, but not to the extent of the countries of the world. We share the kinship of hiding from non-mythicals."

Rebecca didn't expound on how humans would hunt, experiment, or potentially exterminate the mythical population if they were discovered. Even the human-looking mythicals, like giants, would be exploited. Mythicals' unity was strong over their potential abuse if the world at large started believing in them.

Aurora examined a yard out the window. "Are there gnomes?"

"Like garden gnomes? No, Aurora. But yes, gnomes exist." *Question after question after question.* "Your educator will tell you about our many species. And she'll teach you how to interact with them."

Aurora shrunk into her seat. "Are they all nice?"

The million-dollar question. "Like humans, it depends. The mermaids, for example. I have a dozen mermaid friends. But one of their kind has been unpleasant to me since secondary school. Most are nice, but a few are not."

Aurora's shoulders lowered a little at her statement. "I can't see why anyone wouldn't like you."

Rebecca snickered. "You're very kind, Aurora, but I'm not always the best person to be around. Some mythicals aren't happy when I show up."

"Why not?"

She might as well tell her. Sonya would, anyway. "A few mythicals don't appreciate our little country and feel we should inhabit the world with humans. They escape and live among ordinary people, risking the exposure of the rest of us. It's my job to bring those runaways back home. Sometimes, they don't want to return."

"Do you shoot them?" Aurora whispered.

Oh, Hades! What kids watch on the internet. "I don't murder people, Aurora! I bring them back alive."

"But if they're going to tell humans about you. I mean about us. Don't you have to stop them?"

Rebecca kept an eye on her rearview mirror. "Yes, some have tried to tell the others about us. Some have gone so far as to upload videos. But let me tell you something remarkable about humans."

Aurora's finger picked at her left nostril. "What?'

Rebecca grimaced at the child's habit but didn't comment. Leave it to Sonya. "They don't want to believe in us. And if they don't want to believe, they don't believe. It's that simple."

Aurora leaned forward. "But if they loaded a video of you turning into a centaur, wouldn't people believe?"

Affecting her schoolteacher's voice, Rebecca explained. "DEED intercepts and changes a video before it receives many views. Fuzzy Abominable Snowmen? Mermaids who could be seals? Most of the time DEED doesn't have to interfere because humans themselves deny the reports. But sometimes, one of our own decides to speak out. Then, DEED gets involved."

"Are those people punished?" Aurora's lower lip protruded.

Kralston did a number on this girl. "The way your guardian treated you—it wasn't right. You're worried you'll be punished for something."

Aurora puckered her mouth.

"Aurora, please tell me."

"Some people saw my legs. A doctor and a nurse." The child swallowed, close to tears.

Rebecca asked, "And did they identify you as a faun? Or maybe they said satyr?"

Aurora blinked. "No."

"To them, we don't exist, Aurora. The most open-minded human might think you have a medical condition. They may guess people in the past had thin, hairy legs, and ancient people called them fauns. Most humans would diagnose you as having a bone condition, and they'd go home and tell their families and forget all about you the next day."

"But...but..."

"Did the doctor or the nurse treat you? Recommend an operation or give you medicine?"

Aurora's words tumbled out confession-style. "They wanted to operate, but Mom wouldn't let them. She threw away the pills."

"Good for her." *Thank Chiron for Aurora's mother.* "Nothing is wrong with you, Aurora. I find it curious. Even smart humans trust what they believe to be reality. They forget what has yet to be discovered. They think they know it all. They deny an answer on the edges of possibility for the comfortable, and most likely, answer."

The truth is humans don't want to believe in mythicals. They ignore what Occam's razor, the simplest answer, tells them. Rebecca wanted to put this in terms Aurora would understand, but a sign ahead for a rest stop became the priority.

"Are you ready for a break? I'm going to have to cut and style your hair."

Sitting at a picnic table, Rebecca showed Aurora's passport to the young faun. DEED had supplied it before the agent had started for Canada. Rebecca had used DEED tools to print Aurora's name and insert a picture of her into the booklet. Aurora took the manufactured documentation, eyes widening. "This is neat. It looks real."

Rebecca stiffened. Fortunately, nobody was near enough to overhear her young charge. She leaned down. "Not so loud."

Aurora examined the passport. "I have your last name."

"To enter the United States, you must pretend to be my daughter. Good thing we look similar."

Rebecca's handler had needed to convince her to take the mission. Rebecca's resemblance to Aurora, and a border guard's unlikely probability of stopping a mother-daughter combination made her the ideal candidate.

"I like Eidelweiss. It's a pretty name."

Rebecca nibbled on a potato chip from a vending machine.

"What last name will I have?" Aurora's eyes widened. "May I keep yours?"

Rebecca flexed her fingers, requesting the passport. "You'll be adopted and take their last name."

Aurora hung her head. "Oh. Things work the same way there as it does here."

Reaching for another chip, Rebecca tilted her head. "How did you expect it would be?"

Aurora reached into her candy bag and pulled out a blue-coated sweet. "I dunno. I thought we'd all live together or something. Like at a camp I read about in my books."

"No. You'll have a real home." Rebecca flattened her chip bag after pulling out the last piece. "But unlike the rest of the world, Elysium has a hundred percent adoption rate. And age doesn't matter whether you're sixteen or eight."

"Even for someone like me?"

Rebecca pointed at Aurora's nose and tapped it. "Especially someone like you."

Booping another's nose didn't come easy for Rebecca whose fingers preferred to wrap around her bolas.

Though she had no spouse or children, Rebecca had a charming niece. Liliana was the only person with whom the agent would ever make such an intimate gesture. Yet, Aurora drank Rebecca's kindness as a thirsty traveler drinks at a well in the desert. Rebecca could pretend for a while.

Aurora's smile widened, and then her face fell. "I feel bad for Other-Parent, though."

Rebecca lifted her bag. "You mean your mother?"

"No, *Other*-Parent."

Scowling, Rebecca examined Aurora for signs of joking. She was serious. "Your guardian was horrible."

"Just to me." Aurora pinched an orange candy from the bag. "He fixes up old people's homes around town for free. He also buys extra food for the lady down the street. He thinks she may be eating cat food."

"I wouldn't have expected that of the man."

"He'll be lonely without me," said Aurora. "He doesn't know it yet, but he will be."

Unlikely. Yet, maybe, she's right. Aurora had lived with the man, and perhaps, in his grief, Kralston hadn't perceived how much Aurora meant to him. Because Aurora would be a treasure for another family soon.

Rebecca nodded at the M&M bag. "Eat those in the car. Let's go."

THE EDUCATOR

February - Bangor, Maine, United States

North of Bangor, Rebecca turned off a paved road onto the driveway of a compact, white-sided prefabricated home. This residence, designated as belonging to Sonya Gale but owned by DEED, hid away from most traffic and prying eyes. Sonya's home was a perfect place to acclimate a young student to the denizens and land of Elysium—the mythicals' refuge.

Rebecca counted the months she had been on assignment since embarking from her home country. Six. Elysium's rolling, green hills, vast cerulean skies, and salt-tinged scents now beckoned her back for a short reprieve. Her country lived up to its name. Despite Elysium's comfort, Rebecca still enjoyed crossing its borders into the world at large and helping mythicals.

A metal decoration of the sun with its rays zigzagging away from the circular center hung on the house's exterior front wall. A thin copper pole, laden with snow but used to support plants in the warmer months, was rooted next to the house, a United States flag rustling from a bracket next to it. Rebecca smirked to herself. Sonya loved the United States. She once called it her second country and paid taxes from her funds. Rebecca doubted the people around here would tolerate Sonya if they discovered she was a verdurian.

Rebecca turned off the VW Passat, eyeing her rearview mirror. Aurora squirmed but returned her gaze. The agent affected an excited tone. "We're here."

Aurora's attention shifted to the entrance, and Rebecca turned around to see Sonya standing behind the screen door. Sonya wore a stocking hat, a black jacket, and jeans as if she had just come in from outside. Her pink face peeked out from all the clothing, and she flashed a broad smile.

Aurora unbuckled her seat belt. "Doesn't she have green skin?"

Rebecca also removed her fastenings and pocketed the Passat's key fob. "She's wearing makeup. We must be careful among humans. Someone could pass by and notice her."

Unlikely, given the weather, but DEED employees took no chances. Rebecca opened her door, and brumal air swept into the car. Who would brave this cold? Her natural body had a thick coat of hair. Her human form didn't offer the same protection.

Rebecca grabbed Aurora's hand as they approached the house, clomping through the thin crust of snow. Each footfall sounded as though they were stepping on Styrofoam. Aurora hung back slightly from matching Rebecca's pace. The guardian understood. So many strangers in so short a time.

When they reached the concrete steps Sonya had cleared of snow, the home's owner opened the door. "Hi! You must be Aurora."

Diffident, Aurora blushed and nodded. She nudged Rebecca. "How does she know the name you gave me?"

"I texted her before we left Nova Scotia." Rebecca patted her pocket with her cell. "Until I renamed you, DEED called you Jane Doe."

Sonya snorted. "You are certainly not a Jane. Aurora suits you fine."

Rebecca ascended the steps. "Sonya, you're completely breaking protocol."

"Oh, Rebecca." Sonya's breath made a white cloud. "We've worked together for years."

"I could be a doppelganger, Sonya."

Sonya put her hands on her hips. "Go."

Rebecca hummed a few notes from "Always." Sonya responded, whistling a tune from another song—Stephen Sondheim's "Somewhere." Aurora tilted her head, and her mouth dropped open.

She thinks we're crazy. Who would blame her?

Rebecca explained, "We each have songs we hum or whistle to each other to ensure we are who we say we are."

Sonya pushed the door open further. "And now that we know we're each other, come in. Come in."

Rebecca didn't move. "Second protocol."

"Oh, for Chiron's sake, Rebecca." Sonya had pronounced "Chiron" as "Chiryoon." She was inheriting the dialect of the Maine residents.

"Are we invited inside?"

"No." Sonya crossed her eyes and stuck out her tongue as she responded negatively.

Rebecca turned to Aurora. "To ensure an agent isn't compromised, we always lie when answering the first question."

Aurora laughed. "You talk in code. Like in the movies."

Sonya stepped outside and held the door. "Not nearly as exciting. Let's go in. It's cold."

The newcomers entered the front of the house, Sonya following behind. Warm and inviting, the entry, with bright yellow walls, contrasted with the darkness outside. At least a dozen plants covered the tables and shelves in the living room. In one corner, a plinth supported a massive fern. A wall-mounted television and couch across from it were the only modern conveniences in the crowded space.

Sonya stepped in front of Aurora. She didn't bend over in the condescending way some adults do in greeting children. Instead, she welcomed her as if she were family. "My name is Sonya Gale. Has Rebecca told you about me?"

Rebecca bit her lip, suppressing the urge to answer. The bond between an educator and a pupil was necessary, and the relationship had to start from the first conversation.

Aurora's hand tightened on Rebecca's. "A little," the faun answered.

"I'm what's called a verdurian." Sonya winked. "I'm kind of like a plant. I'm a mythical but different from most of our kind, who are similar to you and Rebecca. For several days, I'll teach you about our sort so that you'll know what to expect when you go to our homeland."

Rebecca realized then she hadn't told Aurora how long her training would be. "Four days, Aurora. And I'll be the one escorting you to Elysium."

Aurora's attention shifted between the women.

Sonya leaned in for a conspiratorial whisper. "Did Rebecca give you that goofy line that she was your deed?"

Aurora glanced at Rebecca. Rebecca remained stone-faced.

Sonya declared, "She's so silly. She called herself a piece of paper."

Rebecca suppressed a laugh. Sonya and she had done this routine before. The humorous insight succeeded in putting the younger ones at ease.

Rebecca said, "I was referring to the department. And it's a good tagline, Sonya."

Sonya rolled her eyes but remained focused on the faun. "Now, I've read about you, Aurora, and your life in Amherst. But I want to know more. Why not talk over dinner in the kitchen?"

"How do you know about me?"

Rebecca squeezed Aurora's hand. "Remember when we stopped for lunch, and I had my laptop out? I wrote to Sonya about you."

Aurora's hand trembled in Rebecca's.

I must make her feel safe. "I explained what a charming young girl you are."

Aurora blushed, and Sonya led the way into the kitchen. The room was decorated in an old-fashioned way, Americana circa 1950. Chrome on the refrigerator, tiled counters, and green draperies on the window. A homelike room with plants everywhere.

Sonya went to the windows and drew the draperies. "Let's have some privacy. We may be ourselves here."

Once no one could see inside, Sonya ran water over a cloth. She applied it to her face, removing the makeup and showing her green skin underneath. Aurora leaned forward, fascinated. Sonya gestured to Rebecca. "You, too."

"She's already seen my trick."

Aurora turned to her. "But I'd like to see it again."

"Sure." Rebecca's eyes crinkled. She loved this part of the job.

The forelegs grew out of her midsection, and her hindquarters extended backward. Her stretchy pants bulged outward, still covering a portion of her body. In seconds, Rebecca folded her arms and struck what she called her "centaur pose."

"That's so awesome!" Aurora's voice lilted in wonder.

Sonya pointed at a small table where mist was rising off a brown stew. "Aurora, you may or may not keep your legs covered. It's up to you."

Aurora hesitated, then stepped out of her boots, revealing her cloven hooves. She clip-clopped on the tiles while lowering the ski pants Rebecca had given her. Her shorts came to her knees, exposing her brown, coarse-hair goat legs.

Aurora's ears reddened. "Maybe I shouldn't have."

"Whatever makes you comfortable." Sonya examined the child's knitted hat. "Have you sprouted the nubs of your antlers yet, dear?"

Aurora gaped. "Antlers?"

"Too young." Rebecca removed her jacket.

Sonya pulled out a chair for Aurora. "She's close to that age, though."

Aurora's head swiveled back and forth. "I'll have antlers?"

"I'm sure they'll be beautiful." Sonya reached for a pile of plates on the kitchen counter. "Many fauns decorate them with jewelry, and a few paint their antlers."

Rebecca grunted. "I'll never understand why they paint

them."

Sonya set the plates out on the table. "They're trying to attract someone special, Rebecca. You remember how we were when we were young."

And stupid.

Rebecca set a hand on Aurora's shoulder. "Similar to reindeer, female fauns sprout antlers, too. They grow and fall off seasonally. In Elysium, everyone considers fauns' antlers and legs beautiful."

"Losing their antlers allows faun families to take vacations outside Elysium." Sonya retrieved the cutlery. "Now, everyone, sit down. Let's eat, talk, and learn more about each other."

Sonya's stew was delicious, but Rebecca longed for lobster bisque. Not on DEED's per diem, she knew, but she might splurge her own money on dinner in the next three days. Sonya's meal, however, succeeded in pulling Aurora out of her reticence. By dessert, the faun trusted Sonya. Rebecca was pleased to spy a confident girl peeking out behind the lost and lonely child.

When the time came to say farewell, Aurora grew lachrymose. Tears filled her eyes, and she hugged Rebecca. The agent wrapped her arms around her charge.

"Hey, none of that." Rebecca thumbed a teardrop. "You're off to a great start."

"Ever since Mum died, I..." Aurora faltered.

Rebecca pulled her again into a hug. "I know. But I think your mom would've wanted me to show up today. And she would want you to learn from Sonya. Your mom loved you and would want you to be happy in Elysium."

Rebecca let Aurora go. The girl hoofed back. "Thank you."

Rebecca put a finger under the faun's chin. "DEED or no DEED, I'm happy to have guided you here. You're the reason I do my job."

"A secret agent." Aurora grinned.

"That's me. Now, I must return to my glamorous life of saving the world."

Over Aurora's shoulder, Sonya mouthed, "You saved hers."

"I'll be back in four days," Rebecca reminded Aurora.

As Rebecca opened the door and met the chilling blast of winter, she wrapped Sonya's words in her heart. They warmed her against the cold as she made her way to her Passat.

OH, THE GLAMOR

February - Bangor, Maine, United States

Rebecca's four-star hotel room in Bangor was the size of Sonya's house. Yes, her job was dangerous. Yes, she traveled the world, sacrificing personal time. But still. Couldn't they have afforded better accommodations for Sonya than a tiny house in northern Maine?

Rebecca changed her clothes and secured the room before checking her messages. She trashed filler emails from DEED, such as the St. Valentine's Day online party notification and a few entries related to her travel plans back to Elysium, where she wouldn't disembark. Near the bottom of her list, one message caught her attention.

"Hi, Rebecca. I'm off on my first solo assignment. I just wanted to say thanks again for taking me under your wing. You recommended Fred as a partner when DEED reassigned me. I didn't think he and I would get along, but he taught me a lot. Anyway, wish me luck. Diana."

Oh, that kid!

Rebecca swallowed her guilt. She had requested the reassignment, not DEED. After her first partnership dissolved, Rebecca preferred to work alone. But the DEED council wanted her to take Diana Cantropy under her wing. Diana had been a go-getter from day one, and Rebecca didn't have the patience for an inexperienced operative. After a few missions, Rebecca had petitioned the council to work alone, and they reassigned Diana. "A step up," they had told her. Rebecca was surprised Diana hadn't figured that out.

Or perhaps she had? Maybe Diana realized she had been sidelined, and her message proved she was better than Rebecca thought. Rebecca reread the note. The tone was earnest, not hostile.

Diana was too innocent to be political.

Rebecca wasn't proud of what she had done to the young woman. Working alone was about *her*, not Diana. Her former partner was skilled, and she wished Diana success on her mission. But was Diana ready to be on an assignment all alone? Rebecca doubted it.

Did I push her into this?

She wasn't going to take responsibility for Diana's decisions. If Diana had sought her guidance, she should have reached out to her. Early on, Rebecca had confided in senior agents like Freyarsha, a well-known female DEED enforcer. Freyarsha had never been her partner. Diana could have consulted with her, female-to-female, as Rebecca had with Freyarsha in the past, right?

Maybe I should have told Diana to contact me.

Too much regret over the past. Diana, and the tragic event with the partner before her.

Rebecca's eyelids drooped, but she couldn't sleep. What could she do in Bangor?

Not much happens on a weeknight. I'll go for a drink.

She left her room, descended the stairs, and found the lounge. The room had few patrons as not many people visited Bangor in February. She ordered a Moscow Mule and sat in the corner of the room, away from the well-lit counter. The drink came in the traditional copper mug and the coolness of the vodka and lime juice slid easily down her throat.

What everyone thought of the life of secret agents was wrong. This, what she was doing right now, was typical. Spies drank alone in bars. What she had done for Aurora today was a highlight. In fact, she hadn't been assigned an extraction—DEED's term for rescue— for months. Her job mainly consisted of subduing dissatisfied Elysium runaways and forcing them back home, often drugged. Enforcer agents like her called this operation "A Weekend at Bernie's" after the movie. Lugging unconscious bodies around wasn't a scene often depicted in spy films.

DEED called taking willing mythicals to Elysium an extraction, but Rebecca and other agents had a different term: a "wiffle ball" mission. With its low danger, such extractions were for novices. Rebecca was pleased to help Aurora but was more suited to breaking into facilities and erasing evidence of her kind, or rescuing an endangered mythical.

Didn't DEED have more important tasks for her than extracting an eight-year-old faun? And with no evidence Kralston would put up a fight? Yes, the playbook called for ignoring Kralston and driving away with her charge to Maine. But Rebecca didn't follow the usual path. Padre Kralston needed a lesson, and she couldn't pass up giving him one. Besides, most agents would still be calling Aurora "Jane Doe Kralston." She'd never stick her rescued faun with such a horrible moniker.

When she finished her Mule, she asked for another. Two would be her limit. Or maybe three. She had nothing on her agenda for tomorrow. In her long list of emails, her handler had sent a note asking her if she wanted the "Lester assignment." Lester was a chore, not an assignment. And he was on the other side of the country. She had declined, thinking she'd cruise the eastern coast of the States instead. She hadn't visited this country in a long time. A little sightseeing on DEED's dime wouldn't hurt anyone.

The second Mule came, and the waiter told her a gentleman at the bar had paid for it.

Oh, sludge. Are you kidding me?

Rebecca shook her head. "No, put it on my room."

The "gentleman" stood. A lanky man in what Rebecca thought was his early thirties with haystack-colored hair and blue eyes sauntered over. He had his thumbs hooked into his jeans' pockets. Rebecca wished she could vanish. With her Mule in hand, of course.

"Hey, miss. You look like you could use some company."

This was his opening line? "Use some company" was most New York guys' third attempt after striking out twice. "No, thank you."

The man licked his lips. "You could be nicer, seeing as I bought you a drink and all."

"I bought my drink. And I've had a long day and want to be alone."

Leaning over, the man placed his hands on her table. "If you gave me a chance, you'd be surprised."

The smell of beer on his breath was overpowering. Perhaps the liquid courage was talking. Maybe the guy was decent otherwise. But she had given him two chances. Now, she got rough.

Rebecca dug her nails into the back of his hands in one swift move. He cried out, but her force kept his hands in place. "Back off. Comprehend?"

Lifting her nails, Rebecca maintained eye contact with him while he flexed his fingers. He called her a name loudly enough for several drinkers in the bar to hear and turn their heads. Others had called her far worse—his name-calling was amateur hour. Yes, she had overreacted. A bit. Yes, she shouldn't call attention to herself. But Rebecca kept her nails sharp for just such an occasion.

The bartender strode over, but the man returned to his seat. He raised an eyebrow to Rebecca. She judged the broad-shouldered bartender could bounce the annoying patron out of the hotel, but she didn't want any more fuss.

Rebecca nodded at the bartender, and he returned to his duties. She resumed her drinking, finishing off the second mug. Two was her limit after her incident with Mr. Smooth. She set down the copper cup and stood.

Rebecca's phone buzzed. She retrieved it and she glanced

at the name. "Sonya—Secure."

What does Sonya want at this hour? It's probably a cute story about Aurora.

Yet, a phone call this late raised Rebecca's hackles. Was something wrong with the faun?

Rebecca answered, humming a few bars of "Always," but Sonya cut her off. "Humans took her, Rebecca! They took Aurora!"

THE NEW HANDLER

February - Bangor, Maine, United States

Sonya applied salve to her wound while Rebecca pressed on the accelerator of her Passat. The needle hovered around one-hundred-fifty kilometers per hour. She switched the display to miles. Ninety-five.

Try explaining this to the local police force.

Rebecca's phone trilled over the car's speakers to secure a line to headquarters. Her ice-filled Yeti brand cooler rattled with the speed of the vehicle. Beside her, the safe house educator mopped chlorophyll with a napkin on the cloth passenger seat. Fortunately, Sonya had stopped bleeding, and Rebecca was grateful that the verdurian was alive.

A digital voice sang out over Rebecca's speakers. "Connected! The line is triple secured."

Rebecca spun the vehicle sharply onto the expressway. She'd be at the airport in ten minutes. She only needed DEED to get her an e-ticket. "Ring Marie for me."

"Calling Marie Usley."

Rebecca merged onto I-95 while slapping her steering wheel. "Come on!"

Sonya applied a bandage over the salve on her left arm. "We might be able to intercept them at the airport."

The phone announced. "Calling Ray Phist."

"What?" Rebecca jerked backward. "I didn't tell you to call

Ray. I repeat. Dial Marie Usley."

"Calling Marie Usley."

Rebecca put her foot to the floor, weaving in and out of traffic. The voice announced again, "Calling Ray Phist."

Sonya furrowed her brow. "Why does it want to connect you to a council member?"

"And Ray, in particular." Rebecca sped into the right lane to exit the freeway to the airport. "Of all people."

The agent was about to whistle the first notes of "Always" when a gruff voice cut her off. "Rebecca." Ray's unmistakable voice.

Speaking to him again brought her back in time: meeting him in Elysium, calming down the rare mythical not known to humans—a sphrax—at the Cape of Good Hope, and then...

The disaster in Scotland.

Rebecca closed her eyes. "Ray, I need to speak to Marie immediately."

"We know Jane Doe Kralston was taken. Agent Gayle called it in."

Rebecca slowed the car down at the exit. "Her name is Aurora, now. And since you know so much, you should know why my talking to my handler is important. Marie needs to get me tickets before I enter the airport."

"Rebecca, turn around and proceed to your hotel." Ray's voice was heavy, a tone he never used with her.

Stopping at a light behind three other cars, Rebecca demanded, "What are you talking about?"

A grunt. Typical Ray. "Rebecca, you are *not* to pursue Jane Doe...Aurora. Do you understand? She's already on a private flight that just went wheels up. We spotted her entering the tunnel to the plane."

The light turned green. Rebecca laid on her horn. "You may have seen another girl. They could have—"

"They didn't try to disguise her legs. We have visual evidence and confirmation."

Turning on the road to Bangor International, the DEED

agent inched the car up. She eyed the shoulder and considered pulling onto it. "Why take a girl hiding in an attic for nearly nine years?"

"We have to assume the worst," Ray answered. "The prevailing theory is that a shadow operation knows about mythicals and wants to study us. Any mythical will do. They've been following you until they found a helpless subject."

"Aurora." Rebecca gritted her teeth. "DEED has prior cases of kidnapped mythicals. 'Study' could mean questioning, but it could also indicate euthanasia and dissection."

Ray's lack of answer indicated his confirmation.

For all Rebecca's mission successes and failures, she couldn't allow someone to torture Aurora. "I need to stop them. Where are they headed?"

"Venezuela."

Rebecca swung across the double yellow lines into the lanes reserved for oncoming traffic. Sonya whimpered and mumbled something that sounded like a chant. Rebecca floored her car and passed two vehicles before swinging back into her own lane. "Get me a ticket to Venezuela."

"Rebecca, turn around. Do not enter the airport."

"Baelz Bells, Ray. I botched this mission. Not to mention, a little girl's life is at stake. I need to rescue her. What is DEED for if not for that?"

Ray sighed. "I just suspended all your credit. Return to the hotel."

Rebecca eyed Sonya and mouthed, "Credit card?"

"Sonya's, too."

Rebecca slammed her fist against the dashboard, and Sonya flinched. "Ray, what the Hades?" shouted Rebecca. "Why would you do that?"

"Because I know you, Rebecca. You have more determination than anyone, and yes, you're perfect for the assignment. But even the perfect agent will get herself killed if she tries to extract that faun."

Rebecca drove onto the main thoroughfare between the

terminals. "We have a mythical child abduction. They'll never see me coming."

"Listen, this isn't your typical snatch-and-grab," said Ray. "Taking a little girl out of the United States from Maine to Venezuela by air on a private charter? And they knew enough about Sonya to incapacitate her sufficiently to get away. Whoever this is, they've operated in the dark so far."

"Aurora is my responsibility." Rebecca swerved her coupe around a truck. "Our best case scenario is that they've uploaded pictures of her. You know what will happen next."

"Yes, counterintelligence will work overtime disputing the images." A file-transfer whoosh interrupted Ray. "Just sent you an emergency response image. We already have doctored pictures of Aurora with human legs. We're not worried about them showing her off to the world. Aurora looks more human than most of us, certainly me."

"They may kill her—"

"To what end?" interrupted Ray. "This was an elaborate plan, Rebecca. The operating assumption is extortion. They'll contact us somehow, looking for money. Or possibly our tech. We're not sure which."

Rebecca swerved around another car, and Sonya bumped into the passenger door. The ice cubes in the Yeti rattled again. Rebecca's focus remained on the road. "And their leverage if you tell them you can dispute anything they can upload? If you take that away, what use is she to them?"

"Yeah, I won't lie. The situation is tricky."

Rebecca slammed her hand on the dashboard again. She yelled at the cell built into her car. "She's not a situation. Aurora is a little girl."

"Of course she is." Ray's voice cracked, and his professional voice dropped. "What kind of a heartless monster do you think I am? But the facts remain. She was abducted and transferred to a plane headed for Venezuela. Where exactly? Unknown. Venezuela is a large country. We have no boots on the ground in South America close enough to stake out the airports there."

"We have no one in Venezuela?" asked Sonya.

"I didn't say no one. We can't get to the airport in time for the landing. Bear in mind, Venezuela is a chaotic country, Sonya. We don't station people in risky places."

"An extraction." Rebecca passed a parking lot with the sign *Credit card only*. "If I follow her, then—"

"Where? Where would you—?"

Rebecca spoke over him. "I don't know! This is my job, Ray, and I'm the best at it. It's why I'm in the field, and you're not."

Sonya made a face that clearly expressed her thoughts. *Too far, Rebecca.*

Ray's voice had been casual before, but now it returned to a business timbre with a dangerous undertone. "We will proceed as DEED always has. We start with reconnaissance. From there, we enter the ideation stage and then execution. We don't jump to the end."

"We don't have time for DEED's edicts and processes." Rebecca side-eyed Sonya, who gave her a sharp nod of approval. "We need to do something quickly."

When Ray next spoke, he enunciated each word. "Due to recent events, I've taken over as your handler for the foreseeable future. I'll be giving you your next assignment."

"What?" Rebecca shouted.

"The assignment will download to your laptop when you enter your hotel room. Get a good night's sleep and return to the airport in the morning."

"Ray, you can't do this."

"Promise me, Rebecca. Promise me, you won't go to South America. Your word on this."

Rebecca slumped her shoulders, aiming for the exit lane from the airport. "Why? Why is my not pursuing her so important? Worst case, if I die trying, I may find you some intel."

"Because you matter to us, Rebecca."

Only because I'm your best agent. Rebecca couldn't have this conversation with Sonya in the car.

As if reading her mind, Ray refuted her. "*You* are important. We'll rescue Aurora, Rebecca. I swear to you. Just not tonight."

Rebecca merged back onto the expressway. She wasn't in any position to bargain. No credit. In a foreign country. Stuff DEED! But she'd play their game. For now. "I promise I won't go after her, Ray. But I'm not happy about it."

Ray was all business again. "Get some sleep, agent."

"Out." Rebecca punched the button.

Sonya cleared her throat. "Are you simply going to give up on Aurora?"

Rebecca's nostrils flared. "The next time DEED assigns me to South America I'll head to Venezuela. I will use every trick at my disposal to extract her."

Sonya glowed a brighter green. "That's the Rebecca Eidelweiss I know. But what will DEED do to you if they find out?"

"DEED. DEED. DEED." Rebecca accelerated the car, and both women lurched backward. "Sonya, how do we do it? Why do we do it? Take orders from an out-of-touch, remote institution like them. They live in Elysium, so different from the rest of the world, yet they presume to tell us they know best?"

Sonya touched a bruise on her green forehead. "DEED can be frustrating."

"I sense a 'but' in that sentence."

Sonya patted down a tendril of green hair. "Their heart's in the right place. They have a mission, and they carry it out."

Rebecca glanced sideways at her passenger. "Sonya, you almost died tonight. If you had bones, you would've never escaped the ropes they tied you in. If you had human fingers, you wouldn't have been able to pick the lock on the back of the van. And then throwing yourself on the street? Most of us would have died. All for DEED?"

Sonya frowned. "This wasn't DEED's fault. Nasty people live in the world, and you and I know how the world works. We're not only mythicals who restore our dispersed kind to our country. We defend others from—"

"Finding out about us," Rebecca finished. "But DEED has a lack of concern, a lack of empathy. The department leaders could use a different viewpoint."

Sonya picked up the Yeti. "Yours?"

"Not mine, necessarily," answered Rebecca. "The council consists of seven people, and while it's done a decent job of representing different species, males always make up the majority. How ironic for a department whose motto is Lady Responsibility."

"But Janx is on the tribunal."

"Janx is one woman, and she's powerful. Of course, she's on the council." Rebecca veered into the right lane. "It's a two-to-five mix right now. We were better off two decades ago at the three to four ratio when Natal was a member."

Sonya waved her tumbler. "I'm not so sure. Natal was a lamia. Lamias have a bad rap with their scent defense mechanism and their terrifying appearance, but Natal seemed to live up to their legend. With her frostiness, I'd believe she went home and ate babies."

"She wasn't like that in private. She came over and visited my dad a few times."

"Just saying that Natal isn't my definition of caring and empathy." Sonya breathed in deeply. "I can't go back to the safe house. I might as well check into the hotel you're at. That is, if Ray has restored my credit."

Rebecca nodded in her direction. "I'm sure he will when our phones tell him we've arrived at the hotel. We will both fill out reports tonight but don't worry about mine. You're a hero."

"I don't feel like one," murmured the green woman.

After dropping Sonya off at the hotel to check in, Rebecca returned to Sonya's house for a quick cleanup. DEED had permitted her to return and retrieve anything incriminating in Sonya's ranch home. Fortunately, most of Sonya's files were online and encrypted, hashed, and salted. Yet, a few physical items remained. Sonya's gear bag, for one, and a gadget or two that shouldn't fall into human hands.

Rebecca searched the house while mentally checking off the list she had made with Sonya. She nearly passed Aurora's bedroom.

Huh! Can't call it a bedroom if she didn't sleep in the bed.

A small bag sat open on the floor, a welcome package from Sonya to Aurora. A Lego set, an *Anne of Green Gables* novel, a page of stickers, and a hairbrush with a sparkly handle. And on top of all that was Aurora's passport.

The passport. Waves of shame and anger flooded Rebecca as she grabbed it. The girl should be planning her trip to her new home, not crying to herself among kidnappers. Rebecca flipped open the passport. Printed was the child's name, Aurora Eidelweiss, and the picture of her Rebecca had taken. Rebecca's jaw fell open. Aurora had pasted a sticker of a heart under the Eidelweiss name.

"Baelz dust!" Rebecca breathed.

Whoever took her would pay. While "licensed to kill" was only a movie tagline, Rebecca considered the phrase for a moment. DEED would dismiss her immediately if she took a life outside of a sanctioned mission, but she found obeying their orders difficult tonight.

Ding.

Rebecca's phone chimed. That would be her next mission. Rebecca hated incomplete assignments, and the possibility another agent might have to clean up her mess. When DEED sent her somewhere, they could rely on her completing the assignment. She was the total package. She was the one helping out fellow DEED employees, not the other way around.

"Brazil. Peru," Rebecca said to herself. "Fine, don't send me to Venezuela, but send me close. Any country from which I can quickly locate Aurora. Send me somewhere south."

She retrieved her phone. After progressing through the device's security, she read her next assignment. DEED was sending her south, assuredly.

South, as in South Korea.

THE ACCIDENTAL TOURIST

February - Jecheon-si, South Korea

T hankfully, Rebecca's English was far better than her Hangul, and she was able to read the multilingual signs that led to her destination. The little piece she knew of South Korea's countryside consisted only of Jeju. If her mission was in Jeju, she might enjoy it. Instead, she wound around Highway 55, eyeing the next exit.

Rebecca was completely out of her jurisdiction. As a DEED field agent, her primary role was to blend in and not attract attention. She assumed her family tree had south European roots. She could pass for a native there. Yet, with the proper language skills, Rebecca could also operate in northern Europe and the Americas. Assignments in Africa and East Asia were rare for her.

Rebecca had been assigned to missions in Cambodia and the Philippines, though. She wasn't completely in the dark here in Asia. This morning, she had enjoyed a few hours in Jecheon-si while she waited for her destination to open for business. She had to take pictures with only her eyes because any images she captured on her phone were shared with DEED. She preferred to keep her memories private. South Korea was a beautiful country at any rate, and the landscapes and waterways hadn't disappointed her.

Rebecca turned off Highway 55 and quickly navigated the Kia Sorento she was driving onto a dirt trail ascending a hill. After reaching the top, she drove down the other side through a grove of trees. Her surroundings weren't a forest, but the trees reminded her the Sobaeksan National Park was nearby. Her destination wasn't far, and she would arrive about ten minutes early for her appointment. Good. Showing up early might throw off her host.

The house sat alone on a farm with trees delineating the boundaries of the yard. Like most detached homes in South Korea, the single-story residence was compact and rectangular in shape. This building was constructed in a Western ranch style, unlike others where the roofs featured a pagoda. The weatherbeaten siding and a crack in one of the two windows spoke volumes. Hard times, but not desperate. They were making do with their side business.

Rebecca grabbed a large Nikon camera and bag and then exited the Sorento, straightening her blouse under her jacket. She had everything she needed to appear as a tourist. Patting her jacket, she ensured the car remote was in her left pocket. She reached into her bag and pulled out a miniature, quarter-inch, black pebble. When she tossed it in the air, it buzzed and floated there. "Good boy. Around the back."

Who needs a partner when you have technology?

The ebony object zipped around the house, and Rebecca approached the front entrance. A wintry gust of wind ruffled her hair as her boots crunched over a thin layer of snow. When she reached the house, she rapped on the door.

A cry sounded within, and Rebecca grinned. If she kept him off-balance through this visit, she would get what she wanted.

The door opened to reveal an Asian man in his twenties with long, dark hair and a round face. His brown eyes examined her briefly then focused on a spot over her shoulder. His white

45

shirt and blue trousers were wrinkled, and his tie was askew. He had a sticker on his breast pocket identifying him in English as the guide. "Rebecca Eidelweiss?"

"I'm sorry I'm a little early. You are Jun-seo?"

The man bowed.

Rebecca clasped her hands together and returned the bow. She was pretending to be a tourist, but she didn't have to be rude.

Jun-seo stepped aside and gestured to the interior of the house. "Please, come in."

Rebecca stepped onto the mat and immediately kicked off her boots. She placed them next to the door in a larger compartment of the shoe cabinet. Jun-seo nodded encouragingly, and Rebecca wondered how many tourists he had to tell to respect their customs and remove their footwear.

On her right, the room opened into a small kitchen area, and on her left was a wall. She could see the room she entered curve around the wall, providing an expansive view of the rear room. Large, heavy curtains hung from a pole obscuring the sight of the yard. Curtains weren't the first choice of window coverings in South Korea, but the backyard was what she and other tourists came to see.

Rebecca's nose wrinkled as she stepped onto the worn carpet. She caught a lingering scent of chili sauce and onions in the room. Other than a small table holding brochures and a fold-out, single-person tray with a chair in the kitchen, Jun-seo had no other furniture. The room was an open space, large enough to accommodate about a dozen people.

Jun-seo had walked backward as she entered. He folded his hands and spoke in a squeaky voice. "I must ask for payment first. You understand some do not pay after seeing it."

"Of course." Rebecca retrieved the requisite won from her purse and handed him three bills. "Keep the change."

She hadn't tipped him much, but Jun-seo put on an appreciative face and bowed again. He pocketed the money, and Rebecca did her best not to roll her eyes. What a small operation. Beside a few brochures in her hotel and an internet site, how did anyone find this place? Bad for tourists, but great for DEED.

Jun-seo stood ramrod straight and cleared his throat. "Did you read the brochure?"

"Yes."

"Allow me to remind you of the rules. First, no photography. I must ask you to put away the camera."

Rebecca held up the Nikon. "I don't have anywhere to put it. Will you hold it for me?"

Jun-seo smiled and presented his hand. Perfect. Rebecca assumed, in situations like hers, he would ask to hold the camera. Being offered it was his best option. Little did he know, she wanted him to have it.

"And two, you may observe the statue for no longer than two minutes. My ancestors view our treasure as sacred, and it is written in ancient texts that allowing strangers to gaze on it longer could bring a curse upon our family."

Oh, please. What dribble. This man didn't believe in curses any more than he believed in aliens. Or centaurs. Wouldn't he be in for a surprise if she changed in front of him? But such antics were off-limits. Rebecca put on her amazed expression—thank you, one year of drama studies at the academy—and blinked her acknowledgment.

"Excellent. Please, stand here."

Jun-seo led her to the center of the room in front of the covered window. He pointed at the floor where Rebecca noticed the carpet tamped down in a rough circle. Jun-seo walked over to the corner of the room, near the line and a pulley. With Rebecca's camera in one hand, he put the other hand on the line.

"You will have the best view from there. Are you ready?"

Rebecca nodded.

In one motion, Jun-seo pulled on the line, and the curtains parted. He had to pull again to supply the full view, but Rebecca spied the object in the backyard with the window half-uncovered. A ten-foot statue sat on a pedestal in a Buddha pose. The bald man wore an iron band around his forehead. His eyes were closed and hands folded on his lap. His face was painted with streaks of blue war paint. Apart from a robe, the rest of the sculpture was naked. The muscles on the man's forearms and shoulders displayed intricate detail. The brochure had called this "a lifelike construction, a piece of art, a wonder." Rebecca agreed with the last description.

Folding her hands, Rebecca observed the rural attraction closely. Her task here would be much easier based on what happened during the two minutes. She waited and examined every aspect of the statue. She affected a gawp of someone who was truly taken in.

Near what she assumed was the ninety-second mark, she spoke.

"He's so lifelike."

"A testimony to my forefathers," said Jun-seo. "The family has had this for ages, but only recently decided to display it to the world."

"I see why." Rebecca blinked. "He's truly worthy."

Jun-seo brightened. "Perhaps I may quote you for a future brochure?"

"Perhaps."

"I am sorry, but two minutes have elapsed." Jun-seo pulled the cord again, and the curtains swung shut. "I appreciate you choosing us on your vacation. Will you tell your friends? And kindly leave a good review on TripAdvisor?"

Rebecca turned her back as if to leave. "Oh, I will."

Jun-seo strolled up to her. "And if you would like to make a donation, you may do so at the box near the brochures."

He had positioned himself between her and the rope. Rebecca had to draw this out. "Could you tell me how to get to Birdsong Peak?"

Jun-seo put on a tight smile. "Google Maps may direct you better than I could."

"It didn't." She reached into her pocket and pushed the button on the remote. "I tried to visit it before I came here, and I became hopelessly lost."

Jun-seo offered Rebecca her camera back. "I'm sure, once

you enter Sobaeksan Park, someone will know the way. Your camera?"

The camera's timer chimed, and the device emitted a cloud of smoke. Jun-seo was caught off-guard. Rebecca could have easily overpowered the gaunt host, but violence was her least favored option.

Expecting the distraction, Rebecca dashed past Jun-seo as fast as a gazelle. Jun-seo cried "Miss," but he was two steps behind her when she parted the curtains with one hand. In the backyard, the statue had its head tilted and its eyes open.

Jun-seo shut the curtains, eyes narrowed. "Leave, or I shall call the police."

"Let them come. I'll report you for fraud."

The color drained out of the young man's face. "If you leave, we don't have to report anything to anyone. I will refund your money."

"Open the curtain."

"No." He pointed to the door again. "Leave."

"I know about giants." Rebecca folded her arms. "I've seen them before. You have one in your backyard."

Jun-seo reared back. "I don't know what you are talking about. It is merely a statue."

"That opens its eyes and moves its head. Are you going to call it an animatronic next?" Rebecca nodded to the curtains. "Open them, or I will. I want to talk to the giant."

Jun-seo grimaced. "There is no such thing as—"

Rebecca leaned forward. "Do you think I came unprepared? I want to talk to the giant."

"If there was a giant in my backyard, and I'm not saying there is, maybe he doesn't speak English."

"*Naneun dangsin-ui eon-eoleul sayonghabnida,*" she told him. Translation: "I speak your language."

Jun-seo's eyes widened.

"You have no idea who you're dealing with, and I promise I won't hurt him." Rebecca took the camera from Jun-seo. "My goal is to keep your secret at all costs. I have a reason to keep him out of the public eye."

Jun-seo sighed and allowed his shoulders to sag. "This way."

The guide led her to the hallway along the back of the house. All windows in this building had heavily frosted glass to prevent anything but sunlight to filter in, or anyone to peek in the backyard. He unlocked a door that led to a five-by-five room with hooks for coats. Grabbing one, Jun-Seo opened a door and walked into the backyard.

Trees surrounded the backyard, leaving no visibility to the outside. An elongated shed, capable of holding a sleeping giant, sat against the back of the barrier.

The giant sat still on the pedestal, eyes closed, and motionless. Rebecca followed Jun-seo to the patio. He spoke to the still man. "You may stop, Seung-min. She knows."

The giant opened his eyes and glared at Rebecca. Though she had a powerful stun gun in her clutch, she didn't open it. He looked more afraid than angry about her exposing his secret. He wrapped his arms around his body. Cold or insecure. Rebecca assumed the latter.

She spoke in Korean, enunciating each word. She had spent most of the prior evening and night practicing. "I won't hurt you. Your secret is safe with me."

Seung-min's eyes flickered to Jun-Seo then back to Rebecca.

She continued, "You aren't the only giant in the world. I know many of your kind and would like you to meet them."

The giant spoke. Rebecca had trouble translating it. She thought she picked up the word "family" but his dialect was so heavy that she wasn't sure. She turned to Jun-seo. "Could you translate for me?"

Jun-Seo sniffed. "I thought you knew Korean. He says he doesn't want to meet others. He wants to remain here with his family."

"You?"

"I'm his older brother." Jun-Seo crossed his arms. "My

parents found him on their doorstep. My mother died two years ago."

In most cases when humans adopted a mythical, the subject wanted to leave. Yes, tears were shed, but the bullying, the hiding, or the constant worry of discovery had scarred them. Many ended up in orphanages or as runaways on the streets.

Yet, occasionally, a mythical ended up in a loving family. While DEED had a job to do, it recognized the potential harm of tearing a family apart. They used the same word for forcibly removing a mythical as everyone else. Kidnapping. The targets would likely try to find a way back to their home, with the associated risk that DEED might be publicly exposed. Though the policy sounded humane, Rebecca often wondered if all DEED cared about was secrecy.

Rebecca addressed Seung-min. "You may be happy where I take you. And your needs will be provided there." She wanted to add "better than here" but thought it tactless.

The giant waved his arm around the yard. She caught the words "happy here" and didn't need a translation.

Rebecca turned to Jun-seo. "If word gets out that a giant lives here, they'll take him away."

"What do you think you're doing?" asked Jun-seo.

"Far less humane people than me will put him in a cage, or worse, a lab. He's not just a tall human. He's a giant. They are physically different from us."

Jun-seo stiffened. "You're not the first. Others know."

This complicated things. Rebecca sighed. "How many?"

"The neighbors who watched him grow up." Jun-seo unfolded his arms. "And a couple of trespassers who came across him sleeping."

"And they didn't report him?"

Jun-seo leaned toward her. "They were nice. They too said they knew about giants and were making sure they were taken care of." He pointed back at himself with his thumb. "I take good care of Seung-min."

Rebecca couldn't deny it. She could see no bruises on the

giant's nearly naked body. He appeared generally distressed at the idea of being separated from his brother. How would Rebecca like it if someone came and disrupted her safe world? Poor or not, Seung-min appeared content.

Rebecca stepped closer to Jun-seo, intruding on his personal space. "You listen to me. Others will come periodically and check on Seung-min. He had better not be harmed or misused in any way. Making him a statue for money borders on exploitation. I understand you're trying to make a living, but consider what you're doing to Seung-min."

Jun-seo stepped back. "Acting as a statue was Seung-min's idea. And I work enough to pay the bills. The demonstration gives us a little extra. It's the spice in a meal."

"Remember. The people I represent are going to watch you." Rebecca turned to Seung-min. "If you ever change your mind, write something on the roof. We'll see it, and we'll come."

Rebecca held out her hand, and the little black orb flew down into it. The device had captured images of Seung-min she would include in her report. "And I'm sorry I had to bother you."

She turned and started for the line of trees that surrounded the yard. Jun-seo marched next to her. She spoke without looking at him. "If Seung-min writes something on the roof and we see it removed, we'll assume you did it. We'll be back in force."

Jun-seo lifted his chin. "He's my brother. I would die for him."

The sincerity in his voice convinced Rebecca. "I'll see myself out."

In Seoul, Rebecca thanked the country for its lightning-fast internet. Absolutely no delays. In some countries, internet connectivity was sketchy.

Her fingers flew over the keyboard as she finished her

report with her final recommendation. Seung-min should stay in South Korea for the time being as an extraction would likely do more harm than good. Sure, someone could figure out he was a real giant, but if that came to pass, DEED could spread misinformation about giants roaming around South Korea. Imagine the sensational blog posts coming from a country that placed such a high value on its progressive culture. They wouldn't want to be portrayed as stuck in the imaginary past.

She attached images from her spy orb and saved the report in three places. Time to upload it. Now, she must navigate the DEED maze of bureaucracy to ensure their search engines could retrieve it. The top directory was corporeal. Then land based. The category was confusing when reporting on flying mythicals, but the directory meant lived on land, not walking on it. Next was the binary choice of dynamic or static. Could they pass as humans? Not in Seung-min's case. Another couple of directories, another two choices, and time to name the file. Use the full name, never an abbreviated name.

Rebecca carefully spelled out the giant's name and selected the finish option. Her laptop came back immediately. "File exists. Rename?"

What?

Rebecca reviewed the name. Yes, she had spelled it right. Again, she selected finish, and the same message reappeared. No, that would mean—

Gritting her teeth, Rebecca added a "-1" to the name and selected finish. This time her report saved as expected. She entered Seung-min's name into the search box. Two reports returned—hers and another one dated a year ago. She retrieved the older report.

Two field agents—a kitsune and an amabie—had visited Jun-seo's property and Seung-min at that time, and they had made the same recommendation Rebecca had just filed. The mythical should remain where he was.

Of course! Jun-seo had said a couple of people had discovered Seung-min was a giant. They were DEED agents.

Why had they sent Rebecca? Checking on a mythical was a perfect opportunity for a new field team or a social agent, not an enforcer like her. Someone with her qualifications, at this point in her career, received first contact missions.

Unless.

DEED wanted her out of the way.

JORGE CORTO

February - Seoul, South Korea

Rebecca whipped out her phone and secured the line three times per DEED's standards. She wanted to believe her assignment to South Korea was a bureaucratic mistake. Was DEED so disorganized that it was sending field agents on the same mission?

The automated voice responded, "Triple secure. Connecting to Ray Phist."

Ray's voice. "Rebecca? Do you know what time it is?"

No song or question. He had broken protocol. He knew exactly why she called. "You're the one who sent me to South Korea."

Ray sighed at the other end. "Did you find the target?"

Did she! Ordering her not to pursue Aurora was one thing, but she was still an enforcer agent with exquisite skills. Her typical missions were sabotage, rescue, or information gathering. "How dare you send me on a check-in assignment! Apparently, I wasn't the first agent assigned here. What's going on? You never told me this was a follow-up."

A significant pause came through from the other end. "Rebecca—"

Rebecca sucked in a breath, letting the air whistle through her teeth. "You lied to me, Ray. Why would you lie to me? Wait... you sent me on this bogus mission to get me far from Venezuela, didn't you? If I were closer and went rogue, you couldn't intercept me."

"The council thought Seung-min was the best option for your next mission," Ray replied.

"Don't give me that line." Rebecca gripped her cell so tightly she was afraid she would crush it. "And stop avoiding my questions. How could you do this to me?"

Ray snorted. Rebecca pictured him scraping one of his feet across the floor, a nervous tic he used when upset. "If we had sent you to Colombia, what would have you done? If you want me to be honest, then show me the same courtesy."

"We'll never know, will we?" Rebecca switched the phone to her other ear. "I can't believe the council sent me here."

"For the record, Janx voted against it."

"And how did you vote?"

"I voted for the option that would give us more time. To keep you safe." Ray must have opened his laptop because she heard keys clicking in the background. "We wanted to obtain intel on the abductee in Venezuela, and we did."

The high tide of her fury receded at this revelation. If Rebecca wanted him to share, she had to calm down. Time to switch to her professional voice. "Tell me."

"She's been abducted by Venezuelan thugs reporting to Jorge Corto," reported Ray. "Jorge's official title is high court judge, but he hasn't heard a case in years. Connected to terrorists on one side and the street gangs on the other, Corto hides out of the spotlight. He's filthy rich and holds clandestine parties that only the wealthy, powerful, or famous attend."

Rebecca paced the room. "What would someone like Corto want with little Aurora?"

A long pause. "He collects mythicals, Rebecca."

Rebecca reared back. "I'm sorry. Could you repeat that?"

"You heard me right. He collects our kind and holds them in pens to display to his clientele. He learned about mythicals from cryptids. And he's exposing us to the world for profit and who knows what else."

No. This was impossible. "He can't know about us. He'd post videos of us all over the internet. We'd doctor and discredit that sort of thing."

A powerful figure with government backing was DEED's nightmare scenario. While the mythicals had advanced technology, they weren't impervious to a global threat.

"Exposing us isn't his game." Ray took a heavy breath. "His objective is money and lots of it. No cameras, no phones, no recording devices of any sort are allowed inside. He tells the wealthy about us, and when they don't believe him, Corto offers them a look-see. They pay him on their way out, not in. He's going to put Aurora in a cage, but he won't kill her. Eliminating her would ruin his business."

Rebecca strode along the perimeter of the tiny hotel room. "For how long? When they tire of seeing her, tire of calling her a freak, then what?"

"I assure you we're treating Aurora's case with urgency."

Ray didn't deny the girl's life could be in danger. Rebecca took on her lecturing tone of voice. "By DEED's decrees I must go to Venezuela to bring Aurora back to Elysium."

"And if I had a guarantee you would succeed, Rebecca, I'd buy the tickets myself." Ray sniffed. "But tell me, are you going to take on the small army of thugs Jorge Corto has assembled in his compound? We have high-tech gear, but so does he. And we're blind as to what you'll find there."

Sacred Lightning! She wasn't prepared to take on a mission of this magnitude. "We have some experimental tech. The stealth suit."

"The stealth suit isn't foolproof and certainly won't transform with *your* body. I can't think of any of our equipment that will help one person storm a compound. Aurora's life isn't threatened. If he abuses her, the wealthy will see it. Harming her would be bad for business."

Bad for business? "Abuse? She's caged! She's just a little girl!"

"Rebecca, stop for a moment. Let's say, by some miracle, you figured out a way into the compound. And say, by a different miracle, you found Aurora and managed to free her. They would kill you *and* her while you tried to escape."

Ray was right. But he didn't have to talk to his field agent that way. "Oh, I'm sorry. I'm not on the council, so I'm an idiot and didn't think of that. If I had a plan to get in, do you think I'd leave it to chance on the way out?"

Ray didn't answer. The council poke had hurt him. He didn't deserve it, but she had to get his attention. Who was he to give her orders? Officially being on the council gave him the right to boss her around, but she was the better agent when they were in the field. And he knew it.

His response was surprising. "I know you don't think I deserved my promotion to the council."

"It should've been me." Rebecca couldn't stop her mouth from speaking the words. They had gone unsaid between the two of them for years.

Ugh. When I hang up, I'm going to regret hurting him.

Rebecca didn't hate Ray. He had been her partner, had her back multiple times, and knew her secrets. How could she forget jumping from the plane with him over Yemen, or the pursuit of the harpy through the back streets of Portugal, or the night they spent talking and shutting down that honky-tonk bar in the southeast United States?

Ray's voice became low. "Perhaps. Is that what you wanted?"

And the small regret she had hurting him vanished with his response. She mimicked a little girl's voice when she answered. "Oh, you're right, Ray. Having my life in danger every day is exactly what I want. Why would I want a council seat?" She resumed in her adult voice. "You don't know me at all."

"Obviously."

Rebecca put a hand to her forehead. She had to be the better person, or Ray would remove her entirely from the Aurora mission. "How about a truce?"

"I didn't want to be your handler, Rebecca. The council wanted it."

Rebecca paced faster in a circle. "They could've made it Janx."

"Janx? She's never been in the field. They thought you'd listen to me. I told them you wouldn't. They outvoted me."

Why? The current council was a mess. None of this made sense. The council knew about their history. Why make him her handler?

Rebecca's eyes narrowed. "How do you know Aurora is in no danger?"

"You'll have to trust me on that one."

"You have an agent there." Rebecca's jaw dropped. "How could you assign another agent when you know I want this mission!"

"Rebecca, they were following you after you picked up Aurora," replied Ray. "We have to assume Corto knows of your existence. I told you we had an agent in Venezuela. That agent is now undercover and inside the compound. So far, the news isn't as bad as I thought."

Taking a seat on the hotel bed, Rebecca didn't sink far into the firm mattress. "I'll follow orders for the time being, but I need your promise you'll get me to Venezuela as soon as you can. I mean I need you to propose it every day, Ray."

"I know Aurora is an innocent child, but you seem attached to her."

"She's an unfulfilled mission. A blotch on my record. I took her from her home and promised her a better life. Look what happened. If another agent rescues her, I'll never forgive myself. She'll never trust DEED." Rebecca grimaced. She couldn't end it there. "And by extension, me. *I* wouldn't trust me."

Ray didn't speak for a few seconds. "I'll propose that you go to Venezuela as soon as possible."

"Thank you."

"But for now, I have a new assignment. I'll send you the details."

"Is this a follow-up from some other agent's assignment?" she asked. "Another wiffle ball task?"

"After this talk, do you think I would do that again?"

"You better not. Over and out."

Rebecca hung up on him before he could respond. Yes, protocol was for the handler to finish the conversation—a show of respect. She had to let him know all was not forgiven. Having him be her handler! What an insult! The council knew what had happened in Edinburgh.

Rebecca wouldn't call Edinburgh a complete failure. She and Ray had captured the rogue barghest. Barghests weren't animals. They certainly weren't ghosts, as if ghosts existed! No, Ian the barghest was mentally unstable, and their job was to bring him in, even if they had to kill him. And Rebecca had killed him, while Ray took the brunt of the attack. If she had been alone, she would've subdued Ian. Ian would be alive, and Ray would have been...well, not as he was now. Yet, Ray received the promotion, leaving her behind as an enforcer agent.

And then came the Diana mess. Fortunately, Rebecca had convinced them she didn't need a partner soon after DEED reassigned Diana. She played to DEED's council members' guilty consciences and convinced them to bend the rules for her. Only face changers like Riju, a fellow agent, didn't have partners. Alone in the field? Unheard of. Yet, not for Rebecca Eidelweiss.

Rebecca reached into her bag. Her fingers clutched her passport and pulled it out. But when she examined it, she realized she had retrieved Aurora's by mistake. She opened the minuscule book, eyes falling on Aurora's smiling face.

I'll get this back to DEED. The agent onsite may use it to fly her out of Venezuela.

But why? DEED printed passports as a Pez dispenser pops out candy. This wasn't Aurora's real passport, not that she had a real one. Reclining on the bed, Rebecca held the object above her head. If another agent rescued Aurora, DEED would issue a new set of credentials. They'd replace her name, of course. Gone would be the fabricated name of Aurora Eidelweiss. Instead, she might be called Janet Esperanzo or Holly Graham.

Sludge on that. I should be the one to help her escape. I should bring her home as Aurora Eidelweiss. And DEED?

DEED couldn't stop her. Rebecca's reputation was on the line.

And so was a little girl's life.

DEED might call itself Lady Responsibility, but Aurora was this lady's, Rebecca's, responsibility. The entire reason she was an agent was to make people's lives better. She had screwed this one up, but she'd get Aurora's life back on track.

Rebecca set the passport on the bed and sat up. Leaning over, she retrieved her laptop. She spotted the message Ray had sent—her next assignment. Reluctantly, she opened the file and read the details.

When she was done reviewing her next mission in Greece, Rebecca eyed the passport. *Before I go on my next assignment, I'm off to Venezuela. Losing Aurora is on me, and I'm going to fix it.*

ROGUE AGENT

February - Somewhere in Venezuela

Rebecca shouldn't be here. DEED's instructions had been clear about her next assignment. Intercept and retrieve a mythical in Greece. Instead, she had re-assigned her tracker to a pre-programmed Roomba in her room, making her appear to be pacing. DEED thought she was there, but she wasn't. No, she was in the trunk of a car, bound and gagged, with a bag over her head. Rebecca didn't know when the car would stop. Though, when it did, the soldiers who had grabbed her would assassinate her.

She wanted to blame DEED. They hadn't allowed her to follow Aurora to Venezuela when the girl was first abducted. Rebecca could've caught up and taken them by surprise as they transported the child to Corto's compound. But DEED hadn't allowed her to go after Aurora. The giant assignment was the final straw. They were wasting her, benching her when she should have been in the game.

Now she was in the game, but not the one she wanted to play.

Where had everything gone wrong? The airport or the rental car agency? Were the soldiers who had eyed her at the airport the first to suspect? And the rental car agency had changed her vehicle at the last moment. "Upgraded," they had said. "All new technology." Including, to Rebecca's dismay, a remote kill switch to disable the engine. The rental agency neglected to tell her about the remote that could stall her car, or that the device was in someone else's possession.

The DEED agent had tried to escape the approaching military vehicle when her car had died. The next step was theirs. She had to play along, waiting for an opportune moment to slip away.

Rebecca was at a disadvantage. Yet, she had faced similar situations many times: the ambush in South Africa and the gulag in Russia. Rarely had she risked exposure. Of course, the best strategy was deception. Right now, make them think their plan had no chance of failure. Let them believe she was scared and couldn't think straight.

Of course, they had the advantage, but she still had weapons at her disposal. And the best weapon in her arsenal was her intelligence.

A muffled, chirring cry came from outside of the vehicle. There one instant; gone the next. Her mind raced to identify it —a nightjar. Nocturnal and loud, nightjars usually occupied the countryside. The lack of horns or other vehicles tipped Rebecca off that they had driven out of the neighborhood where they had caught her. They had to be close to their destination, and the location where they'd kill her.

The razor blade sewn into her cuff sliced through the bonds, and the ropes fell away from her wrists. No handcuffs? She was lucky. She removed her hood while assessing how much they knew about her. They likely thought she was an American spy. Rebecca fit that profile, but she had better not give them that impression. She didn't want to start an international incident.

Now that her hands were free, she rolled up her sleeve. On the inside of her bicep where frisking often didn't probe was a fake layer of skin. Slowly, she peeled it back and pinched the thin board. This would be difficult in the dark while hitting pothole after pothole, but that was why the instructions were in Braille. Her fingers brushed over the raised bumps, "reading" what she needed. When she found the inset switch, she dug her fingernail in and flipped it. The machine vibrated in her hands.

Immediately, the car slowed down. Voices of alarm came from the front, first the driver's then that of the woman who had frisked her. The woman had been referred to as *Violencia* and the man as *Chuleta de cordero*, or Lambchop. Rebecca didn't hear a name or nickname for the sneering man who had spoken the most. This fight would be three against one.

In the movies, heroes overcame those odds with their eyes closed. In life, defeat was one bullet away. Inadvertently, they hadn't left her defenseless. Odds were she'd die on this road —but not if she could help it.

Rebecca had abilities beyond her tech and training at her disposal. The world had claimed centaurs half-human and half-horse, but her physiology wasn't so simple. She wasn't fully human above her waistline, nor fully equine below it. Unlike human eyes, hers possessed a tapetum, or layer, in the back that allowed her to see in the dark much better than a human could. She traded night vision for a loss of certain colors. But her natural night vision might give her a slight advantage for what came next.

The car came to a halt, and doors opened. Rebecca grabbed the spare items in the trunk and shifted into position, only her rear and elbows touching the floor. She had found the instruments of her potential salvation in the trunk. Two items in her hands, and one balanced between the heels of her boots. She'd have to chance that the person opening the trunk was in front of her and wait to see how many had flashlights or phone lights. They'd have guns trained on her, but they'd have to avoid shooting the person directly in front of the trunk, so they couldn't fire immediately. At least, she hoped they wouldn't.

Footsteps sounded on the cement, moving around the car. Rebecca closed her eyes for a moment, readying herself. Even if she survived this, DEED would take her out of the field once they found out. If this worked, she'd have to play by their rules for a while.

Oh, Hades! I hate their rules.

A click. The trunk opened on its own. In a split-second, Rebecca spied two lights. Both of her hands clutched lug nuts she had found left in the netting against the side of the trunk. She aimed at the lights and threw the metallic nuts at once. The sting of the projectiles striking their hands forced the soldiers to drop their lights. As the trunk darkened, Rebecca kicked out, the heels of her boots leading.

The three soldiers hadn't expected her to be unbound so they hadn't prepared their guns. The sneering soldier exclaimed when her heel found his gut, and he took stuttering steps backward. A grunt from Lambchop behind the sneering soldier indicated she had pushed two out of her way. The sound of metal hitting the ground also told her she had succeeded in hurling the tire jack's lever out of the trunk. She'd pick that up when she exited.

Rebecca had ruled out transforming. Not enough room, and too much resulting body mass of a target. She'd have to remain in her less powerful but wiry human shape.

Violencia had flipped off the safety and unleashed two bullets into the trunk, but Rebecca had already escaped and crouched under the line of fire. She was on her stomach, crawling toward the woman soldier. Rebecca grabbed one boot and pulled, knocking Violencia off balance. The gun shot skyward.

The woman soldier landed on her back; Rebecca turned to her two male adversaries. She no longer had the element of surprise, so she remained crouched and on her feet.

Lambchop was readying a pistol while the sneering man, who had dropped his weapon, was throwing a punch. Rebecca shifted her head to the left, avoiding the fist, and kneed him hard below the belt. As he doubled over, she grabbed his shoulders to keep him somewhat upright. Using the sneering soldier as a shield from Lambchop, she ran with him in front of her. Lambchop discharged his weapon, and her "shield" screamed. Perfect! The man had shot his companion. The wounded abductor fell to the ground.

Lambchop stopped shooting. Out of the corner of her eye, Rebecca noticed Violencia climbing to her feet. Time for the jack's lever.

Scooping up the metal bar in her hand, the agent rose in front of the stunned male soldier, Lambchop, and hit him hard. Killing was never an objective and was against DEED's rules except in life-or-death circumstances. Yes, this warranted it. Lambchop fell to the ground without anything passing from his lips.

Two down.

Rebecca turned to the woman and leaped to the side as the Venezuelan's unsteady hand tried to aim. Poor thing. Violencia didn't know the extent of her disadvantage. Rebecca weaved as she approached her opponent, and the soldier realized at the last minute that this was going to be a fist fight. Violencia raised her free arm in front of her face as Rebecca readied her punch. The agent knocked her opponent's arm into her own head.

The woman successfully deflected the blow. Violencia then brought the gun around. Rebecca grabbed her wrist, keeping the weapon's barrel away from her. Rebecca's right hand held Violencia's left wrist at bay. Rebecca fisted her other hand.

No doubt, Violencia had been trained in hand-to-hand combat. Rebecca had too, so the advantage would come down to who landed the first incapacitating blow. Which one of them would execute the most unexpected move?

Violencia was lightning fast and aimed her knuckles at the bridge of Rebecca's nose. Rebecca lifted her forearm, deflecting the blow upward, which then knocked Rebecca on the top of the head. That jab hurt and rocked Rebecca's head backward, allowing the other woman a second chance. The soldier went to rabbit punch Rebecca in the neck. Again, Rebecca used her free hand to deflect the blow. This time, the punch only brushed against her skin.

The blow to the head had rattled Rebecca more than she wanted to admit. Her skull flared with pain, and she struggled to focus. She had to finish this soon. Violencia was a formidable enemy.

Humans automatically preferred to start a fight with their hands or feet. Centaurs, being half-horse with four equal appendages, instinctively chose the limb that would do the most damage. Even in human form, Rebecca had this advantage. While the woman soldier readied her free hand, Rebecca lifted her boot heel. As Violencia adjusted her aim to target Rebecca, Rebecca kicked at the other woman's knee with the heel of her boot. A crack of a kneecap, the sound of a lone firecracker, exploded through the night. Violencia roared with pain and fell.

Rebecca grabbed the gun before her opponent lost her balance. A quick shove threw the woman soldier off her feet and onto the ground. The DEED agent pointed the gun at her.

Cradling her knee and with blood trickling from her mouth, Violencia hissed a command in Spanish. "Do it."

Rebecca aimed at her captor's forehead, and Violencia gritted her teeth. But this was a distraction. With the heel of her boot, Rebecca connected with Violencia's head and the woman stilled.

Rebecca didn't take a moment to recover but wiped and threw the gun into the surrounding woods. The trio of Venezuelan soldiers had likely communicated with backup or had at least told them of their situation. She had to disappear. She scanned her surroundings.

Rebecca knew the woman, and potentially Lambchop, if he survived, would claim their abductee was lucky. They weren't wrong, but they didn't realize she was a centaur, a trained agent, or skilled with technical gadgets. Yet, she still was fortunate.

But Rebecca didn't rely on providence to achieve her missions. She preferred preparation and backup options. Standing in the middle of a hostile country, the agent reconsidered her plan. In the past, she and DEED had carefully studied the factors when planning an assignment. DEED also had her back when events went sideways.

For Chiron's sake, I don't know what I did or didn't do to tip off the people who abducted me. I don't know whether they're associated with Aurora or not.

Rebecca hadn't even made it to Corto's compound, the easy part of the plan. If she encountered five more criminals like these three along the way, she would be dead. And of no use to Aurora.

I must leave the country and regroup with DEED.

Though the decision made her want to retch, Rebecca sprinted into the surrounding woods to become a ghost. With her training, obtaining a new identity, changing her appearance, re-entering Caracas, and boarding a plane wouldn't be a problem. She recalled what she had promised back in the trunk of the car, hating every step she took away from Aurora.

Fine, DEED. We'll do it your way for a while. Back to the mission in Greece that Ray assigned to me.

She'd return for Jorge Corto, though. Of that, she was certain.

HACKERS AND ATTACKERS

February - Mumbai, India

After the disaster in Venezuela, Rebecca caught a break. For once, DEED's bureaucracy had worked in her favor. Ray had sent her to Greece, and Rebecca had gone to South America, instead. But, at the last minute, the council had reassigned her to Mumbai. Fortunately, some hapless employee hadn't informed everyone else. Rebecca went missing, but her contacts in Greece thought she was in Mumbai, and the DEED agent in Mumbai assumed she was in Greece. The assignment in Mumbai wasn't nearly as exciting as her usual missions, but at least it had relevance to Aurora's plight. And with that in mind, Rebecca was all for going to Mumbai.

Rebecca discovered this clerical error before she boarded the plane in Brazil and switched her plans to go to India. She cleverly chose a flight with a layover in Greece and reassigned her tracker to herself in the airport. Upon closer inspection, someone might report Rebecca had teleported from her hotel room to the airport. Fortunately, the bureaucracy of DEED wouldn't examine the matter carefully.

In her room at the West River Hotel, Rebecca reviewed the upcoming mission on her laptop when she heard a knock on the door. She strolled over to the eyehole and peeked out. Not that what she saw mattered. She had no idea what her contact would look like.

A young man, slight of frame with a thin mustache stood outside. He resembled most of the people in this populated city, except her visitor was dressed as a bellhop. She had met the man before but not in this form.

Rebecca whistled "Always," and he hummed a few notes of "Gham ki andheri raat mein." She cleared her throat. "Are you an employee of this establishment?"

"Room service at your disposal," he answered.

Rebecca opened the door, and the young man slipped inside. After she shut the door and turned around, she spied a different looking man in her room. Thicker hair, green eyes, no mustache, and hawk-shaped nose. She had met this form of the enforcer agent before. "Riju."

"Rebecca. Good to see you again."

"Same. Shame I don't see you more in Europe or the Americas where I'm based. With a rakshasa's abilities, blending in shouldn't be a problem."

Riju placed a hand over his heart. "India is my home away from Elysium. I would stay here if DEED would allow it."

"Mumbai is busier than New York, and that's saying something. I prefer our wide-open fields."

Riju snorted. "Of course, *you* would. Overpopulated, yes. But the lights of Diwali, the grandeur of the architecture, the simple pleasure of finding something handmade in a market, for all of that, India has my heart."

Rebecca moved to the laptop on top of her desk. "I've reviewed our mission twice, but DEED said you would inform me why we're meeting Arjun Jain. What did he hack into now?"

Riju strolled to the window and moved a sheer to peek out. "Nothing. He has information we need."

"Of what kind?"

Riju kept his eyes on the street below. "Someone stole a software algorithm from Nystar Technologies, and they

70

auctioned it off on the dark web. Arjun was there and knows who won the bid."

Rebecca shut her laptop. "Who?"

"A man named Jorge Corto. I've never heard of him."

Rebecca rose quickly to her feet. "I have. He's central to a mission I'm on."

Riju let the window covering drop, giving his attention to Rebecca. "The reason why you and I are paired this time. I know the country and have Arjun's confidence, and you need to know what was bought. Though Corto isn't my mission, I'm glad to assist."

The rakshasa didn't explain any further. Rebecca guessed he had asked DEED, as she had, why she needed a partner on this assignment. She rarely partnered with other enforcer agents. With Riju's abilities to shape change, he, too, was often alone on assignment.

This time, I'm glad DEED assigned us together. "When do we meet?"

Riju rubbed the back of his neck. "Arjun has recently grown fond of ancient weaponry. He wants to see a demonstration before he divulges what he knows."

"What kind of demonstration?"

Riju eyed her luggage. "Did you bring your bolas?"

Riju and Rebecca approached Arjun's meetup location, a gymnasium on the outskirts of the city. Rebecca retrieved her bolas while waiting for Riju to override the security system. They entered as quietly as phantoms with slippers on. The lights were off, and equipment lined the room beyond the foyer.

Riju jerked his thumb to a chamber in the back. "He said he would meet us in the volleyball court."

They strolled through an area stuffed with treadmills and bench presses. The low lighting cast the machines in shadows, so that they resembled robots from a mechanized world. The odor of sweat overpowered the air filtration and freshener systems. Rebecca was tempted to hold her nose. Even in human form, she had a heightened sense of smell.

Rebecca followed Riju through double doors into a massive volleyball court. The emergency lights illuminated just enough for her to see a polished floor and folded stands. The net was missing from its place in the center. But before she could observe anything else, Rebecca braced herself as a group of men rushed at them from dark corners of the court.

The four attackers immediately split into a group of three and one. The group of three cornered Riju, but the fourth raised his arm. Rebecca saw the balls at the end of a bola whip around with the whoop-whoop-whoop of a helicopter blade.

Rebecca snorted, grateful she had her weapon handy. She jumped to the left to avoid being ensnared by the cord of her opponent's bolas. For Chiron's sake, this wasn't the friendly meeting Riju had described. Where was Arjun? Who were these men?

Riju was weaving and retreating from his attackers. He had already knocked one of the three unconscious.

Rebecca twirled her bola as her opponent lifted his own weapon in the air. She had to time this right. She didn't practice much with sparring partners skilled with the rare weapon. Only a handful of other agents ever handled her instrument of choice.

The man aimed the balls at her head this time! Dust!

Bolas were for lassoing, not striking. This guy wanted her in a grave. She ducked, the orbs hitting the wall behind her with a crack.

Time to end this.

While avoiding the charge, Rebecca had maintained the helicopter motion of her bolas. She whipped the weapon at the attacking man's legs. He had sidestepped most of the bolas, but one found its target and encircled a leg. Yanking, she pulled with both hands. The man toppled to the ground.

Rebecca retrieved her stun gun as the man untangled

himself. She shot him just as he freed himself, and he jerked and went still.

She turned to examine Riju standing over the last of his opponents. Riju grinned at her. She could almost read his mind with that expression. Four? Come on, they were top agents. Whoever was behind this should have sent at least six.

Someone clapped from a dark corner, and the lights came on. Rebecca and Riju jumped into defensive positions.

"No need to attack me. I only wanted to see a demonstration."

Arjun Jain stepped out of the shadows, a grin spreading over his face. He was a heavyset man with the type of white hat one often sees in the tropics. A broad face with a cauliflower nose, Arjun's smile displayed one gold tooth in front.

Riju straightened. "What is all this, Arjun? You asked me to have my accomplice show you how to use bolas, and you attack us?"

Some of the men on the ground groaned as they shifted. Arjun said, "You were never in any harm. I paid them handsomely to keep you away and see *her*—" Arjun's eyes glittered as he focused on Rebecca—"in action. She didn't disappoint."

Riju had told Rebecca Arjun's hacking had made him rich and a bit eccentric. The technical genius knew nothing of DEED except that Riju worked for a secret organization. He had asked Riju if one of his members knew sword fighting or lassoing. Riju had thought of Rebecca.

Rebecca squared her shoulders. "I'm not something to entertain you."

Arjun bowed. "I apologize, but I wanted to see action with heart, not an education lesson. You've inspired me to learn to use bolas myself."

Rebecca eyed Riju. He cleared his throat. "The information, Arjun?"

The man put his hands together behind his back. "Oh, onto business, then. Yes, your Mr. Corto bid the highest to retrieve a proprietary Nystar software algorithm, stolen by a Romanian cartel."

"And what does it do?"

Arjun stepped forward, eyebrows raised. "It allows machines to think."

Arjun invited them to a small room where he detailed the intricacies of the technology. With each passing word, Rebecca grew more concerned.

THE CEMENT CITY

March - Athens, Greece

T he woman in the car ahead of Rebecca spotted her.

Baelz Bells! Rebecca floored the accelerator as the car in front of her rounded a corner. Fortunately, most of Athens' boulevards stretched straight a considerable distance, allowing her to race forward. And at one a.m., she didn't have to contend with traffic either.

Rebecca's electric-blue Ford Puma jumped to one-hundred-twenty kilometers an hour. She couldn't lose the Peugeot now that she had verified Dimitra Kotzidakis was a passenger. Bribing the landlady had paid off. Dimitra had indicated to the rent collector she was moving out that night—leaving the perfect opportunity to collar her.

Before turning, Rebecca decelerated to avoid losing control and sliding into a bakery. With the squeal of the Puma's tires, she prayed the Hellenic Police weren't nearby. Her Greek was terrible. If they suspected she was a foreign agent, they would throw her in jail. The authorities didn't know Dimitra was the dangerous one. Not her.

At any moment, Dimitra might wield her powers on the citizens of Athens. The police wouldn't believe Rebecca until it was too late, and DEED's attempt to hide Dimitra from the world would be ruined. Talk about a rough day at the office.

Why had Dimitra left Elysium? She had seemed happy at

home as a nurse. She'd surprised everyone when she fled.

The Puma shortened the distance between the two automobiles. They raced between the Grecian capital's concrete columns, reminding Rebecca of the trench on the Death Star. Yes, Athens' government tried to plant islands of trees here and there, but this city had a way of inducing claustrophobia.

In the back seat of Rebecca's target sedan, Dimitra's avocado-green babushka bobbed when her car rumbled over the uneven street. The single lane broadened to two. If Rebecca sped up and pulled alongside the Peugeot, she could nudge the other car to the side of the road.

However, Dimitra started to unwrap her scarf. Rebecca gasped and touched a tiny button on the frame of her glasses.

I have to go to camera mode.

Viewing through the camera limited Rebecca's reaction time, forcing her to slow down. The Peugeot sped away, and Rebecca slammed the palm of her hand against the steering wheel. What was Dimitra doing unwrapping her headscarf? Rebecca was driving! Did Dimitra want to kill her?

No. Rebecca couldn't turn to stone now. Her main goal in Greece was to pick up tech she needed in Venezuela. Catching Dimitra was a side mission.

Don't panic.

Turning to stone happens much slower than in the movies. More importantly, the effects were temporary. But the gorgon didn't know the gyrating vipers on her head couldn't affect Rebecca, thanks to her glasses. Her quarry would assume that as her body hardened, Rebecca would have to pull over and stop. And then freeze. Statuesque.

Wait, I can use this to my advantage.

Rebecca pretended as if Dimitra had succeeded and decelerated. She'd let the fugitive assume the agent had fallen victim to the petrifying gaze.

After the Peugeot completed a right-hand turn, Rebecca pulled out, maintaining a stealthier distance.

Five minutes later, Rebecca spotted the sedan down a

cross street. A harried Dimitra exited and climbed a set of stairs to a townhouse.

Gotcha!

Rebecca parked around the corner and proceeded to the house. A quick lockpick later and she stepped inside. And now for the "delivery" part of DEED. The "emigration" in DEED meant escorting home mythicals who were willing to go. A much easier task than a "delivery" job.

Rebecca crept from the vestibule to an adjoining room. The front room was small—with only padded chairs and a round table. Dimitra stood near a fireplace, her babushka replaced.

The woman of Medusa's lineage whirled around when Rebecca entered the room. "Eidelweiss." Snakes hidden under the headscarf hissed, prolonging the "s" in Rebecca's last name.

"Enough. You're coming with me."

Dimitra stepped away. "You don't understand. I didn't leave our home to cause trouble."

Rebecca unlatched the holster on her belt. "No one leaves Elysium, Dimitra. If they discover you're a gorgon, they'll learn about the rest of us. Your kind, centaurs, dryads, all of us. Do you know what they'd do?"

"It's not like that, Rebecca." Dimitra's face pinched.

"Our kind belongs together, not with humans." Rebecca set her hand on her dart gun in its holster. "We're free at home —not here. These people would think you're a freak. Now, don't make me drug you and—"

"Do we have a problem here?"

Rebecca turned around. A robed, middle-aged man with gray hair stood in the doorway of an adjacent room. She opened her mouth to warn him about Dimitra but swallowed her words. The man's glossy eyes stared in the gorgon's general direction.

Dimitra rushed past Rebecca and into the man's arms. Though off-balance, he received her gently. The fugitive returned her attention to Rebecca. "This is Tito. He accidentally washed up on the shores of Elysium. I nursed him, and…" She put her hands on his cheeks.

The man removed her babushka. "You don't need to hide yourself from me," he whispered.

He brushed his fingers down the skin of her snakes, and they swayed back and forth. Tender and caring, his hands moved to her face. Tears ran down his craggy cheeks. "I've missed you."

The scene wouldn't have swayed a younger Rebecca. But the look between them now affected her. She had seen her parents stare at each other with similar longing. She couldn't deny this feeling to someone else.

The man cleared his throat, his head swinging in Rebecca's direction. "Who is here?"

Rebecca's hand dropped from her dart gun. "I was just leaving."

With her lover's arms enfolding her, Dimitra mouthed, "Thank you." Rebecca nodded and let herself out. As she descended the steps, her phone chimed. The text read, "Get her?"

She typed, "Got away. Not in Athens any longer."

She returned to her Puma, examining the concrete buildings lining the streets. Who would've thought a heart beat so strong beneath this stony exterior?

INTERRAIL

March - Somewhere in Albania

T he train swayed from side to side, throwing Rebecca against the wall in the restroom of the deluxe cabin section. She dialed the number for a Polish company's head office, awaiting a response. The answering voice was high and perky. "Hi. I'm on my lunch break. May I call you back later?"

Rebecca jostled back and forth, speaking in Polish. "This is your employer—the other one. I assume the line isn't secure?"

"I don't know what you're talking about" was the curt reply.

Rebecca cupped her hand around the receiver end of the cell. "Your song is 'Three Blind Mice,' and you won't sing it. You're forced to cluck it. We both know why."

The person on the other end shuffled, signaling to Rebecca she was moving. "Now, I'm in a safe space. Who is this? And why are you contacting me this way instead of using normal protocol?"

"I'm not in a secure location, Celisa. And I'm calling you because we have a narrow window of time. The Protection is going to contact your boss, Aleksy, again. I need him to set up a meeting. Can you do that?"

Celisa whispered, "The Protection is one of Poland's most dangerous—"

Rebecca finished her sentence. "Organized crime families.

79

We know. Set up the meeting."

Someone rapped on Rebecca's door. "Hey, are you almost done in there?" a brusque voice called to her.

Oh, for Chiron's sake! Not now!

"Who is that?"

"Ignore that voice. Celisa, will you do as we ask?"

"How do I know I'm not being set up?"

Rebecca didn't blame Celisa for not trusting her. No secure line, no proof she was from DEED where they both worked. Celisa wasn't even an enforcer agent. By all rights, she should hang up on Rebecca.

Ray suckered me into this when I asked how I could help with the Aurora mission. Next time, I decline acting as a handler. "What's the harm in setting up the meeting? Aleksy can decline any offer they make. And if you become involved, they'll never show up again."

A fist banged against her door. "One minute!" shouted Rebecca, first accidentally in Polish, and then in English.

Ray had told Rebecca not to call from her cabin until she secured it, but the cleaning crew had delayed her admittance to her quarters. The bathroom seemed a better option.

"Yes, I'll do it." Celisa interrupted her thoughts. "But tonight, someone had better explain what is going on."

"Excellent. *Do widzenia.*"

Rebecca hung up and opened the door, slipping out into the hallway. She received a dirty look but ignored it and proceeded to her cabin.

The moisture collected outside Rebecca's Interrail window. She traced a finger down the rain streaks. The train sped by a two-story mosque with a round dome across the street from a cell tower. Though she had traveled through Albania multiple times, Rebecca'd never had an assignment here. She wished she'd had. Maybe she needed a vacation.

Another stamp on my passport.

She reached under her inside vest to a breast pocket. Not one, but two passports brushed against her fingertips. She should store away Aurora's. But not yet. Not until Aurora herself was in a safe place.

Someone knocked on her sleeper door, interrupting her thoughts. Wrinkling her brow, Rebecca whistled to her empty cabin six notes of Irving Berlin's "Always"—the sound carrying past her washbasin and folded-up bunk. In response, the person in the hallway hummed a series of musical notes. The tune lifted at the end. Sondheim.

Impossible. Yet...

Rebecca crossed her small accommodations in several steps and peered through the peephole. Elations! DEED had reassigned Sonya to Europe. Should she feel bad for the verdurian? Sonya was safely in Maine when the two women last parted, but of course, her own situation had changed.

Rebecca had to think of a question. She said the first thing that came to her mind. "Do you drink with your feet?"

"Ugh, Rebecca. That's gross. Of course not."

Wrong answer, right person. Rebecca quickly opened the door.

Sonya entered without a greeting. Wearing a wide-brimmed, velvet rose-colored hat with a veil, a white three-piece suit with red buttons, and a violet knee-high skirt, Rebecca's fellow agent looked poised to command a board office. Sonya's high heels crossed the room with a click-clacking sound while Rebecca closed the door.

"Do I drink with my feet? Really, Rebecca? Are you going to announce my species to the world next?"

Rebecca leaned against the wall, examining her friend. "I'm underdressed."

Sonya took off her hat. "The clothes draw attention away from my face."

A heavy application of makeup covered Sonya's green

complexion, yet a slight avocado hue lingered around the edges. The verdurian shook out her green curls, far shorter than the last time she and Rebecca had been together. She caught Rebecca's eye. "Dimitra got away."

Rebecca returned to her bench seat near the window. "You may read that misadventure in my report."

Sonya crossed her arms. "A rare failure for Eidelweiss?"

"A string of failures for Eidelweiss." Rebecca blew out a puff of air. "As you well know."

"Hong Kong. Peru. And who could forget Chiclayo?"

All successful missions. Bless Sonya for reminding her. But Rebecca remained emotionless. "How about Edinburgh? Lisbon? And now the mess in Maine?"

Sonya waggled her stilettos in the air. "Do you mind if I kick these off? They're so tight. And Lisbon was a draw."

Sonya was right about Lisbon. "Make yourself at home."

The plant woman reached down and pulled off one shoe. "I wish I could. Agents get deluxe cabins. Educators get sleepers."

Rebecca grimaced. "I'm sorry. We can switch."

With her shoes removed, Sonya stretched out her tendril toes at the end of her stumps for legs. Her roots all wiggled in satisfaction. "I wouldn't dare switch with you. You do the hard work. You deserve it."

Rebecca leaned forward. "I lost Dimitra. I checked on Seung-min, a bogus assignment. Someone had done the work before me. And poor Aurora." She turned and faced the window. "Out there, all alone."

"It's more my fault than yours. She was under my care when Corto's thugs took her."

Rebecca fisted her hand. "You know that's not true. You were her educator. I was to escort her after initiation. They even followed me to St. John, Sonya. And I thought they were after me when they were after her."

The verdurian paced over to the bench. "You did your best."

Rebecca's shoulders slumped. "Which wasn't good

enough."

Sonya took a seat on the window bench and removed her gloves, revealing her green hands with abnormally long fingers. She placed her tendrils on Rebecca's shoulder. "Stop blaming yourself, Rebecca. I know you. You will right this."

"DEED won't let me. They keep sending me these sludgy, rookie assignments."

Sonya's brows raised. "A gorgon?"

Rebecca avoided looking at Sonya. Had DEED reassigned the verdurian to Rebecca to remind her of her failure? If they had, they'd failed. Sonya was the exact tonic she needed right now.

Nonetheless, Rebecca resisted Sonya's logic. "I shouldn't be leaving Athens empty-handed."

"You're not leaving empty-handed. I read you received new tech. Tech that will help you in Venezuela."

True, Rebecca had been given a new toy. The creature—a cross between a pig and a man called a higpin—who had handed her the bolas said he had never installed smart chips in such an ancient weapon. She was excited to try them out.

Still... "Dimitra was the main objective. I should be handing her over to you."

Sonya snorted. "I'm an educator handoff, not an enforcer. Dimitra would turn me to stone in two seconds. You know it's true."

Rebecca didn't answer her, so Sonya continued. "I'm not you, Rebecca. You handle naiads, giants, gorgons."

"I can't be trusted with a simple faun."

"Aurora's situation is not strictly about her," said Sonya. "She's part of a larger mission DEED hasn't figured out yet."

"You trust DEED that much?"

Sonya placed her hand on the window. "Ever since a DEED agent found a young, homeless girl in a Liverpool slum and told her that her green skin wasn't a fatal disease."

The verdurian had never before shared her past with Rebecca. "You were a rescue?"

Sonya stood. "You're some hostess. You didn't offer me a drink on DEED's tab."

Laughing, Rebecca gestured to the small mini bar.

Sonya said, "Yes. A small community of verdurians lived outside of Liverpool with DEED's permission. We had to scatter after a fire broke out in our settlement, and I lost my family." Sonya opened the mini bar and retrieved two small bottles of white wine. "I begged on the streets, unaware of Elysium or the rest of you. And then, agents Banc and Freyarsha found me."

Rebecca interrupted. "You met Freyarsha?"

Sonya handed her a bottle and returned to her seat on the bench. "She's wonderful, isn't she? Yes, they found me and told me about DEED and our home. I was on our native soil within a week. I lost my family and many friends. I was horribly sad, but DEED helped. They couldn't cure what ailed me, but they gave me hope when I had none."

Rebecca and Sonya opened their bottles, and they clicked them together. Sonya raised hers. "Here's to you, Rebecca."

Before drinking, Rebecca said, "Here's to us."

"Salut."

Sonya placed her bottle at her root toes, and they snaked through the neck to the liquid inside. Rebecca had witnessed her friend drinking many times. She also knew that alcohol didn't affect Sonya's plant sensibilities.

"Does all this travel wear you down?" Sonya's roots pulsed while she spoke. "Don't you wish you could live in safety for a day in Elysium?"

"Don't talk with your mouth full." Rebecca winked.

"Ha. Ha. Haven't heard *that* one before."

Rebecca leaned back. "Elysium's a lonely place for me."

"Didn't you recently buy a house?" asked Sonya.

"I shouldn't have." Rebecca sipped her fruity wine. "Houses are for families. I'm just me."

Sonya shook her head. "Perhaps you should rescue the most important person of all."

Aurora? No, she couldn't mean her. Rebecca wrinkled her

forehead.

"Yourself, Rebecca. The time has come for you to rescue yourself."

"Too late for me." Rebecca grimaced. "Anyway, I'm now focused on Aurora."

"Of course you'll rescue her. And I'll help you in any way I can. We'll be the Banc and Freyarsha to her. But, for now, I'm involved in your next assignment, not your prior one."

Rebecca returned her gaze to Albanian landscape. They would be moving out of the country soon and into Montenegro. "My rail ticket ends in Venice. Are we flying out from there?"

Sonya shook her head, and her green curls bounced. "No. We have more rail adventures ahead of us. We're headed north."

Good. Rebecca enjoyed northern Europe and northeast Russia. Perhaps they'd end up in St. Petersburg, a place she had never seen. "And you know my next assignment?"

Sonya hummed more Sondheim as she drank. She nodded.

"Well, don't be so mysterious!"

"Why not?" Sonya's eyes brightened. "We're going after one of the most mysterious species of our kind."

CRONIES

March - Gjøvik, Norway

Spy paperback in front of her face, Rebecca observed the teenage girl seated across from her. She examined her target through a small viewscreen she held against the pages with her thumb. Rebecca had placed the camera on her lap when she took her seat in the bustling Norwegian station. The camera was disguised as one of the googly eyes on a plush unicorn toy. The device captured the crystal-clear image of the girl in real time.

After departing from the train the prior night, Rebecca had checked into a four-star hotel in Stockholm. A note had been delivered with her morning breakfast. "Gjøvik bus station. Two hours." Fortunately, the message hadn't dictated that she had to eat this particular note.

When she had arrived at the bus station, Rebecca spied a green-haired adversary checking her phone across the street. Ms. Colorful Hair was a bounty hunter of some renown. Pulling down her hat, the DEED agent slipped inside the station, hoping she hadn't been noticed.

As was customary, Rebecca proceeded straight to the second stall of the ladies' restroom to find her mission. Everything she needed to know had been scribbled on the inside of the cardboard of the toilet paper roll.

The world thinks that the espionage game is all high-tech. If they only knew how it really works.

The description of the girl had helped, but the pimple medicine gave her away. At least three tiny, pink dots littered the blonde girl's face. Rebecca had picked her out and taken a seat across from her. She hoped her subject's bus wouldn't arrive soon.

With her target identified, Rebecca made her move. She took a deep breath and without lowering the book, she cleared her mind and sent the girl across from her a message. *I know you can hear me, Sigrid.*

The teenager jolted, flaring her nostrils. Her head swiveled back and forth.

I'm sitting directly in front of you, reading a book.

Eyeing Rebecca across the aisle, Sigrid reached for her bag.

People are here who want to take you someplace far worse than the home you're fleeing from. Rebecca's Norwegian was rusty, and she hoped she had used the proper term for "fleeing." She had either warned Sigrid about her current situation or said her safety smelled like a banana. Hopefully, she'd sent her message correctly.

Sigrid's hand clutched the bag, knuckles turning white.

Rebecca switched to English. *They'll kidnap you before you board the bus to Oslo. Before you'll be able to see your mother.*

Sigrid's jaw dropped. *How do you know I'm going to see my mother?*

Out of the corner of her eye, Rebecca spied the lime-green-haired woman from outside, chomping bubble gum. She marched up and down the rows of waiting bus travelers. Most people might have thought the woman was nineteen or twenty, but Rebecca wasn't fooled. Joelle was nearing thirty. This woman was an early cog in the human trafficking machine.

You don't have time, Sigrid. They are about to make their move.

The teenage Sigrid stood. *I'll take my chances.*

Your mother is not in Oslo. I know where she is. Now, go to the restroom, and I'll meet you there in two minutes!

Through her viewscreen, Sigrid rocked back and forth on her heels. The DEED agent hadn't wanted to reveal so much so rapidly to Sigrid. However, if Joelle wandered closer, the bounty hunter would recognize her target. Sigrid had to move. If she went left, Sigrid would be heading for the bus queue. The restrooms were to the right.

Please, go right.

Wavering side to side, the young lady turned and strode toward the restrooms.

Mentally, Rebecca sighed and lowered her book. Touching the putty nose she had masked herself in before entering the station, she stored the book in her backpack while keeping Sigrid in sight. The bathroom was interior to the station with no windows and one exit.

Crossing the floor, Rebecca bit her lip when Joelle's attention fell on her. Did her nemesis see through her disguise? The agent hadn't had time to do an elaborate design on her face, and her features weren't much changed. She and Joelle had last confronted each other in Switzerland, and Rebecca winced at the memory of the two of them circling each other. The battle had taken place on the roof of a ski resort. Only a snowdrift had saved Rebecca from being seriously injured.

Yet, Joelle continued her examination of the passengers as if she hadn't recognized the DEED agent. Protocol stated that Rebecca had to take a circuitous path to the restroom, but if she did, she wouldn't make it there in two minutes. Sigrid might leave if she was late. Rebecca had to risk going directly to her destination.

Shoulders back, Rebecca strolled to the bathroom at a steady pace. She reached into her bag for a sign in Norwegian and produced it as she approached the door. She slapped the official sign onto the door, '*Toalett stengt* / Restroom closed,' and pushed her way inside.

The agent moved the trash receptacle inside to bar the door. It wouldn't prevent entry, but if anyone pushed the door, she'd hear the can scraping across the tile. She stepped around a wall that blocked the view of the interior of the cinderblock room which was made up of standard sinks, dryers, stalls, and mirrors. There, at the far end, stood Sigrid.

The girl had her arms crossed. She glared at Rebecca and spoke with a Bergen accent. "Who are you? And how do you know my mother?"

Rebecca fumbled around in her backpack. "I'm Rebecca, and I was part of her rescue team."

"Rescue?"

The DEED agent produced scissors from a hidden compartment. "I must cut your hair for you to get away. Do you understand?"

"I want to know—"

"Sigrid Magdal, do you understand? I will tell you everything while I cut your hair."

Sigrid pouted and nodded.

Rebecca moved to the girl's side and gently took her hair in hand. She had done this dozens of times, and the same thought accompanied the action every time. *If I ever lost my job as a spy, I'd make a decent hairstylist.*

The agent worked her magic with the scissors as she talked. "Sigrid, you have recently discovered your telepathy after puberty, but you didn't tell anyone because of your mother. She heard voices, too, and she went away to Oslo for treatment. Your mother discussed her condition with you before she left. What she didn't know was that you inherited her gifts."

"They aren't gifts," spat Sigrid. "I have a psychological condition where I hear voices. I'm bipolar."

Snip. A large tress fell to the floor. "Those are your father's words. No, you and I communicated through your telepathy. I heard you. I'm sure you've known for a while you can project your voices into other people's minds. This ability scares you."

Rebecca paused and gave Sigrid her most encouraging motherly expression. *But you don't need to be frightened. You're normal, and there are others like you.*

Sigrid started, and Rebecca almost dropped her scissors.

The teen's eyes bored into the agent's. *I'm not alone?*

The scissors flashed, and the girl's hair drifted down. Rebecca cut as straight a line as she could. *No. Sigrid, you're what's known as a crone, and others like you live all around the world.*

"A crone!" screeched Sigrid. "Like those old hags?"

Rebecca never stopped cutting. *Forget what the world tells you about crones. Crones are people, usually women, with extraordinary mental abilities. Telepathy, telekinesis, thoughtography, clairvoyance. The list goes on. In the past, people with these powers were often thought of as witches and given the names enchantresses, weird sisters, or hags. But some used the correct name—crone. Unfortunately, culture spun the word from its original meaning to indicate an old, ugly woman.*

So, crones aren't evil? Sigrid fiddled with a ring on her pinky finger. *I thought they threw curses on people.*

Crones aren't inherently evil. Crones choose who they want to be, and I'm delighted to say that most choose to be kind and thoughtful people. They have all sorts of careers. With their talents, they are an important part of our society.

Sigrid gasped. Rebecca's revelation was a lot to take in. Sigrid wasn't bipolar but gifted. She could have a future where she was respected, even admired. Rebecca would've eased into this conversation—spread it across an hour. But they didn't have time.

Your mother is a crone, Rebecca continued, eyeing Sigrid's bob cut. *I'm sorry to admit you've been under observation for a while to see if you exhibited any abilities. You are good at hiding it.*

Where is my mother? Will you take me to her?

Of course. Eventually.

Sigrid frowned and stepped away from Rebecca. "What do you mean by 'eventually'?"

The agent was done with her work and began gathering the hair left on the sticky floor. "Help me pick this up."

Rebecca couldn't talk about the subject openly. *You must understand who you are, what you're capable of, and what place you have in the world. First, I must take you to a safe house. There, they'll answer your questions, and you'll be allowed to video chat with your mom. She'll explain the process. And then, only when it's safe, we'll take you to her.*

Sigrid didn't help Rebecca, again folding her arms. *Why am I in danger?*

Rebecca wanted to answer, "Are you kidding?" but refrained. *You have so much power, yet you aren't an adult. Think of the ruthless people who would want to exploit you for their gain. Countries could use you to learn secrets; criminals, to acquire wealth. Sigrid, mentally you're strong, but you haven't developed your telekinesis or pyrokinesis, or any power that could help safeguard you in a dangerous situation. People like you will help you nurture your skills at the safe house.*

"Oh!" Realization crept into the Norwegian's eyes. *I can do telekinesis?*

The agent had an armful of Sigrid's hair and rushed to a stall. *Most crones can, among other talents.* Rebecca released the hair into a toilet and flushed. *Please, don't clog.*

"We need to hurry." The hair swirled around the receptacle. "Bounty hunters will sell you to a man who wants to put you in a cage. Others like you are trapped there. People I'm trying to help."

Rebecca left the stall and froze. Standing behind Sigrid was Joelle, the bounty hunter's hand over the teen's mouth, and a stiletto pointed at her neck. "Hey, Rebecca. Did you think a garbage can would be an effective alarm?"

Joelle's tone of familiarity, as if they were old friends meeting for coffee, wasn't lost on Rebecca. The DEED agent wasn't going to lose Sigrid after working so hard to travel here and contact her. Baelz Bells, Sigrid would end up in Venezuela over her dead body. Yet, Rebecca wouldn't underestimate the woman who held the young Norwegian's life in her hands.

Rebecca remained silent. Joelle's eyes were focused on her. Fortunately, the bounty hunter didn't know Rebecca was a centaur. Rebecca could transform and upset everything—a possibility. And they were in a restroom. The location provided many options.

"Unlike in St. John," said Joelle. "You're not going to escape."

Ah! Joelle had been the driver in the gray sedan in New Brunswick. "Joelle, don't do this."

"I'm going to leave now." Joelle tugged Sigrid backward a step. "I suggest you don't follow. Not if you want to keep this young girl alive."

Joelle wouldn't kill her. Rebecca had studied the woman enough to know the bounty hunter wasn't an assassin. The knife was to keep Rebecca at bay. Joelle wasn't tempted strictly by money; Rebecca wouldn't even offer it. Her opponent was motivated by success, the thrill of hunting and finding runaways. But that wouldn't stop the woman from hurting Sigrid, possibly incapacitating her.

And Joelle didn't know anything about crones.

Sigrid! Focus on the woman behind you and send her this message. 'You're a failure, and Rebecca knows it.'

The bounty hunter and her hostage were nearly around the privacy wall of the restroom. Sigrid started to nod, but Joelle applied slight pressure to the long-bladed knife. "Don't move, girl. When we step out of here, the knife goes into your back hidden by my body. No time for heroics if you know—"

Sigrid must have transferred the message because Joelle's mouth curled down. Overconfident Joelle forming a negative thought about herself? The bounty hunter must have believed Sigrid's messages were from her subconscious mind.

Rebecca threw another thought Sigrid's way. *Now send her this. 'Rebecca must have backup. A trained assassin will kill you before you leave this station.'*

They were at the door, out of Rebecca's sight, when Joelle cursed.

Last thought, Sigrid. 'Give the girl back to Rebecca and meet them at the first bus stop. You grab Sigrid on the platform, away from Rebecca's allies.'

The door creaked open and then stopped. Instead, it shushed closed, and Joelle and Sigrid appeared again around the partition. Stiletto poised at Sigrid's neck, Joelle glared at Rebecca. "How many agents do you have out there?"

"None." Rebecca's voice was steady as a calm lake.

Joelle glanced over her shoulder. "Her bounty is too large for you to be the only one."

After a moment of indecision, Rebecca readied herself. If her deception worked, she had to anticipate her adversary's next move. Everything depended on it.

She had to be careful. While they were matched in height, Joelle had at least thirty pounds on her and was trained in several fighting techniques and martial arts. Rebecca had been on the receiving end of her pugilistic skills at the ski lodge.

Then, Joelle fell into her trap. "I know when I'm beaten."

Joelle was fibbing, of course. The bounty hunter was attempting to convince the DEED agent to lower her defenses. Removing the stiletto, Joelle shoved the teenager forward for Rebecca to catch. But Rebecca wasn't there.

Rebecca had jumped on top of a sink at the same moment. While Sigrid was trying to keep her balance and losing, the DEED agent was leaping around her like a cat on a fire escape. Joelle hadn't expected the sudden move. She raised the knife in defense, the blade horizontal. Rebecca launched forward, pushing the knife back against Joelle's chest.

Without wasting a second, Rebecca rabbit punched Joelle between the eyes. Pain flared in her knuckles at the sound of a twig snapping. Rebecca had broken her opponent's nose. The agent pushed her right upper forearm at Joelle's head. The one-two combination produced the effect she had hoped for. Joelle's skull rebounded against the wall, and her eyes rolled up.

Rebecca fell in a heap onto the unconscious woman. Rapidly, she untangled herself from the bounty hunter and kicked away the stiletto. She backed away, crouched in case her adversary was playing possum. No, Joelle was out like a light, and Rebecca thanked her years of training. With someone like

Joelle, a prolonged fight almost certainly meant a defeat.

Sigrid was on her hands and knees, staring back at the results of the fracas. Rebecca quickly went to her and took her hands. "We're leaving now."

Sigrid pulled away. Her eyes were wide with horror at what Rebecca had done, and the agent could read the question in her eyes. Again, using her matronly tone, Rebecca said, "Which one of us pulled a knife on you? I'm a friend, Sigrid. Please, we must leave now. She'll be up at any minute."

The girl glanced at Joelle and then squeezed Rebecca's hand. Rebecca and Sigrid stepped over Joelle and hurried out of the restroom.

THE GLOVE

March - Gothenburg, Sweden

After chatting about her future, Sigrid snapped photos of the unusual architecture of Gothenburg. Rebecca envied her, having only traveled to the city twice before and never having stayed here as much as a few hours. Would DEED allow her to remain here tonight? Of course not. Rebecca had to board the Interrail bound east.

Their Volvo purred along the busy streets as the agent wound through traffic. Though instructed to take the girl straight to Sonya, Rebecca made a few detours for Sigrid's benefit. The red splendor of The Cog, the spherical wonder of the Universeum, and the impressive heights of Karlatornet contrasted with the older Götaplatsen's square's Poseidon and the charm of Tomtehuset's al fresco murals. Some of the cathedrals and landmarks were on Rebecca's bucket list as well, and the young girl didn't seem anxious to arrive at her destination. Rebecca had informed her she would be secluded for several weeks of instruction.

Rebecca had lived among crones all her life, but driving with Sigrid in the car from Norway to Sweden had caught her off-balance. Sigrid had used her gift to communicate, now that she thought of telepathy as a talent. The two of them hadn't spoken out loud; instead, Sigrid had used her mind to fire off questions. Rebecca had done her best to answer them. Sigrid would be a perfect field agent if DEED ever came to use crones for her line of work. How much more secure could a line of communication be?

When Rebecca found parking near the safe house, she powered down the Volvo and thought to Sigrid that they should speak in public. *Mentally talking to each other might look odd to the people around us, and we want to blend in.*

A crease appeared at the bridge of Sigrid's nose, but she opened the car door. "Understood."

Rebecca and Sigrid strolled down a street beside a long building of three-story, cement houses. Rebecca mentioned that these apartments had been constructed more than a hundred-twenty-five years ago. They stood out because of their faint red coloring on the outside and cement base.

Doors led inside to the ground floor. When Rebecca came to Sonya's unit, she punched in the combination code to enter and opened the door for the girl.

The ground floor was all stone with a narrow staircase leading to the higher two stories. The DEED agent led Sigrid up the stairs to the top level where the floors were wood and watercolor paintings of still-life flowers hung on the walls. Laying a hand on Sigrid's shoulder, Rebecca directed the teen down a hallway to a pine-wood door and knocked.

A count to ten to allowed Sonya time to approach the door while Rebecca hummed a few bars of "Always." She placed her hand on her taser until Sonya returned her tune. Sonya called through the door. "Are you here to sell me a horse?"

Sonya must have been getting back at her for her drinking-with-her-feet question. Sigrid put her hand over her mouth, stifling laughter.

"Yes," lied Rebecca in Swedish. She rolled her eyes at the teenager.

The door swung open to a smiling Sonya. With her makeup applied, the verdurian blended in nicely with the residents of this country. A wig of curly blonde hair and just a faint blush on her cheeks, artistically done, completed the disguise. "Please, come in."

The doorway opened into a living area with another door to a kitchen. Further back was a sitting area near the windows that looked out over a field. Two more closed doors were on the same wall, likely bedrooms.

Rebecca, with one eye up and down the hallway, ushered in Sigrid first. After entering herself, Rebecca put up a hand and caught Sigrid's eye. *This is Sonya who we spoke about in the car. I have to check out the apartment. You may talk to her while I look around.*

Again, Rebecca noted how odd it was having two people standing in front of each other without speaking was. Sonya had interacted with as many crones as Rebecca had, so the wordless communication wasn't anything new to her. Out of the corner of her eye, Rebecca watched as Sonya held her hand out, palm upward, and Sigrid shook it.

Protocol mandated that field agents entering a new area search for listening devices. Rebecca knew that Sonya had already canvassed her temporary home, but DEED required the procedure be done by all enforcer agents. Lowering shades and ensuring the access to the attic was locked, Rebecca searched the domicile. She came away five minutes later satisfied no one was listening. Then, she affixed a magnetic interrupter to the wall to scramble long-range listening devices.

When Rebecca rejoined the verdurian and crone, she placed a hand on Sigrid's arm. "We need to speak out loud now with the three of us."

Turning to Rebecca, Sigrid nearly shook with excitement. "I want to see it."

Rebecca had told her all about her own true nature. Sigrid was skeptical, but the field agent was insistent that she was a centaur.

"Maybe another time. Sonya has a lot to do, and I dropped you off late."

Sonya had a handkerchief in her hand, wiping away her makeup. "Oh, go ahead, Rebecca. I confirmed what you are. Let the girl see it."

"Oh, all right."

The Velcro on Rebecca's pants was worn down, and she didn't want to send for new trousers. She efficiently removed her lower clothing and then allowed her body to transform into her true shape. Sigrid swore telepathically, and Rebecca suppressed a laugh.

Sigrid walked around Rebecca at arm's length distance as if the DEED agent was a sculpture. "How do you hide this? Don't people see you through windows?"

"I'm rarely in this form in the outside world."

Sigrid furrowed her brow. "What do you mean 'the outside world?'"

Sonya locked eyes with Rebecca. Though they couldn't speak telepathically, the two held an unspoken conversation using only their facial expressions. Sonya raised her left eyebrow, asking wordlessly if Rebecca had revealed to her anything about their culture. Rebecca's head shake confirmed she hadn't.

Sonya stepped forward. "Our kind's native land is somewhere hidden away from the world."

"Your mother is located there," added Rebecca while transforming back into her human form.

Sigrid's attention bounced between Sonya and Rebecca. "So, you'll take me to see her, and then the three of us will return home?"

Sonya laid a hand on Sigrid's shoulder. "No, you're going to live with her."

Sigrid shook off Sonya's gesture. "What? No, I'm not!"

Rebecca pulled up her pants. "Elysium is where your mother lives. You'll be residing with her now."

"But my father? What about him?"

Rebecca released a shaky breath. "Your father was about to commit your mother to an institution before I rescued her. He visits her online and in person twice a year. We have an agreement with the institution where we fly your mother when

98

the meeting is in person. The same will be true for you."

Sigrid took a step backward. "I have to keep this from my dad?"

This part of the job was truly horrible, but DEED was adamant. The less the outside world knew about them, the better. Most mythicals were mistreated like Aurora, or abandoned like Sonya, and they welcomed the news they had a home where others of their species would accept them as they were. But a few, like Sigrid, had closer ties to the human world. The idea that they'd have to give up everything and everyone in their past could be heartbreaking.

"But I don't look like you." Sigrid nodded to the two agents. "I can live in society with my dad and my friends."

Sonya removed her gloves, revealing her chlorophyll-colored, boneless fingers. Eventually, the educator would explain how crones age rapidly, and how her mother had disguised it for years. Most crones used makeup, but on close examination, one could tell.

Instead, Rebecca had agreed to lower the bomb. "Think of Hedda and her daughters."

Sigrid's father had started seeing another woman, Hedda. The agents watching the situation had reported that Sigrid's father and Hedda had been shopping in jewelry stores.

Sigrid froze at the woman's name.

Sonya dabbed a tear from her eye. "Sigrid, even if you and your mother weren't crones, she and your father would have divorced. You'd be in your mother's custody."

Sigrid's eye twitched. "You don't know that. He might be seeing Hedda because he thinks my mom is in an institution."

"Your father has known Hedda longer than he's let on, Sigrid." Rebecca held up her hand to stem Sigrid's protest. "We're not saying he was seeing her when your mother was living with you. We're suggesting your mother might have divorced your father, and you'd be living with her now. This is the same outcome."

Lips trembling, Sigrid said, "My father loves me."

"He does," affirmed Rebecca. "With the information DEED has gathered, he didn't want to put you in the institution. This wasn't about getting you out of the way. He has tried many avenues. But he now believes this was the best way to protect you. Your mother thinks differently, and we're on her side."

Sonya set her hand gently on the girl's right shoulder. "We don't often allow mythicals to return to the rest of the world after they go to Elysium. This deal, allowing you to see your father twice a year, is rare."

Tears appeared in Sigrid's eyes. Sonya opened her arms. "May I?"

Sigrid nodded, and Sonya pulled her in for a hug. Rebecca observed the scene, thankful for Sonya. Rebecca wasn't comfortable embracing people she hardly knew, unlike her verdurian friend. But, for a moment, she pictured herself hugging Aurora. She vowed to embrace the faun after she rescued her.

Sigrid's voice was muffled against Sonya's sweater. "My friends? What about them?"

Sonya sighed.

Sigrid buried her face deeper. "I'll never get to see them, will I?"

The crone didn't require an answer because Sonya and Rebecca had said enough. For a moment, Sigrid cried in front of the two agents. Rebecca remained still, hating herself for extracting her. But what choice did she have? If only DEED would loosen some of the rules. If the council could see this poor girl weeping at her loss, maybe they would have the heart to permit her to see her friends from time to time.

Sigrid stepped back and wiped her face. "I want to be alone for a few minutes. Please."

Rebecca had Sigrid's phone—standard protocol—so the girl couldn't contact her friends. Escape? Possibly, but Rebecca would keep an eye on her. The enforcer agent debated what to do, but Sonya answered for her. "Of course. I prepared a bedroom for you."

Sonya pointed to a door off the seating area, and Sigrid nodded. She turned and hurried through the doorway, shutting the door after her.

Rebecca rubbed her face. "I hate this part."

Staring at the closed door, Sonya responded, "She'll recover. I've read her profile. She wants to see her mother more than anything, so she won't try something drastic at this point. She's thinking now how she can convince her mother to escape with her, but Zara will talk her out of it."

Sonya's mother, Zara, had been elated to escape the institution. Yet, like Sigrid herself, her mother was also committed to her family. "Yes, I suppose she'll make it work."

Sonya frowned. "I guess I won't be seeing you for a while. They want me to keep Sigrid here until DEED establishes all details of her stay at the mental institution. I hear you're headed for the United States."

Rebecca took out her phone and checked. "No, I declined that request."

"You don't want to see Lester?"

"The so-called Lester mission is anything but. It's a chore."

Sonya's eyes glazed over. "'Chore' is not the word I would use for Lester. Remember how he painted himself gray at DEED's summer party and stood still. Poor Mei thought she had accidentally turned him to stone."

Rebecca stashed away her phone. "As I said, 'chore.'"

Sonya walked over to a couch and her purse. "While we have a few minutes, I have some things for you. More information on the operation in Venezuela, provided to me by a local field agent."

Sonya reached into her purse and retrieved two items. First, the verdurian handed her a small, circular disc about the size of a matchbox. The removable drive could only be accessed by a DEED laptop. Rebecca accepted the disc in the palm of her hand.

"And I have this, too."

Sonya grasped a plastic evidence bag, pinched between

her fingers. Inside the bag was a leather driving glove.

Puzzled, Rebecca accepted Sonya's offer. "What should I do with this?"

Sonya held out her hand. "Give it back to me for one thing, but the glove is proof from Ray that things aren't standing still in Venezuela."

Rebecca shrugged, dropping the bag in Sonya's thin fingers. "And that means?"

"The glove belongs to Jorge Corto. Let's say someone replaced his gloves with duplicates so he didn't know they were missing. On the inside—"

"Are fingerprints for a scanner." Rebecca snapped her fingers. "Ray sent me blueprints of Corto's compound from the same source. We have boots on the floor in the compound itself?"

Sonya placed the glove back in her purse. "Ray had this sent to you after lifting the fingerprints. He wanted to show you DEED hasn't forgotten Aurora. And he told me to say the tech agents have constructed a glove with Corto's fingerprints on the outside."

Rebecca put a hand on her hip. "You didn't answer my question. We have an enforcer agent there?"

"I don't know the answer." Sonya tucked her purse away in a locked cabinet. "But I would assume so."

Rebecca folded her arms. "Why not me?"

Sonya flashed a look at Rebecca. Okay, so Rebecca had gone off the radar and hadn't been successful. DEED didn't know about it, however. No matter. She would get to Venezuela sooner rather than later. She would carry the gloves with Corto's fingerprints to bypass security and bring Aurora home at last.

SIRIN

March - Warsaw, Poland

After an entire day on the Interrail, Rebecca entered DEED's rented apartment, dropped her bags, and flung herself on the bed. Why couldn't she have stayed in Sweden? But no. Drop off Sigrid and then hop on the train again the next day. She wondered if DEED was full of busybodies making schedules instead of doing actual work. Agents in Mission Impossible never lived like this!

Using only her feet, Rebecca loosened her pumps so that they hung from her toes. She flung each of them off the bed, one at a time, and heard them land in a clump against the rug. The one-bedroom apartment was spacious for downtown Warsaw with colorful, abstract art hanging on the walls. Still, it lacked a personal touch. "Personal touches" weren't in the cards for people in her profession, only traveling, working, and dying.

Great mood we're in today!

Rebecca had beat out twenty of her classmates in the academy to become an enforcer agent. The rest applied for other jobs—handlers, researchers, educators, technicians—most envying her role. Even regular field agents thought highly of the thrilling adventures enforcers had. What few of them knew was that much of her time was spent hurrying to board trains, eating fast food, or reading reports until her eyes hurt. This was the true life of the enforcer agent. Though, to Rebecca, her missions were better than sitting at home, solitary and bored.

The kitchen was attached to the living room and viewable over a half wall, but Rebecca declined to cook that night. Normally, she'd find a local recipe to experience a little of what the country had to offer. Her "pork" pies in Nova Scotia were a keeper, and dates were a clever substitute for pork. Little Aurora had lived her life in Nova Scotia. Her father had been so cruel to her. Was she ever allowed to eat the local specialty?

Aurora.

Rebecca needed a plan. Most of her downtime had been spent reviewing the documents on the disc she had received from Sonya. Even if Rebecca could turn invisible, which none of her kind could, Corto's compound remained a fortress. Optical scans, ever-changing keypad entries, and electronic eyes were only a few of its defenses. The judge was paranoid. And why wouldn't he be? He had a treasure trove in the cell area.

Rebecca's head swam. She engaged in a mind game she often played when attempting to fall asleep. The exercise was her way to dreamland. She thought of trivial "what if" scenarios, often something outrageous, to keep from focusing on her current problems. A typical one was to imagine what her life would've been if she were another species. At times, she'd even imagine herself as human.

As a human, she'd have even more trouble breaching the compound. But not if she was a crone. A crone might be limited physically, but not a gorgon. She could stop anyone approaching her, yet this wouldn't get her past the keypads.

Rebecca's eyes flitted behind her eyelashes, approaching sleep. The tendrils of slumber massaged their feather-touch fingers around her face just before her phone rang. She sat up and clenched the bedsheets as her eyes focused on a nondescript spot on the wall.

The phone display scrolled Ray Phist across the viewscreen. She answered and went through protocol to triple-secure the line. When they were safe to talk, Rebecca said, "No mints on the pillows, Ray. You know how I like my mints."

Ray snorted at the other end of the line. "Mint sends you into a sneezing fit. I have an assignment for you."

Rebecca rubbed her neck. "How many kittens do I have to rescue from a tree this time?"

"Just one," answered Ray. "But she's no kitten. And you'll wish she was up a tree."

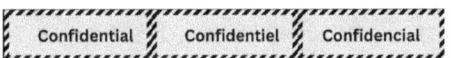

A centaur in a wool cap stole through the shadows of the back alleys of Warsaw. The agent galloped off the beaten path, at least where she could avoid being mugged. Thanks to a cloth covering on her feet, she trotted without sound. She stole from a dark corner to a dim doorway. For stealth missions, Rebecca preferred her natural form. Her control as a centaur was intuitive. And stealth was all about control.

Rebecca stopped across from a metal warehouse with Polish markings. Her top outfit was a flap jacket. She patted down her pockets for a specific tool. Her taser, knife, ah, the goggles. All her equipment along with a Kevlar covering went over her equine half.

Retrieving her multi-use goggles, Rebecca slipped them on and read the sign on the side of the building. "Property of *Dobre Wieści*," she whispered aloud. "A shipping company."

Dobre Wieści meant glad tidings, though nothing glad was going on inside.

Dangerous. High profile. Rewarding. All the elements Rebecca could hope for in an assignment. No more riding the Interrail or checking to see if a mythical stayed hidden. Missions like this were how she earned her pay. And she would earn her pay tonight.

Two guards patrolled around a corner of the warehouse, stopping next to one of the loading dock doors. Rebecca spotted their sidearms. One stopped and lit a cigarette. She might be able to bypass the code for the door once they moved around the corner, but Rebecca couldn't take the chance. The newest technology for combination locks made them smarter than in the past. "Smart" combination locks bounced against a cell tower, and the tech to interrupt that signal and send back a successful outcome was a new challenge for DEED. Getting past the locked door might take time.

She would have to knock the guards unconscious.

Reaching into a satchel around her neck, she retrieved two small orbs no larger than ball bearings. As far as she could, she threw them in the direction of the guards. When they hit the road near the door, the guards turned toward them. One of the sentries started to speak. The balls exploded in a silent puff of blue-colored smoke while Rebecca fastened her gas mask. The agent couldn't see through the haze, but the sound of bodies hitting the pavement told her all she needed to know.

The smoke obscured her vision, but she reached forward with her fingers until they grasped the lock. Retrieving a camera-shaped box from her satchel, she counted to ten to let the smoke dissipate. When she could see the lock, she pointed the box at it and entered a code into its keypad. The tech whirred and clicked for a few minutes while Rebecca removed her gas mask, eyeing the unmoving guards.

The combination lock clicked. Rebecca shoved the camera back in the satchel and reached for the door handle. She had scoped the interior of the building earlier with her heat vision goggles and knew nobody was stationed on the other side. The door opened on rows of crates, a perfect cover to enter and survey the interior situation.

Closing the door quietly, Rebecca flipped a switch on her goggles to change them from heat to night vision. She cocked an ear before moving inside. From the noises within, several people stood on the other side of a row of crates, discussing matters in Polish. She caught the tail end of a question.

"...zapłacić za ciebie?"

Translation: "pay for you?" As in, how much someone would pay for someone else. Was that their game? Blackmail?

A female grunted in response. This likely originated from her main target, the woman Rebecca had talked to days before, Celisa. Get in, get Celisa out, and don't reveal your species or hers unless necessary.

"Not in money." This statement floated over the wares, spoken in Polish, from the same man. "He already pays you for your services, doesn't he?"

Of course, they would assume Celisa was romantically involved with her manager, Aleksy. Criminal minds couldn't conceive that Aleksy was happily married to his wife of ten years, or loved his two children. Celisa was, and would always be, his administrative assistant and a friend. In these modern times, society conditioned people to believe a businessman was cheating on his wife. If Aleksy was romantically involved with Celisa, he had to know her species. And he would never keep that secret. Few humans would.

Rebecca carefully hoofed to the end of her row, the soft padding keeping her footfalls silent. She had to maneuver into position before she enacted her plan and that meant coming closer to the action.

Another voice cut in. "Perhaps she doesn't return in the same condition, huh?"

Rebecca didn't translate the answer, knowing it would be crude. But another statement caught her attention. "We don't want Aleksy's money. We want his loyalty to us. If he doesn't commit to us, we kill you and make your death appear as if he did it."

Ah, so that was the Protection's game. Aleksy, with Celisa's assistance, had kept the crime family from extorting money from his company for years. Aleksy was squeaky clean. They were going to use Celisa to get to him.

Kidnapping Celisa? They picked the wrong woman.

Rebecca rounded a corner, pressing buttons on her watch. A row of crates was all that stood between her and Poland's most wanted. She peeked between two large boxes and counted three men with Celisa. Her target was tied to a chair in the middle.

Extracting her would not be an easy job. But Rebecca didn't have much time as someone might soon find the two guards she had left outside.

Celisa's muffled response indicated they had gagged her.

All three men laughed. "This one is a gold mine."

The mobster's joke was accurate. Celisa was a large part of the company's success. And one of the charities of that success? A front for an operation called DEED. Well, someone had to fund their activities and tech, like the brooch Celisa was wearing. A brooch that sent a signal pinpointing her exact location.

When Celisa's brooch started broadcasting her distress signal, DEED had kicked into action. Ray had made a brief phone call to Rebecca. Rescuing Celisa was no sleepy assignment, and she'd show her talents to the DEED council, proving that she was ready for Venezuela.

Rebecca didn't know Celisa personally and had never met her kind in Elysium. She was not only eager to show off her talents but excited to meet a real sirin. This might be fun.

But Rebecca couldn't think of it that way. She was a professional, and her first line of business was to rescue Celisa without discovery. But these guys were sludge of the highest order, so if she could go a little further, she'd take the chance.

Celisa tried to speak through her gag, but a broad-shouldered blond man cut her off. "You sit tight. I'm sure he'll play our—"

A door at the side of the building opened, and a tall, mustached man called inside. "Something's happened to Daniel and Kris!"

Rebecca gritted her teeth and headed for the end of the crates. No time like the present. She tapped her watch.

The lights in the warehouse went dark. Amid calls of alarm, Rebecca galloped at full speed toward the location of the abduction. Her night vision goggles picked up that two more people had entered the warehouse. She could handle three, but five? Five was a big ask.

The padding on her hooves still muffled her footfalls, but

at full speed, she wasn't silent. One of the red images before her raised his gun. "Someone's here!"

The bullet whizzed by her left ear. Close, but she was on them then, rearing up. Another man raised his gun, but her hooves kicked him hard, and he flew against two other guards. Like pins in a bowling alley, they scattered over the ground.

So much for the original three. Rebecca landed near Celisa, and she retrieved her pocketknife. She cut through the material of Celisa's gag and let it fall. When a hail of bullets sprayed overhead and pinging off darkened light fixtures and walls, Rebecca stopped.

"The next time I fire," sneered a voice from the doorway. "I decorate these warehouse walls with your insides."

Rebecca and Celisa weren't bulletproof, and the enforcer agent considered her actions. Before the lights came back on in a minute, she'd transform into her human form. She would be taken hostage or killed. Perhaps Celisa too.

Rebecca still had knockout gas if she could get to it. If they spotted her move, however, would they shoot her? And carrying Celisa around would slow her down.

The second figure near the doorway tilted his head. "What is that thing over there? It looks like...a horse?"

"Eidelweiss," whispered Celisa.

Rebecca's reputation preceded her. She considered galloping away. If they shot at her, the bullets would be away from Celisa. At least, Rebecca would save her companion.

"I don't care what it is, I'm—"

And then, Celisa started singing. While not entirely on-key, the music filled the warehouse with a light melody. If words accompanied the tune, Rebecca didn't hear them. She was too busy enjoying the notes.

The men dropped their weapons, the only discordant sound in the warehouse. Celisa continued to belt out her tune, gaining more strength. All Rebecca wanted to do was listen. She wanted to sit down and bask in the enveloping lightness the sounds made. The world was beautiful, and life was amazing.

Rebecca recalled all her favorite sights, sounds, and scents. They were all here, in this warehouse, all at once. She was overwhelmed with pleasurable sensations, her body tingling in response.

The song was a physical melody performed by the perfect masseuse. No, rather, it was the perfect symphony executed with precision. Not quite. The music filled her with thoughts of those closest to her, expressing their love through embraces and words: her grandfather, her niece Liliana, Sonya, even little Aurora. Yes, Celisa's tune was music's love language. How could Rebecca ever be unhappy again?

"Eidelweiss." A voice. Far off.

She could never feel sad again. She had reached the pinnacle of what being fulfilled meant. The experience was not just a cherry on top of a sundae, but the entire sundae itself. It tasted divine, perhaps the way sugar had first tasted to her as a child. Delightful. Amazing.

"Rebecca!"

Who was this person interrupting her high? Why interrupt her when she had now achieved what so many had sought? Pure nirvana.

"Rebecca, cut me free."

Me? Oh, Celisa. Yes, she should cut her free, so she could continue her singing. If only the music could fold around her like a blanket on a cold winter morning.

Absent-mindedly, Rebecca stooped down and cut through the ropes. The sirin's hand took Rebecca's to help her stand. "Thank you for removing my gag. It muffled my voice. We can walk right past the men. They won't bother anyone for a while."

The lights came on.

Oops.

The men stared at Rebecca as a centaur. The two times human men had seen her in native form, they had naturally been surprised by her equine half. Not so this time. These two men's eyes were glazed over, and they swayed to the music Celisa had sung.

Celisa led the way. "Come on."

Rebecca obediently trotted after her. "Sing again. Will you?"

Celisa grinned. "For them, not you. You must cover your ears."

As they passed the men, Celisa sang, "You two will go to the police and turn yourselves in, exposing this cartel."

They smiled back at her. And the other said, "Have you ever seen such a beautiful woman in your life?"

"I like the centaur," replied the man as they left the warehouse.

"Must I keep drinking this vinegar? I'm going to throw up."

"Just sip it."

Three hours later, in a bathrobe after a freezing shower, Rebecca eyed the shot glass of white vinegar warily. She had "sipped" about half of it. True, its bitter taste had restored some of her equilibrium, but she knew the thrill of ecstasy still slid through her veins. Her emotions roller-coasted. Recalling the song tempted her to view the world through a honey-colored film. Rebecca would then think of the night in Edinburgh or Maine, and her spirits would crash into the ground nose-first.

Rebecca sipped the drink and forced herself to swallow. "Yuck. Distract me from this torture. Tell me how they kidnapped you."

Celisa eyed the apartment. "Are we secure?"

Rebecca waved around the room. "Yes, I followed all the protocols when I arrived here."

"Good. I'm getting out of my work clothes." Celisa slipped off her blouse over her head. "The Protection, as they call themselves, has invited Aleksy to many dinners, trying to wheedle their way into his business. He and I have fended them off, but this time DEED instructed us to agree to a meeting. He thought I should attend on the phone with him while they negotiated. Wonderful idea. Aleksy is a smart man."

Celisa had removed her undergarments, and if she had been human, would've been naked from the waist up. But she wasn't human. Instead, a spongy, pink-colored substance covered her body with a zipper extending from the neckline to the belly button. She grabbed the zipper and pulled down, and the skin suit peeled away.

"I was in an adjacent room of the same restaurant. They drugged my food."

Under the suit was brown plumage with red-tinged feathers. Metallic appendages were strapped to her shoulder joints, and they retracted from the suit as the pink-colored "arms" draped uselessly. Unfolding behind her, her wings spread and rippled as if stretching.

"Gagged, I couldn't use my voice," Celisa finished.

Starting to feel high again, Rebecca took another sip. She grimaced. "I'm not sure why they called me in. You handled them yourself."

"I couldn't untie myself from the ropes, Rebecca. And my singing couldn't lure people under my spell the way the songs of my cousins do, the sirens. I'm a sirin."

Rebecca nodded. "Capable of heralding great joy to all." She tapped her temple. "Exploding the dopamine in their heads."

"Yes, sometimes confused with seraphs." The sirin's claw flexed. "But we're more like you centaurs." She gestured to her head. "Human." Then her midsection. "Avian." And then her lower extremities. "And human again."

"You're quite a marvel," remarked Rebecca.

"As are you." Celisa flushed. "I can't believe they sent Rebecca Eidelweiss to rescue me. I've heard so much about you."

"I'm glad we had a chance to meet." Rebecca fiddled with her vinegar drink. "But for a full confession, I'm the one who put you in danger."

Celisa's wings shifted. "What?"

"I was the one who contacted you on your lunch break. On DEED's orders, I asked you to contact the Protection. The mob here has been hiding money for a thug down in Venezuela. A man imprisoning mythicals."

Celisa put a claw on her breast.

Rebecca continued, "Our goal was to have Aleksy call in a favor and provide us transport when we executed our mission there. But the entire thing went sideways with your kidnapping. Thank Chiron, you wore the brooch."

"Standard procedure," Celisa answered.

"Wearing a tracer is standard for an enforcer agent, but you had the foresight to suspect you might be in danger."

"I wanted to be an enforcer agent." Celisa brushed the ends of her claws on the table. "I have a rare talent. I failed my psychological tests, though."

Celisa couldn't deal with the pressures of a mission? "You seemed to handle yourself quite well tonight."

"Yes, well, not according to DEED." The sirin nodded toward the glass of vinegar. "I think you won't need this any longer. You'll have a headache in a couple of hours. You may want something stronger than over-the-counter medicine. I'm sure you have something in your field pack."

"Yes, something that helps with bullet wounds."

Celisa sat down. "If you don't mind, I'd appreciate staying for a bit before I must put my stuffy suit back on and then go into hiding. Will your partner mind?"

Rebecca waved at the second bedroom. "You can stay all night. I don't have a partner."

Celisa nodded. "That's right. Wasn't it Diana? I remember reading the memo that the two of you would be individual agents. Unusual."

A pang of guilt shot through Rebecca. Her junior agent should be paired up with someone else. Best to change the subject. "A shame you have to lay low until this blows over."

"I received the call from DEED this morning," said Celisa. "A doppelganger from Latvia is on her way and will impersonate me. We can't take chances. Imagine if they call me in for questioning and pat me down."

Rebecca sympathized with mythicals like Celisa who couldn't shapeshift.

Celisa continued, "My double can stand in for me, and feign an illness with Aleksy until I return. How about you? Do you have to abandon this apartment?"

Rebecca stood and walked to the window. "Until my next assignment, I'll wait here. Watching over Warsaw unless they call me."

DEED called. Rebecca left the apartment six hours later, heading southwest.

FREYARSHA

March - St. Jean-D'Angle, France

Rebecca approached the elderly man and the horse, wondering who to talk to first. She wanted to address the horse, but she had to take care no one was watching. She wouldn't be stroking the ungulate's mane and speaking in baby tones. No, the man would have to be first. Noticing his glare, Rebecca prepared herself for the difficult conversation.

Under his tweed cap, the man's wrinkled skin folded down as if every portion of his face frowned at her. "Are you the one?"

He spoke in provincial French. Rebecca had to take a moment before answering. She was far too used to Parisian French. This man swallowed his "l" perfectly.

"*Oui.*"

"If you think I'm going to hand her over with such a simple response," snarled the man. "You'll witness a man *péter un plomb.*"

Rebecca wasn't sure of the translation, but she understood the meaning. The irony was she knew more about him than he knew about her. Her intel told her he didn't know anything about DEED, the creatures who lived in the world around him, or that she was a field agent. He only knew he had a talking horse, and she was there to take that horse away. The reports didn't have to record that the man loved his horse very much. This much was evident.

Rebecca glanced at the horse. "She'll go to a land where she'll be loved and admired every day." Though fumbling for the order of the sentence, Rebecca still made her point.

The old man's eyes filled with tears. He turned to the horse and threw his arms around her. "Freyarsha, are you certain?"

"It's time, Lucard. It's time," the horse responded.

The man wept on the horse's neck, and Rebecca stepped away in a failed attempt to give them privacy. She noticed a dandelion growing by the side of the dirt path and toed it, averting her eyes from the tender scene. Then, with a soft step, the man approached her. Though not glancing her way, he murmured, "Take good care of her."

He strolled off and into a barn. Rebecca hummed a bit of "Always," and Freyarsha responded with "As Time Goes By." Then, Rebecca approached her and held her hand out. Freyarsha eyed her. "What am I going to do with that?"

"I'm greeting you. Others may be watching."

The horse rolled her eyes. "Just say hello."

Rebecca lowered her hand. "He loves you."

"I was here when he was born." The horse tilted her head toward the barn. "He and I have been on many adventures."

Rebecca, not knowing what to do, folded her hands behind her back. "Are you ready?"

"I'll never be ready for this. Come with me for one last run around the pasture." Freyarsha nodded her head backward. "I have a beautiful sight for you to see."

Rebecca leaned away. "The last time you said to accompany you, we ended up racing out of a gulag in Russia in the middle of the night."

"Gulags don't exist in Russia, Rebecca," snorted Freyarsha.

"Neither do talking horses. And yet, there we were."

Rebecca started jogging next to the horse as it trotted further into the field. The horse put her face to the sun. "Beautiful day in beautiful France. Will you be returning here?"

Rebecca increased her gait to keep up. "Ray has been pressuring me to deal with Lester. What a chore."

"Lester is a chore, but the best kind, don't you think? Go see him."

Rebecca shrugged.

This mission had come out of the blue. And while Rebecca recognized it as a wiffle ball she appreciated that DEED had chosen her for it, though the danger level on the assignment was low.

"When we trot far enough, you may transform," said Freyarsha.

"Freyarsha, my clothes can't accommodate my natural form. I'm wearing nylons for Chiron's sake."

"Lose it all." The horse lifted her head. "No one will see you."

No amount of arguing would persuade Freyarsha. The fact the agent was taking the horse from her assigned location after spending one hundred ten years there, deserved a final request. Yes, DEED had sent her to accompany a legendary field agent to her retirement. While Rebecca appreciated the task, she couldn't help but feel she was ill-suited for it. She excelled at subterfuge, not ceremony.

After they had walked for ten minutes, Freyarsha nodded. Rebecca removed her clothes. Instantly, she allowed her back to elongate into her centaur form. Releasing her equine side never failed to quicken her pulse. She noticed Freyarsha had extended her back too. Now, three adults at least could ride her.

"Show off," Rebecca remarked.

"You like that?" the horse asked. "Then catch me if you can."

She raced off at full gallop, and Rebecca gritted her teeth. She'd catch the old girl, certainly, but that wasn't the point. This wasn't a game of catch-me-if-you-can. Rather, the point was to follow the leader. Rebecca hurried after her.

The wind whistling through her short hair and along her back, her steady hoofs beating down the soil, the smell of heather and spruce swept cares away from Rebecca's mission-organized mind. She was a young adult again, galloping through

Elysium, out with others her age. She sped across meadows, fields, and heaths with the joy of the sunshine on her back. She had forgotten such a simple pleasure. The circus tunes of nature —she hadn't heard it over her technology. The blurring effect of running so fast that you wonder how you ever stood still in your life. Her centaur heart beat hard against her chest in perfect synchrony with her natural form.

Rebecca passed Freyarsha and focused on a location in the distance. The terminal point was a ravine, merely a dip before rising again to a new meadow. But the older gal might need help, so she slowed down as they approached the precipice.

Freyarsha wasn't far behind her and called out for her. "Just beyond that meadow is the property line, and I can't say what we'll encounter if we cross it."

Rebecca pulled up to a stop, and Freyarsha capered to a similar halt. Both panted hard, and sweat beaded on Rebecca's face. Breathing in deeply and smelling the soil, she asked, "How did you know that's what I needed?"

"You don't live one hundred and twenty years without learning something about others."

Rebecca eyed the older agent. "Freyarsha, how did you survive out here for so long without revealing how intelligent a horse you were?"

"Some say I inherited my talents from my ancestor Bayard." The horse switched her tail. "He was so smart he never let the humans know he could talk. They found out he understood English, though. His great downfall."

"That's not what I meant." Rebecca drew a deep breath. "How did you stand being an agent for so long?"

Freyarsha sidled along Rebecca's equine body. "Let's talk while we overlook the ravine. I sometimes stand here for hours, observing nature."

They stood side by side. A breeze blew back Rebecca's bangs. Somewhere below, an unseen frog croaked.

Rebecca wanted to confess her recent thoughts about their organization to the retiring horse, but she couldn't ask

Freyarsha not to tell DEED. A request like that would insult such a high-ranking companion. She would have to trust her to keep it to herself.

"I'm thinking of leaving DEED." There she said it. "I'm not happy."

The horse, without looking at her, responded, "Is this about Aurora Eidelweiss?"

"Her last name isn't Eidelweiss."

True, Rebecca had named her Aurora, but DEED created the surname on her passport to help her transfer over the border. Freyarsha naming her Eidelweiss made Aurora family, and Rebecca's failure to rescue her even worse.

Freyarsha nickered. "'Eidelweiss' is how they recorded it in the database."

Rebecca kicked up some dirt with her hoof. "Yes, my resignation has to do with Aurora."

Freyarsha didn't speak.

"Don't tell me the fault wasn't mine that I lost her," warned Rebecca.

"I would never." Freyarsha's large black nostrils flared. "But why leave DEED?"

"Because I must get her back, and DEED would never sanction my plan." Rebecca side-eyed Freyarsha, hoping for a reaction. She didn't get one.

"If the plan was solid, why wouldn't they?"

Rebecca was unsure what she wanted from Freyarsha. Her blessing, maybe, but the question wasn't the one she was hoping for. She turned away. "Really, Freyarsha. Don't you see what DEED's about?"

"DEED is about ensuring our kind is safe, free, and fulfilling our destiny."

Rebecca expected more from the horse than to be DEED's tool. "DEED is too often a council of men deciding the fates of others around the world. Their goal is not safety or freedom, but about power. The *best* I could hope for is for one of them might allow me to go through with the plan and tell the council the idea was his. But mostly, they won't like a field agent—let alone a woman—thinking independently."

During her tirade, Freyarsha had turned to her. By the end her eyes were wide. "Do you believe that?"

"Don't you?"

Freyarsha swayed back and forth. "What is DEED's nickname, Rebecca?"

Rebecca frowned. "Lady Responsibility."

"Yes, *Lady* Responsibility. Not Lord Responsibility. Why does DEED characterize itself as a woman?"

Rebecca wanted to answer that DEED thought of women as submissive. She decided against it. Instead, she gave the textbook answer. "The founding members of DEED thought responsibility better represented by the feminine title. And so, they proclaimed, 'For society to function, Lady Responsibility must bear the world's burdens.'"

"All genders, all DEED's employees, all council members proclaim DEED's responsibility oath. The work of the department—saving mythicals and humans, keeping our kind hidden, sowing peace where we can—is a heavy burden," said Freyarsha.

"But the council is mostly men," objected Rebecca. "And they only make decisions. They don't have to carry them out."

"Many think of the council as pompous, ignorant representatives, yet they adhere to the truths we hold dear. DEED wasn't built on the shoulders of men but men and women together."

A breeze ruffled Rebecca's hair. "I don't need a history lesson."

"No, you need a philosophy lecture." Freyarsha's tail twitched. "Do you believe the women agents who have gone out into this world with missions were ignorant or shallow?"

Rebecca turned sharply toward her. "Of course not!"

"Do you think those who have died for our cause were wrong to do so?" asked Freyarsha.

"No."

"Do you think no other female agents have had the same thoughts?"

Rebecca pulled back and stared into Freyarsha's eyes. Had *she* thought of abandoning DEED?

Freyarsha moved her long snout closer. "DEED is not an institution. If it was, we—all of us—would be doomed. We might as well hide in our corners of the world. DEED is a transcendent movement, a golden umbrella above the globe, with only one foot in this world."

Centaur children were all taught this at one time. Rebecca remembered the meadow where her sixth-year teacher lectured similar words. She was mesmerized then. How easily she had forgotten.

Freyarsha stepped closer to her. "The humans mustn't find us. We are designed to lead them to belief, not be the center of their religions. If they capture us, the good ones will converse with us, the bad, dissect us. If discovered, we become a different culture from them. Familiarity breeds contempt. Hidden, we are so much more."

Most who lived in Elysium believed that humans would eradicate them if they discovered them. Freyarsha spoke of the ancient emigration from all corners of the world to Elysium.

Rebecca licked her lips. "I have nothing against humans. My complaint is DEED. It has lost its way. Institutions fail, Freyarsha."

"And why do they, Rebecca?"

Freyarsha even sounded like her college professors with her quick question. Rebecca failed to give a plausible answer, so Freyarsha continued.

"Rome fell internally as most empires do. The Ottoman Empire was in decline before World War One. Crones had predicted the United States' demise if the South had won their civil war. DEED is not a sword, but a shield against such divisions. It's not Lady Justice but Lady Responsibility. Our higher calling is what separates us from humans, but no biologist with a scalpel will ever write about that in a journal."

Freyarsha sidled alongside her. Rebecca gulped. A horse's presence so near was its way of embracing another.

Rebecca whispered, "I can't help but feel DEED is corrupt."

"Of course it's corrupt," Freyarsha said quietly. "We're all corrupt, Rebecca. That's precisely why DEED exists. DEED's core principles aren't corrupt. And as long as a council is beholden to those principles, an institution of corrupted men and women won't fall."

Rebecca bit her lip. "You were tempted to leave?"

"As I grew older, I could've made an excuse to stay with Lucard and ignore DEED's summons." Freyarsha paused. "With my reputation, they would've left me here if I desired it. I could've retired in this meadow years ago and cast off DEED as a snake sheds its skin. But then, I would have never met a brash young agent in a Russian gulag."

Rebecca recalled her delight when Freyarsha had first spoken to her, kindling a flame of freedom from the prison. A spark of hope.

Freyarsha winked. "A gulag that doesn't exist."

Rebecca almost laughed. "You think I should trust DEED?"

"I do." No hesitation in Freyarsha's answer. "Furthermore, I would only be too glad to go on one more mission with you, Rebecca, if these old bones would carry me. But I pass on to you my dedication to making the world a better place."

Rebecca shuddered at the burden of responsibility.

Lady Responsibility.

"My dear, we should return." Freyarsha turned her head. "Lucard will be worried. And then you and I shall walk through a beautiful country to a boat that will take us to another beautiful country. And there, I'll be put out to pasture."

Rebecca squared her shoulders. "I'll never put you out to pasture."

Freyarsha tilted her head. "I know, my dear. That part of you is the true calling of DEED."

LAYOVER

March - Boston, Massachusetts, United States

When in Rome, do as the Romans do. When in Boston, eat clam chowder.

Good clam chowder wasn't available in Logan International, so Rebecca left the airport during her three-hour layover on her trip to San Diego. She headed for The Captain's Table, a small eatery twenty minutes away. This restaurant was clean, efficient, and had the most delectable clam chowder in the area. The Captain's Table made the dish just right, not soupy like fine dining, or oversalted like the dives. Rebecca ordered the meal with oyster crackers, and soon, with a full stomach, exited the building a happy woman.

For three seconds.

Across the street, a male teenager pushed an older woman and grabbed her purse. The woman shrieked as she smacked into the wall and tumbled to the ground.

Rebecca's first thought: *Do something.*

Rebecca's second thought: *I have another mission after this layover. I can't get involved.*

Rebecca's third thought sounded like Freyarsha. *What is DEED about, if not helping people?*

"Baelz Bells," Rebecca murmured while darting off after the purse snatcher.

The store-lined street was mostly empty with a few

pedestrians gazing at the scene in shock. Rebecca would have to cross the street to catch the young thief. The Black kid spotted Rebecca and turned down an alley. Two cars, headed in different directions, were racing down the two-way road. If she waited, she might lose the little purse snatcher.

The cars were approaching at different speeds, and Rebecca calculated the physics in her head. She rushed in front of the car closest to her. The driver leaned on his horn as she did so. The other car was speeding; she couldn't outrun it. Rebecca halted on the yellow line and stood like a statue. The drafts from the two vehicles whisked past her in opposite directions. The agent planted herself like a tree. As soon as the second car cleared, Rebecca resumed her pursuit.

When Rebecca arrived at the alley, she discovered it turned behind a building. She rushed to the end and put her back against the wall. Carefully, Rebecca stole a quick glance around the corner. This section dead ended. She spied a six-foot, slatted fence with the posts ending in sharp diamond heads, resembling spears pointed to the sky. A teenager could easily vault it with the help of a trash can.

Centaurs had a heightened sense of smell compared to humans. As she entered, her nose picked up offal and mold, but one more scent. She caught the smell of sweat in the air.

Rebecca stomped down the alley, scooping up a chunk of brick discarded on the ground. Her quarry was at the end, hidden behind garbage cans. He rummaged through his purloined prize. She grabbed the hoodie of the young thief and turned him around. The boy screamed.

"You're going to restore the purse and apologize to that lady."

Rebecca expected the kid to either pull a weapon on her (she was prepared) or to drop the purse and jump the fence. Instead, the punk shook his head. "No, you don't understand."

I don't have time for this.

Assuming her tough cop persona, Rebecca pushed him against the wall. She pinned him to the bricks with her forearm.

"I understand all too well. What is it? Drugs? Gambling? Or are you going to give me some sob story that you don't have anything to eat?"

The boy gulped. His eyes filled with tears. First-timer.

He released a shaky breath. "My name is Jawal Robertson. My dad's a detective on the force. At least, he was."

Rebecca turned her head. This was new.

Jawal continued, "The lady I stole the purse from? She killed him. I was looking for evidence."

Rebecca removed her arm. "You're telling me that a sixty-year-old woman killed a police detective."

"My dad said she's unhinged." Jawal shivered. "Dangerous. She's killed other people. My dad had a lead on her—"

"And he told you?"

"Yeah," answered Jawal. "He wasn't supposed to, but he always talked about his cases with me."

Jawal's father had broken protocol. Rebecca liked him.

The boy held up the purse. "If I can find something... anything...in this purse to—"

A light footfall, the sole of a sneaker, on the pavement behind them. They weren't alone. Rebecca was about to hush Jawal, but the next noise alarmed her even more. Snick. Someone released the safety of a revolver.

Without words, Rebecca grabbed Jawal and pulled him down. Bullets whizzed through the air, striking the bricks where they had been. Jawal cried in pain. Rebecca hadn't been quick enough.

A series of words flashed through Rebecca's mind as she dropped to her hands: Silencer, snub-nose, six-shot. Was this a Jorge Corto hit? Another one of Rebecca's enemies?

No. She had made the same mistake with Aurora. The bullet hit its intended mark. The gunman was after Jawal. But the shooter wasn't a *man*.

Rebecca zeroed in on her possible options in less than a second. Her mind discarded useless ideas as if they were sand falling through the holes on a sifter. The best defense was a surprise offense.

First, she had to use the brick in her hand. If Rebecca threw the brick at the shooter's head from her angle, she'd likely miss. But the hand holding the pistol was an easier target.

From the ground, she launched the bit of masonry at the weapon, striking the woman's hand. The gun fell to the ground. Success, but they weren't out of danger, yet. If Rebecca stood and ran at her, she gave herself a fifty-fifty chance of surviving. No, she had to think like a four-legged creature, not a two-legged one.

The agent positioned herself on her hands and feet. She scrambled on them backward, toward the shooter. The unexpected move would either surprise her opponent or result in her death—hopefully, not the latter.

As Rebecca moved, her target scrambled for the snub-nose six shot. The gun was within her adversary's reach.

Rebecca crawled backward like a scurrying beetle. She had been through numerous obstacle courses where she had to execute complex maneuvers. Her training gave her the advantage. Judging the distance of the alleyway, she estimated she was within range of her foe. Before her opponent could aim the revolver, Rebecca had one more trick up her sleeve. Unleash the centaur.

At least, a small portion of it.

Rebecca transformed only her feet into her beloved horse hooves. The semi-transformation was tricky. Her instinct demanded she change into her full centaur form, but she didn't have time. Changing partially was like taking a large drink of something you enjoy then swallowing a few drops and keeping the rest in your mouth. But she only needed hooves right now.

Bracing her hands against the ground, Rebecca pulled herself in at the waist and immediately launched herself backward, hooves-first. Her shoes remained on the ground. The sides were too wide. The hardened structure of her hooves struck the woman in the stomach. Her target exhaled a large breath and fell, the pistol clattering to the ground.

Rebecca was on her hooves in seconds. She twirled around and clip-clopped to the shooter. The sixty-year-old woman was conscious but trying to catch her breath. Rebecca's assumptions were right. The woman was Jawal's victim.

Jawal.

Rebecca spied the boy on the ground, groaning. A small pool of blood was spreading over his clothes.

Rebecca's attention returned to the woman. Time to end this. She made a fist and cross-punched the shooter on the jaw. The woman's head hit the ground, and her eyes rolled up.

Rebecca hurried to Jawal. Walking on hooves was not the same as galloping, but steadying herself on heels had given her experience. She crouched down next to the boy when she reached him.

The bullet had entered Jawal's shoulder. The woman had shot him with a small gun, so the bullet hadn't exited. Jawal cursed, clutching his arm.

The agent opened her purse. An emergency medical kit took up half of the space inside. She retrieved and opened it, grabbing bandages. "Turn your head. You may throw up and I don't want you choking on your vomit."

Jawal complied.

"I've patched bullet wounds," said Rebecca. "You're going to be okay, but this will hurt."

"I don't feel like I'm going to be okay."

Rebecca ripped his shirt and grabbed the antiseptic. "You have a phone?"

"Pocket." Jawal gritted through his teeth. "I—"

He howled as the liquid landed on the wound.

Rebecca capped the bottle. "When I'm done here, I'll call for an ambulance. With the assault, she'll go to jail for certain. Tell them everything you told me. The police may find more evidence, and your father may be vindicated."

Jawal breathed heavily but didn't answer.

Rebecca grabbed the bandages. "You must promise me something. Don't describe me to the police. Say that the woman over there showed up, you dropped to the ground, and she shot you. I came and knocked her out. You didn't get a good look at me. With the pain, you were out when I treated you. Understand?"

Jawal nodded and shut his eyes. His face tightened with an agonized expression.

"Good. Your father would be proud, Jawal."

"He's not here anymore to be proud."

The sorrow in Jawal's voice loosened Rebecca's tongue. "I know a little more about the afterlife than—" She couldn't say "humans" so grabbed the nearest substitute. "...most people. He's still here."

"How do you know?"

Rebecca wrapped the bandages. "If you see the impossible, would you believe me?"

Jawal winced with pain. "What do you mean? Impossible?"

Rebecca nodded, finished with the bandages. The agent reached in Jawal's pocket and retrieved his phone, then stood. Rebecca lifted a pant leg and showed off her transformed horse's hoof.

"Now, not a word about me to anyone," she instructed.

Jawal's mouth opened. Rebecca winked and rushed over to her shoes. Restoring her human feet, she slipped on her pumps while dialing emergency. Rebecca gave a brief explanation of what happened and hung up on the operator despite his advice.

Jawal sat up and braced himself against the wall. "What did I just see?"

Rebecca put her hands on her hips. "No more involving yourself in your father's cases. Sometimes, you must trust the authorities to do their job."

What a laugh coming from you, Rebecca.

"I'm trying," she whispered to herself.

Rebecca vaulted over the wooden slat fence. She remained there, listening to Jawal curse, stand, and examine the shooter. She waited until the ambulance sirens were near and doors opened. Then, she retreated silently.

Rebecca pulled her luggage behind her while navigating Logan International Airport. Her cell rang and she retrieved it with one hand. Ray.

Rebecca drifted to the side of the walkway and faced the wall to triple secure the line. Rebecca hummed "Always," waiting for Ray's song. Instead, he growled at her.

"Eidelweiss! What the Hades! Boston was supposed to be a layover."

Rebecca merged into the crowd and headed for her gate. "I decided to have a delicious dinner at The Captain's Table. At my own expense, no less. The department can't be upset at that."

"You know what I'm talking about. The boy who was shot, Rebecca. Why did you get involved?"

Freyarsha came to mind. "DEED's mission is to help this world, right? We're not limited to our own, Ray."

"You know what I mean. You could've enjoyed a massage in the Diamond Club! I asked you to engage in a technical objective in San Diego and then interact with our guard in Oregon. These are two simple missions, Rebecca."

Rebecca shimmied between two slower airport travelers. "Indeed. Two tasks even Hans could handle."

"Don't start—"

"My last assignment in France reminded me how important making a difference is." Rebecca spotted her gate. "I made a difference today, Ray. If you want to yell at me about it, let's continue our conversation in San Diego. I'm about to board."

Ray huffed at the other end. "Jawal Robertson says he can't remember the person who saved him. I suppose no harm done."

"One life saved. One criminal jailed. Rebecca's having a good day."

"Rebecca, file the paperwork."

"What paperwork? This wasn't an assignment."

"Rebecca—!"

"I'm boarding the plane. Talk soon."

LESTER'S BUSINESS VENTURE

March - Oregon Wilderness, United States

When facing a wayward mythical, Rebecca understood that espionage missions didn't have to be lethal. Hopefully, this was one of those times.

Rebecca knocked on the cabin's entrance, foregoing protocol in this remote area. She squared her shoulders and put on her *I mean business* face while waiting for the creature to answer.

A bushy-haired, seven-foot man with rugged skin and eyebrows extending halfway up his forehead answered the door. His plaid shirt stretched across his muscular frame, which towered over his visitor. Rebecca—with her professionally styled hair, red suit jacket, and gray pressed pants—stood tall in his shadow. She poked him on the breastbone. "Remove the disguise, Lester."

Lester rubbed his square jaw. "What are you doing here, Rebecca?"

Always the same question. As if they didn't know.

Rebecca didn't wait for his invitation and brushed past him, entering Lester's mountain cabin. She detected a pine scent and a moist earthy smell.

After shutting the door, Lester adopted a sarcastic tone. "Won't you come in?"

Rebecca noticed a package containing small plush toys next to the door. "You know why I'm here."

Lester stiffened, then eyed an adjacent kitchenette. "I only now put on tea. Take a seat."

Rebecca walked to the small table while Lester made for the kitchen counter. She selected a chair with a view of the cabin's owner. While she didn't expect him to run, she couldn't be entirely sure. Her eyes darted to the fake family photos on the walls and the porcelain knick-knacks. The setup screamed domesticity. "You have a cozy place here, Lester."

He returned with the kettle in one hand and two teacups in the other. One cup had an oversized handle. "Thanks."

"Though you shouldn't be living here at all."

He placed everything he was carrying onto the table. "Beats a cave."

Lester chose a chair that groaned under his weight. Rebecca pulled a doily close to her seat. "Did you make the mask?"

Lester huffed. "Mask! I'm insulted! I would think you enforcer agents would recognize prosthetics. The process takes time to apply."

Lester set a teacup, spoon, and a variety of teabags in front of her. With his bare hand, he grabbed the base of the kettle, steam flowing from its spout, then tipped hot water into her cup.

Rebecca examined the tea bags. "Nice selection. Nice house. A little too nice on a yeti's salary."

Lester lifted his teacup with his beefy fingers, pinky extended. "I recently came into money."

Oh, come on! "Yes, selling merchandise about yourself. What a setup."

Slurping, the yeti peered at the agent over his cup's rim. "Oregon hasn't outlawed capitalism... yet." He furrowed his brows. "That reminds me. I need to register to vote."

Rebecca used the spoon to agitate the water. "The head office sent me here. You're not my normal assignment, as you well know. But I like you, so I agreed to it. Feelings aside, I'm here to demand you shut down the website, Lester."

"Oh, Rebecca, be reasonable. The store's not hurting anything."

She pointed at him. "You're selling T-shirts of yourself emblazoned with 'Have you seen this creature?' and 'Oregon's Most Wanted.' Your job is to hide, not draw attention."

Lester waved at her, shooing away her objection. "No one believes it."

"Tourism in the area has increased forty percent." Rebecca tapped her spoon on her saucer. "You're not fooling anybody, Web Admin B. Foote."

Her host grinned, displaying his jagged teeth.

Time to switch tactics. "This isn't only about you. Shandlai had her foal yesterday. Six months from now, the nub on her head will sprout."

The yeti reared back in surprise. He didn't know.

Thought so.

Slumping his shoulders, Lester hung his head. "I wasn't aware. I'll visit Shandlai tonight."

"You're a DEED guard, Lester. Your duty is to keep people away from those unicorns." She changed her tone of voice to disappointed mother. "What happens when some tourist discovers them?"

Lester shifted, and the chair groaned again.

Rebecca wrapped her knuckles on the table. "What if they're captured?"

Lester set his cup on the yellow, flowery doily. "You've made your point. Tell the office I'll resume terrorizing the countryside tonight. But, Rebecca, must I take the website down?"

Rebecca sipped her tea. "Not my call. But you know what the office will say."

The yeti bit his lip, then beamed at her. "I guess it's not so bad."

Uh oh.

Rebecca took a deep breath. "What're you scheming now?"

Lester spread his hands as if flattening out an invisible banner on a wall. "A going-out-of-business sale."

TEAM PLAY

March - Flint, Michigan, United States

"**M**ichigan? What are you doing in Michigan?"

Rebecca ladled a second helping of tomato soup into a bowl in her tiny room. "Jealous?"

"Yes." Sonya pouted across the screen of Rebecca's cell. "You know how much I love North America. And I've never been to Michigan. Are you in the northern part of the state?"

Rebecca reached for the pepper shaker shaped like a Trojan warrior. The saltshaker was shaped like a small wolf. A mismatched pair. "Lower peninsula. Flint's closest to Lake Huron. Residents give directions here by holding up their hand and pointing at their destination. Imagine if people did that in Italy with their feet!"

Sonya clicked keys on the other side. "I found you. Mother Earth! You could see four of the five Great Lakes within a day's drive from there. Why Michigan?"

"Reports on the Internet of faeries in the woods. DEED sent me to investigate. They were worried some of the dryads from Shadow Oaks had migrated north. When I looked into it, I found a weird human cult. While they didn't seem dangerous, I anonymously sent some tips to the local police."

"Doesn't sound dangerous. DEED could have sent a social agent, for sludge sakes."

Rebecca finished sprinkling the pepper into the soup and

set down the shaker. "First contact is always an enforcer agent, Sonya."

"Protocol, sure. But dryads?" Sonya sounded on the verge of laughter. "The poor things are the shyest creatures on Earth."

"They reported faeries." Rebecca held the edges of the bowl and walked to the two-person table in her rental house. "They could've been leprechauns."

"Oh. Right."

"You'd love it here." Rebecca gazed out the window at a small yard. "The snow is ten centimeters deep."

Rebecca lifted her cell and pointed it at the window. Sonya sighed.

The enforcer agent replaced the cell on the table. "I'm going to switch off video mode. Watching me eat is not for the faint of heart."

Sonya snorted. "You've watched me."

Rebecca flipped the button and Sonya's image vanished. "Have you applied to return to the United States?"

"Twice." The disappointment in Sonya's voice was unmistakable. "Rejected both times. I may not be able to move back for years. Maybe never."

"I'm sorry, Sonya."

"You know that Bangor house felt like my home away from home," said Sonya. "I love nature in that part of the world. You'd think, being a verdurian, I'd love Ireland, Italy, or Costa Rica. Someplace where plant life dominates. But I love the northeastern coast of the United States. I've always felt a belonging there."

"One day you'll return." Rebecca hit the mute button while she slurped her soup.

"I don't think so. I think, after I screwed up and lost Aurora, they aren't going to trust me with a long-term assignment."

Rebecca unmuted. "Someplace to put your roots down?"

Sonya tsked. "Your humor is just terrible, Derby Girl."

Kentucky Derby, of course. "That joke was just as bad.

Well, we won't make it as comedians. And we'll rescue Aurora."

"Anything on that front with DEED?" Sonya's voice was full of hope.

"Unfortunately, no. I ask Ray daily for an update on when they'll send me. Same answer." Rebecca mimicked Ray's gruff voice. "Too dangerous, Rebecca."

"He isn't wrong."

Rebecca had told Sonya about her misadventure in Venezuela. She had covered up her absence by claiming to be in stealth mode, and Ray hadn't mentioned any agent had been seen there. Rebecca was savvy enough not to talk about it over a DEED-secured line. If she had, if DEED found out, she'd never set foot outside of Elysium again.

No matter. The next time, she'd be ready. "I'll get there."

"I believe you," Sonya affirmed.

And Sonya did. Sonya and she had been friends before Aurora's disappearance, and they had bonded even more since. If Sonya had enforcer agent skills, Rebecca would choose her as a partner to infiltrate Corto's compound.

Spoon halfway to her mouth, Rebecca stopped. Her mind whirled. Not Sonya, no, but many enforcer agents were within reach of Venezuela. If she waited for DEED, she might retire before they decided to send her. But if she assembled a team…

A team. Rebecca didn't trust teams. She liked the camaraderie of teams and trusted other DEED agents to have her back, sure. But with teams came disagreements. And disagreements begat compromises, and with compromises, rules. She and Ray had instituted rules when they were partners. Ray was all about the rules; Rebecca was all about breaking them. When she had broken one of his rules in Edinburgh, he had been injured. But hadn't it been a lose-lose situation? If they had followed the rules, he might have been dead.

Or maybe not. Ray might have both of his hands now.

But Rebecca wasn't going to play the "what if" game today. She and Ray had put that behind them.

She had always thought of a team as a liability, as DEED

ensuring the odds that they'd succeed because one agent alone couldn't accomplish the mission. And an agent like her? A team around her would enforce DEED protocol. DEED protocol was sludge most of the time in the field.

But a team is the shortest path to Aurora. Isn't it?

Likely. Any other mission? No way. But for Aurora, Rebecca would shove her pride into the coat closet of her soul and lock it. A team was her ticket to Venezuela.

"Ground control to Major Rebecca. Come in, Rebecca."

Rebecca blinked. While thinking, she had placed the spoon back in the tomato soup. "I'm here."

Sonya's video appeared. "Requesting video."

"No need. I just—"

"Video, Agent Eidelweiss."

My, my! How quickly soft-hearted Sonya became bossy. Rebecca turned on her video. "I'm fine."

Sonya's shoulders relaxed. "You went dead silent for a moment."

Rebecca grinned at her. "I have an idea. You're in contact with multiple handlers, aren't you?"

"Yes, we're all in a football pool."

Hope fluttered in Rebecca's chest. "I need to know the status of a few other enforcer agents as soon as you can gather the information. Locations, and how soon they're able to free up."

Sonya's mouth dropped. "You know a lot of that's classified. People will want to know why. Do you want me to tell them?"

"Not just yet." Rebecca chewed a hangnail. "You're right. I don't know how many are in the field. Let's narrow it down. How about Riju and Hans? Uh, no. Not Hans. Um...Ofer."

Sonya's vine eyebrows rose. "Ofer? Good choice."

"Definitely. How quickly can you obtain that information? Not what they're doing, only what country they're in and the deadline for their assignment."

Sonya mimed cracking her knuckles. Her fingers bent all

the way backward, ruining the effect. But she made her point. "Leave it to me."

Four hours later, Rebecca hung up on her second call with Sonya and dialed Ray. On a scratch pad resting on her knees, she had taken down all the information she needed. Sonya hadn't been able to answer every question, but the basic two—where and when—were annotated for everyone.

The line connected, and Rebecca then went through the procedure to triple-secure it. The exchange with Ray was so important to her that she'd quadruple secure it if required. DEED protocol mandated that all missions be on paper, not online, so she had filled eight sheets in a notebook during the four hours. Her plan was rock solid.

Ray's voice sounded on the other end. "Hello, Rebecca. It's late. Isn't Flint in the Central Time zone?"

"Eastern." Rebecca bounced to her feet, pacing. "Not as late as you think."

"Sleep is a luxury."

Rebecca took a deep breath. "I have an idea. Let me talk for three minutes without interrupting, and then you may respond. Okay?"

"Uh...sure."

Rebecca used all her three minutes outlining her plan and flipping pages in her notebook. She highlighted various points she felt Ray would object to and answered them, and she listed key mitigating factors that addressed each risk. The only element she withheld was the names she required for the incursion. Ray had to first be on board with the idea.

When Rebecca had finished describing her plan, she again took a deep breath. She allowed Ray to comment. Now he would rebut her. The plan was too risky, premature, and untenable. She had an answer to any negative assessment he might have. She waited, her heart beating fast.

Ray asked one question. "So, Rebecca Eidelweiss wants a team?"

Rebecca wasn't thrilled with his tone. Would she have to beg? She swallowed down a curt rejoinder. "Yes."

She waited for the "I'd never thought I'd see the day" response, but he didn't start off in that direction. Instead, Ray cleared his throat. "It's a solid plan."

Rebecca nearly dropped her phone. "But?"

"I have to take it to the council," replied Ray. "You know I can't authorize this on my own."

"And why not? You're my handler!"

Rebecca knew she was being unreasonable. Infiltrating Corto's fortress wasn't going to be something DEED left to a handler and an agent. Yet, she wanted to push him to find out how much he'd fight for the proposal. What he honestly thought of the plan.

"Come on, Rebecca. You know how it works."

"If by 'it,' you mean DEED, then yes, I'm fully aware." Rebecca bit her lip. "By the time the plan moves through the bureaucracy, I'll be collecting a pension."

"I'm going to take it to them, and we'll vote on it. But to convince the council, I'll need to know who you want."

"Are you just humoring me?" Rebecca asked. "Because if you are, don't waste my time."

"Humoring? Rebecca, did you think the Mumbai and Greece miscommunication was a mistake? You were supposed to go to Mumbai after Greece, but I entered it wrong after you went off the grid. Did you think I wouldn't notice that you transferred your tracker's signal to a Roomba? What kind of jacktail do you think I am?"

Rebecca's jaw dropped.

Her handler's voice became business again. "I like the plan, but its success depends on the team. So, who are you asking for?"

Rebecca jumped in the air, landing silently like a cat. She

had high vaulted the first gate, and now she was galloping toward the second. "First, I need Ofer."

Sonya had told her Ofer was in Jordan. He had recently completed a mission of recovering stolen technology for DEED and taken refuge in a cave with the restored goods. Ofer was a perfect choice—he was a top-notch agent, and he was available.

Ray snorted. "Why am I not surprised?"

"The fact that he's a dynamic is to our advantage." Rebecca circled the outer edge of the living room, around the end table and chairs. "You know how his and my shapeshifting blend in. His tail is almost as effective as my hooves. He's nearly as strong as Lester. Plus, and I'll admit this but never say I did, he is scary in that half-scorpion mode of his."

"He's also easy on the eyes."

Rebecca grimaced. "Really? Do you honestly think I chose him for that?"

"I'm saying he's charming. Missions sometimes rely on charm."

That wasn't what Ray was implying, but for the sake of the plan, Rebecca let his insinuation go. Ray continued, "Slight problem, however. He's only half finished with his mission. He's re-acquiring some of DEED's goods. He has most of it, but they split the package, and he needs to finish the assignment."

Rebecca set her chin. "What's more important, Ray?"

Papers shuffled at the other end. "I may be able to re-assign him on short notice. And you're right. He's a solid choice. But I have to say, he's so good that all the enforcer agents want to be paired with him."

Another little jab. Yes, Ofer was an obvious choice, but she wanted this mission to succeed, didn't she?

Ray cleared his throat. "In his place, how about Hans?"

"That's an immediate *no*." Rebecca began to pace again.

"He's available. Admittedly, he's a bit far from Venezuela, but if we start soon, he could travel there."

"If he managed to get on the right plane," snapped Rebecca. "No. No. And again, I say no."

"Fine. We can discuss alternatives for Ofer, later. Who else, then?"

Rebecca closed her eyes. "Diana."

Diana wasn't a great choice, but she could serve as backup if everything went to Hades. After the meeting with Freyarsha, Rebecca wanted to mentor Diana again. Not partner, mind you. Mentor.

"Diana? I thought you didn't want to be paired with her."

Ray was pressing all her buttons today. "A team is not a pairing."

"And Diana is not available." Ray exhaled loudly. "She's undercover. Next."

"Riju."

Ray cleared his throat. "Riju is not an option—"

Rebecca threw her notebook on the couch. "Zero for three. Dust it, Ray!"

"Riju is not an option, but not for the reason you're thinking." Ray went silent.

"The plan is sludge then. Ray, come on. Give me something to start with."

"The plan isn't dead." Keys clicked on a keyboard. "Even if the agents you mentioned were available, I'd need time to pitch it to the council. But I may have an assignment for you in the meantime that will further your cause." A final clack of the keyboard.

Rebecca sat down on the couch. "What is that?"

"Agent Eidelweiss, I need you on a 1D-2U."

The code meant "one down, two up" or one agent down and two up. The "two" were to assist the "one" in danger. But Rebecca voiced its more familiar name. "I need to rescue an agent?"

"A hostile 1D-2U." Ray was all business now.

"Huh?" Rebecca knew the meaning of a hostile extraction. She had to find a mythical who didn't want to return to Elysium and force them to go back. She had completed many similar missions. But the word "hostile" never went with "1D-2U."

Unless.

"You mean...Riju's gone rogue?"

"Sludge!" swore Ray. "We can't locate him. I have a few social agents scouring India, but he's disappeared. And we have every reason to believe he chose to vanish."

"Are you kidding me? With Riju's abilities in a large, overpopulated country like India? The odds of finding him are a million to one." Rebecca grinned. "For everyone else, that is. But for me, however..."

"I've booked you a ticket, Rebecca. Detroit to Chicago. Chicago to New Delhi. I'll transmit everything we have. You have your next assignment. Find him, and we'll talk 'team.'"

RETURN THE NATIVE

April - Jaipur, India

Walking through Nehru Bazaar, Rebecca stood out like a sandcastle on an Arctic plain. With her umber-colored hair and white jacket, she contrasted with the crowd of patrons surrounding her wearing scarves, salwars, and sarees. She was never one for disguises, but perhaps she had made a mistake this time. She hadn't wanted to draw people's notice, but she had. The only way to draw more attention to herself would be to transform into her centaur form.

Because of her position in DEED, Rebecca had globetrotted around the world multiple times. However, she lacked fieldwork in India. As such, the department didn't often send her to this area on assignment, the Mumbai mission a rare exception. Rebecca had visited India at least five times before, but this was her first time in Jaipur. And finding this particular renegade wouldn't be easy.

Rebecca stopped and examined a vibrant blue robe. During her career, she had collared a baker's dozen of satyrs, at least three kitsunes, and a Norwegian naiad—under the ice, no less. But a rakshasa, a shapeshifter who could assume any human form in seconds? No, she'd never been assigned someone so elusive. How would she find him in Jaipur among its nearly five million population?

Simple. She'd figured out his secret.

Riju's credit card statements had him shopping at the Nehru Bazaar. The last video of the missing agent placed her target at a merchant's table interacting with a twenty-year-old woman in a ghagra choli. Rebecca had reviewed this thirty-second video and home movies of the creature several times until she discovered an angle, a potential path to her quarry. And now, while wandering around the marketplace, Rebecca observed her surroundings, humming and whistling wherever she went and waiting for a reaction.

The simple pleasure of finding something handmade in a market.

Those were Riju's words. But she'd had no luck all morning. Rebecca's feet were hurting. She shouldn't have taken the detour to the pink city palace, but she couldn't resist. While the swirling, traditional music pleased her ear, a distant car horn would often break the mystical environment of the market. And the crowd made her feel like a number.

Across the aisle, Rebecca spied a stall where a woman facing away from her brushed the dust off tapestries hung on a line. She had seen these wall hangings before. Black fabric with gold tassels and a pattern of swan silhouettes running in diagonal lines. The design resembled a textile she had seen in the last video of Riju.

And the woman beating the tapestry was the same woman. In that video, Riju had walked in, paid for the tapestry, and walked out. The merchant had stayed behind.

But Rebecca had restored the video to its original capture. In this version, Riju had paused at the door and had run back to the counter. He had transformed into the woman, who had walked out.

Riju had never left the stall. A false identity had purchased the selling booth from its previous owner. Whether this was Riju's long-term plan or a short diversion, Rebecca didn't know. She only knew he was here disguised as the woman.

Rebecca edged nearer, out of the tapestry seller's line of sight. She ducked behind the side of the merchant's tent and cut three small holes in the tarp. The ambient sounds drowned out the fabric ripping.

She placed her eyes against the top two holes and her mouth against the bottom one. Offkey, she hummed the first few notes of "Always."

The woman's head jerked, and she swiveled around like a lighthouse spotlight through the fog. She wasn't curious but panicked. Riju knew Rebecca's code song.

Success! She had her rakshasa.

Rebecca cut a line down the tarp and stepped through. The merchant immediately dropped the brush and darted to the back of the booth. If she lost eye contact now, Riju would shift, and she would lose him. The booths were connected in a long row and their backs were against a wall. Circling the wall would waste time.

The woman hurried through the rear door. Rebecca had to make it to the door before it shut.

Her luck ran out when the door cut off her view before she reached it.

Rushing through, the agent sprinted into the backyard of the booths where merchants stored wares. An eight-foot, chain-link fence enclosed this section, keeping thieves on the outside. A set of hanging tapestries hung in front of her and to the right and left.

Rebecca removed her bolas from her shoulder bag. The foremost tapestry flapped as if someone had disturbed it.

"Stop, Riju. I will entangle the next person I see, assuming it's you."

Behind the central tapestry, a boy with a bowl cut stepped into view. His round eyes indicated fear, and he trembled. "I've lost my mother."

"Save it. DEED wants you home."

The boy moved behind the arras to her right. The voice changed, becoming older. "How did you find me, Eidelweiss?"

Rebecca licked her lips. "A lot of patience. You didn't clip the video. You used AI to insert frames of the merchant standing alone over the original footage. You and I have been thoroughly trained in AI and can spot its application. Certainly, an agent should double-check all videos for traces of it."

"Not everyone would think of AI on a security feed. Only someone who hunts others."

Rebecca took his statement as a compliment, even if it wasn't meant that way. "I've been singing my code song all morning. Your reaction, on hearing it, was the final giveaway."

A teenage girl with her hair in braids peeked around the tapestry.

Rebecca had studied Riju's methods. He transformed into people he paid to give pursuers the slip. She was taking the chance he hadn't placed these duplicates in this yard to deceive her.

The girl fingered a braid. "I'm not like the others. I belong here."

"They all say that." Rebecca steadied the hand holding the bola. "We can't risk you exposing us. You know what the world would do if they discovered us. They'd hunt us."

Riju slipped behind the center curtain and appeared in the gap between it and the left wall hanging. Now, he took on the form of an elderly woman. Her voice croaked. "It's not fair. I want to live in the world, not be assigned to it. I want to choose if I go and if I stay."

He had a point. The constant moving did wear Rebecca out, but that was the least of her gripes about DEED. She never thought of a permanent residency anywhere but in Elysium. "It has to be this way."

Sliding behind the front tapestry, the old woman vanished from eye contact. A ripple in the fabric indicated the rakshasa was on the move. A young, broad-shouldered man with a mustache emerged on the other end. "I should live in Jaipur. Before all creatures immigrated to Elysium, my family lived here."

"We're all diasporic people, Riju. Do you think I like this part of the job? You've done it yourself, for Chiron's sake.

But think of the consequences if we re-integrated into human society."

The man's features changed. Bald, white eyes, clean-shaven. A blank slate. "I'm more useful here. I know the culture and could be both an enforcer and a social agent. Not many rakshasas are in the field."

Rebecca's shoulders slumped. "I wish I didn't have—"

Hold on!

Why hadn't she thought of it before? Rebecca lowered her bola. "Riju, I may know of a way for both of us to get what we want."

Tilting his head, he waited for her to continue.

"I have a mission for you," Rebecca said. "And if you agree to it, maybe I could get you permanent residency here."

Riju leaned forward. "Tell me."

Rebecca entered her hotel room, rubbing her eyes. The day had been a long one, and though the shopping was interesting, keeping her senses peeled for Riju had taken a toll. She wasn't used to the crowds and the hustle of India, either. Rebecca threw her handbag on a chair.

Pulling out her phone, Rebecca strode to the window and moved a blind with her finger. Observing the street, she went through the motions of triple-securing the line. She continued to survey the crowded avenue in front of the hotel when Ray answered.

"Assignment completed?"

"Mostly. I made contact." Rebecca licked her lips. "He wants concessions."

"Sludge on his concessions!" cussed Ray. "You haul him back here."

"Let's talk about his demands. He's willing to accompany me to Venezuela if we give him what he wants."

Ray grumbled on the other end. "What could he want?"

"How about a council without grumpy members?"

"Rebecca, I don't have time to play games." Ray breathed loudly through his nose. "You want him on your team, so you have a stake in this, too."

"He wants to stay here. Primary residence, India. Secondary residence, Elysium."

Ray's voice sounded gravelly. "Of all the stupid asks. Well...I shouldn't tell you this, but he wouldn't be the first."

"Really? DEED allows other agents to live in the world?"

"Not many," Ray responded. "Oh, this will be a mountain of paperwork, but I'll see if we can grant his request. But he must come in and go to Venezuela first."

"Ray, whatever I said about you in the past, I take back half of it!"

Ray laughed. "Half? I was expecting a quarter." He paused. "Enjoying India?"

Rebecca observed a man leap onto the remaining open space on a bus's back bumper. "I find it fascinating."

"Unfortunately, I'm sending you back to Poland. We didn't flip the apartment to a new agent, so you should have all you need to return. Do you have a way of contacting Riju?"

Rebecca fingered a slip of paper with the number of Riju's burner phone. "Yes."

"Good. Your flight leaves in four hours. Pack, and we'll continue the conversation there."

The line disconnected, and she hung her head. No rest for field agents. Always on the move.

This is what I signed up for.

Then, Rebecca heard the flattening of the carpet behind her. She hadn't cleared the apartment when she returned. So full of confidence in finding Riju, she had made a rookie mistake!

Rebecca took a short breath as she swiveled around in time for a dart to pierce her neck. She reached up for the thin missile with the jagged edge. The needle hurt, but that wasn't her largest problem.

Green-haired Joelle stood there with her arm extended, dart gun in hand. "Sorry, Eidelweiss. This time, you're the target."

THE HUMAN FACTOR

April - Jaipur, India

J oelle had aimed directly for a blood vessel in her neck. Was Rebecca surprised, given the bounty hunter's talents?

"Gotcha." Joelle stepped forward.

Rebecca couldn't go down without a fight. If she fell unconscious, she would be taken to Jorge Corto's compound. While Joelle might be clueless to Rebecca's true nature, her bosses certainly knew. No, Rebecca couldn't succumb to the drug. Yet, with each second that passed, she was growing dizzier.

I have only one option. DEED isn't going to like it.

Rebecca's idea broke every rule in DEED's twenty-centimeter binder of policy, but she wasn't known as a rule-follower. She couldn't overthink it or worry about the consequences. Aurora's life could be on the line. Hers, too.

Rebecca transformed into her centaur body.

Both her width and her height elongated, gaining more mass, pushing the needle from her neck. Joelle had drugged the dart with enough solution to knock out a human woman, but the same amount against a horse? And even the human-appearing part of Rebecca's body grew more muscular and broad-shouldered when she transitioned to her native form. The drug's effects lessened, and her vision cleared.

Joelle grabbed a shock of her own grass-colored hair, mouth open.

While her foe gaped at her, Rebecca trotted over and grabbed the gun from the woman's hand. The bounty hunter allowed it, surrendering the weapon without a fight. Good. Rebecca had hoped for this reaction, and not the cries of terror, although Joelle never seemed like a screamer to her. Still, when a human sees something impossible, the reaction is unpredictable. To say the least.

Rebecca nodded to a wall away from the door and window. "Move there."

Joelle followed the command, eyes glued to Rebecca. Her face didn't show fear but incredulity.

The gun was a cheap but effective model. Using her centaur's stronger hands, Rebecca jammed it so Joelle wouldn't be able to use it again. She reached under the counter where she had duct taped one of her revolvers.

Standing next to the wall, Joelle struck her head hard against the plaster, creating cracks.

Startled, Rebecca asked. "What are you doing?"

Joelle repeated the action, an ugly red bruise flowering from her temple.

Rebecca grimaced. "Stop."

Joelle closed her eyes, and then rapidly opened them. "I'm hallucinating. I was careful not to touch anything, worried you had coated your living space with a contact poison. You put something in the air, didn't you?"

Perfect. Let her adversary think she was drugged. That would allow Rebecca to escape without compromising her species. Now, she had to put Joelle to sleep.

"Correct. You're hallucinating. Now stop harming yourself."

Joelle snorted. "No. You want me to think I'm drugged. What did you do? Hypnotism?"

Rebecca flipped off the safety. She wouldn't use it on Joelle. The weapon would allow Rebecca to move close enough to Joelle to knock her out. "Yes, that's it."

"Stop agreeing with me, Eidelweiss!" Joelle observed her

horse quarters. "Show me some respect. You can't pull this on me and then put me to sleep."

Sighing, Rebecca knew her opponent was right. The DEED agent didn't owe her anything, but the two had tangled so often, she thought as highly of her as of her fellow agents.

Joelle cleared her throat. "Are you what I think you are?"

Rebecca would love to transform into a human then instill doubt into what Joelle had seen. She had used that trick in the past to great effect, but with the drug still in her system, she had to remain a centaur. "I don't answer questions. You do."

"Are you kidding me right now?"

"Maybe what you're seeing isn't real." Rebecca moved the gun so that it wasn't aimed at Joelle but at the wall to her left. "I have amazing tech at my disposal."

"You're delusional if you think I'm doubting what I'm seeing. You're..." Joelle struggled to form a word and then found one. "Magnificent."

Rebecca suppressed the blush. She had read about this. When mythicals revealed themselves, most humans reacted with fear. Fight or flight dominated ninety percent of reactions upon seeing a creature who shouldn't exist. But the ten percent minority will regard them as higher or lesser beings. About half of the ten percent might view Rebecca as nothing but a horse— an animal to be captured, sold, or enslaved. But others might treat her as a demi-god. Joelle appeared to be in the latter category. Her adversary's take on the situation would make everything much easier.

"Who sent you, and where were you taking me?"

"You haven't answered my question." Joelle didn't sound angry. She sounded more as though she was on the verge of laughing.

Rebecca slightly shook her hand. "I have the gun."

Joelle's eyes roved back and forth over Rebecca's horse half. "You won't shoot me. Everyone knows you aren't a killer."

Gaa! DEED's rules, again! "I could kick you. Have you ever had a horse hoof to the head?"

Joelle touched her nose. "I can't say that I have, but you broke my nose as a woman. I'd hate to see what you'd do with those legs. Truce, then. If I answer your questions, will you answer mine?"

Rebecca kept her expression frozen. "Perhaps. Now why did they send you after me?"

Joelle's eyes flicked to Rebecca's face then back to her equine body. "My contact in Venezuela asked me to bring you in. You've interfered with two other jobs, one in Canada and then in Norway, and he wanted to make you a counteroffer. You'd work for them for a lot more money."

Rebecca's right eye twitched. "What was the plan?"

"I have a private charter waiting for us," replied Joelle. "I was to keep you drugged for the duration of transport and hand you over at touchdown."

"And if you failed?"

Joelle set her chin. "I was warned not to fail."

"Will they come looking for you?"

"Come on." Joelle shifted from foot to foot, like a child waiting for their Christmas presents. "I've answered your questions. Now answer mine."

Rebecca shook her head. "I need to know what the next step is. And you may find this hard to believe, but I want to keep you safe. I'm not going to put you in a cage like they'd do with me."

"They wouldn't do that." Joelle crossed her arms.

"Where do you think the little girl from Nova Scotia is right now?" asked Rebecca.

"How would I know? You have her hidden somewhere."

Wouldn't that be ironic if DEED was behind Aurora's kidnapping? But no, Rebecca had seen her former charges, ones from prior missions, roaming free in Elysium when she returned. "Your people grabbed her in Maine and flew her to Venezuela. And now, she's sitting in a cage."

"No."

"I have confirmation," said Rebecca. "And I know what my

people want with her. My people think she's one of our kind. Your people think she's a freak to be exploited."

"She's not like you."

Rebecca gripped the gun. "She's not human. She can't shapeshift, but she belongs with people like me. She shouldn't be imprisoned with Jorge Corto's thugs."

Joelle shook her head. "Who now?"

Rebecca leaned back. Her impression of Joelle from before Aurora was as a highly skilled bounty hunter. She was one of the best. Corto only sent Joelle on assignment to retrieve human-looking mythicals like Sigrid. That was, until Aurora. The bounty hunter never knew they were mythicals. Her handler might have described Aurora's legs as a birth defect. And Joelle believed her handler's lies. Her contact, Jose Mareillo, kept her real employer secret.

"Jorge Corto is the man you're working for, and he collects and imprisons people like me."

Joelle blinked. "No, I reunite families. I'm careful not to take on child abductors."

Joelle's downward turn of her lips expressed her doubt even after she said it. Rebecca had done enough research on the bounty hunter to know that this was true in most cases. Joelle had built her reputation on finding runaways.

"You didn't dig deep enough this time." Rebecca lowered the gun. "Mareillo is your contact, not your employer. Jose's in Corto's pocket. Mareillo's bribery court case was thrown out thanks to Corto. Take out your phone and search for Brazil's series of articles, *La Libertad*, with both their names."

Joelle did as instructed, thumbs flying over her cell. After a few minutes, she slumped against the wall and rubbed her temple. "I'm not a child abductor."

"No, you aren't."

Eyes glued to her cell, Joelle said, "Why did I ever trust Mareillo?"

"Because you wanted to save children, and he lied to you about financing your deepest desire. When we want something deep in our heart, we're often blind to logic."

Such as running off to Venezuela to complete a mission without preparation.

Rebecca's hooves shifted. "Now, I need you to do two things for me. Disappear, and never talk about what you've seen."

"The first is easy." Joelle lowered her hand. "I have so many questions about who you are."

She had said "who," not "what." Joelle thought in terms of mythicals as people, not things. "I don't know if I can answer them."

"Are you a centaur? If so, where did you come from? You mentioned 'your kind,' so more of you exist? How many more?"

"Most of this is classified." Rebecca rolled her eyes. "Actually, all of it is. But if you reveal it, I'll find and discredit you. My organization may leak false information about you, guaranteeing you'll never find a job again. Do you understand?"

Joelle frowned. "You don't need to threaten me. Who am I going to tell that will believe me?"

Rebecca gestured to the couch. "Yes, I'm a centaur, and yes, more like me exist. I can't tell you anything other than that."

Joelle sat on the arm of the couch. "Why are you hiding?"

"If you reflect on that question, I think you'll figure out the answer."

Joelle focused on Rebecca, unblinking. "You shouldn't hide. You're a work of art."

This time Rebecca blushed. "You almost killed me."

"Because I thought you were kidnapping children." Joelle lowered her gaze to the floor. "Turns out *I* was."

"Not always." Rebecca moved to the side of the couch. "The Perodi twins were runaways. I wasn't after them when we first met. I was after another child, Jackson. But I needed the twins because they knew what Jackson was."

"What was he? A centaur?"

Rebecca pictured six-year-old Jackson, a shapeshifting mer-child. Joelle already knew too much, so she lied. "Yes. The

Perodis were also trying to rescue him, but I needed to talk to them to keep them quiet. So, I had to take all three."

"What about Agatha?"

"I wasn't after Agatha." Ugh, that horrible chase at the ski resort ending on the roof. "My assignment just happened to cross your path again, and you assumed she was the target."

"Oh."

"You brought Agatha home, right?" Rebecca asked.

"Yeah. She knew she was in over her head but didn't know how to get out."

Rebecca tapped her chest. "We're not so different."

"You don't belong in a cage." Joelle waved her hand to indicate her horse half. "You belong out there with us. Like this. Not disguised as a human."

Rebecca smiled. "Thank you. You think differently than most people, though."

"Yeah, I figured." Joelle brushed a stray green curl from her hair. "If everyone grew up poor, having the world say no truth existed in anything, but you *knew* something real was out there somewhere." She regarded Rebecca again. "And then you found it. The world is bigger than malice and self-interest. If everyone grew up like I did and met you, there would be no cages."

Rebecca had known Joelle's history and thought of her as a brutal version of herself. Rebecca had misjudged her. She had to bite back telling her everything to fan that wicker of hope. Instead, Rebecca returned to the immediate situation. "The plane is waiting for you, so I need you to disappear."

Joelle dropped her gaze and stared at a point on the floor. "Yeah, I know."

"I..." Rebecca chose her words carefully. "I can't guarantee I'll see you again, but I'll try. Please, drop your contacts in Venezuela, and don't capture anyone else for them."

Without looking at her, Joelle spoke slowly. "I want to help you."

Rebecca sighed. "I can't allow—"

"Think about it. They trust me."

"I can't involve you."

"Don't discount the human factor." Joelle stood. "I have talents, too. Talents you need."

This was unexpected, but DEED would never allow a non-mythical on such an important mission. "Joelle—"

The bounty hunter pointed at herself. "Foster child to Venezuelan parents. Sure, my birth mother was from the northern hemisphere, but I know the language and culture better than most."

"I can speak Spanish," said Rebecca.

Joelle put a hand on her hip. "Oh, yeah? Say 'very well' in Spanish."

Was this a trick? "*Muy bien.*"

Joelle grinned. "They'll tag you as a foreigner. Venezuelans say *chévere*. Venezuelans like to say things in their way. Because of my foster parents, I applied for dual citizenship and have lived there. Rebecca, I know their culture and ways. You step foot in that country, you'll be marked before you exit the airport."

And thrown into the trunk of a car. "I don't know, Joelle."

"I want in," said Joelle. "I want to make this right. For that little girl who's in a cage, let me help."

Rebecca raised her eyebrows. Ten minutes before, she had been drugged and almost imprisoned, and now she might have the final piece of her plan, a missing piece she hadn't even known existed.

USZKAS

April - Warsaw, Poland

R ebecca rubbed her neck. Jaipur hadn't turned out at all the way she'd expected. However, with Joelle joining her roster of potential allies, she was one step closer to fulfilling her plan. She had spent the plane trip back making notes on how to convince Ray to include a human on her team but had failed to think of a closing argument. She needed inspiration. And when she needed inspiration, she cooked.

Doing something ordinary distracted Rebecca long enough to start her creative juices flowing. Rebecca had decided to cook a Polish dinner in her small apartment in Warsaw. She had rummaged through the well-stocked kitchen and found the ingredients she needed—hooray for small miracles—and was cutting her dough into squares when Ray called her. Her flour-covered hands working on the food, Rebecca answered his call by tapping her nose against the receive button on her device. Afterward, she answered questions to ensure the line was triple secured.

Before speaking, the person on the other end hummed a few bars of "Flight of the Valkyrie." Rebecca responded with "Always." Then, the question. "Rebecca, are you dating that hockey player?"

Protocol dictated a fib. "Yes. We're going out tomorrow."

After security validation, Ray transitioned to all business.

"I'm checking in. Anything to report?"

Rebecca scooped out the mixture to spread on the dough. "Has the council made a decision?"

"I'm not in a location where I can discuss that topic."

Ray sounded as though he was in an elevator, as wordless Muzak floated through the speaker. DEED headquarters was located in a five-story building, the highest in Elysium.

Rebecca dabbed her mixture on several of the flour squares. "Are you in a place where we can discuss Riju?"

The response was calm and even. "I have your back on that subject. Remember that."

"Speaking of remembering, recall how we used to cook for each other while in the field? I'm making uszkas. I already have one batch in the oven," Rebecca said.

On the other end of the line, the elevator dinged, followed by Ray's footsteps. "What's an uszka?"

"A Polish dumpling." Rebecca wiped her hands on a towel. "Stuffed with mushrooms and onions and a few other things you'd like."

"Sounds like a pierogi."

Rebecca leaned against the wall and snatched up the cell. "It isn't."

"Why? It sounds like the same thing."

"It's different, that's all."

A long awkward pause followed. Rebecca considered winding down the conversation, but Ray spoke again. "I know you're frustrated with your assignments. You're a top-tier agent, and someone of your skills shouldn't be babysitting yetis or checking up on errant giants. It's like...I don't know... asking a chef whose specialty is Beef Wellington to cook using Hamburger Helper."

Rebecca let a short guffaw escape.

"But I have to ask you to trust me."

"I do," whispered Rebecca.

The centaur closed her eyes and transitioned back to Edinburgh. She and Ray were on the moors, tracking the barghest. Night was falling, and facing one of them in darkness was a terrible idea. But they both agreed to press on. They were young, idealistic agents—in other words, foolish. And when the hound-like person appeared out of the mists and jumped at her, Ray's arm had cut across its trajectory.

But his act of bravery earned him a spot on the council, hadn't it? The spot should've been hers, but she hadn't contested it. How could she? He couldn't remain in the field any longer, and Ray wasn't someone suited to taking orders at a desk job. Why had he been assigned as her handler? Not only was the history between them awkward, but Ray wasn't well-matched for the position.

Rebecca set the phone back on the counter and picked up the spoon. "This isn't a typical check-in, is it?"

"You didn't complete your assignment."

Rebecca scooped her last bit of the mixture. "It's almost completed."

"Not to DEED's satisfaction."

She threw the spoon back into the mixing bowl and swore. "DEED. DEED. DEED. To Hades with DEED. They need to be more lenient."

Ray's footsteps clomped down a carpeted hallway. "Perhaps."

After finishing her task, Rebecca wetted her fingers and allowed drops to land on the corners of the unbaked dough. She placed the pan in the oven, replacing the one inside. "In the meantime, I'll be here where you put me, stuffing my face with uszkas."

"Sounds delicious."

Rebecca set her pan of completed dumplings on an oven mitt, letting them cool. The mixture of bread, onions, and mushrooms smelled delectable. "I made too many. I always do."

"You're generous that way. I wish I could eat them with you."

Rebecca set a timer. *"Do widzenia,"* she responded, saying goodbye to Ray in Polish.

"Hej."

As she hung up, someone knocked at the door. Rebecca was immediately on alert. No one knew she was here. She didn't know the neighbors, and the hour was late, so this couldn't be a sales call. Who could it be?

She advanced to the door and approached the peephole. Before she could look through, she heard someone whistle "Flight of the Valkyries" outside.

What? Must be a mistake. She had just hung up on Ray. The person outside couldn't be him. But then again, Ray hadn't disclosed his location.

Rebecca couldn't believe it. Her hand reached for the knob but hesitated. She had to answer. She hummed, "Always."

Ray's voice spoke through the door. "What's for dinner?"

Rebecca peered through the peephole. As she suspected, she spied Ray standing outside. She answered, "Pierogis."

Ray chuckled as she opened the door. His build filled the doorframe, droplets of rain dripping off the largest trench coat the brand sold. A stylish dark-brown fedora sat on his head like a ski cabin atop a mountain. His broad, ruddy face, golden-colored eyes, and pug-nose hid the plastic surgery he had undergone when he first ventured into the field. He'd even allowed the surgeons to remove his minotaur horns. His lower forearm extended into his coat pocket. The pocket didn't bulge with an item or even his hand. In the other massive hand, he held up a brown paper bag. "Beware of Greeks bearing gifts."

Rebecca stepped aside. "You forget. Like you, I trace my lineage to Greece before the Great Migration. What are you doing here?"

Ray clomped inside and surveyed the apartment. "It's not unheard of for handlers to visit their agents."

"Even when the handler is a member of the council?" Rebecca shut the door. "Come inside."

Ray tipped the paper bag so Rebecca could see inside. "A friend, then."

In the sack was a slim bottle of vodka. "I have ginger beer

and the other ingredients with me," Ray said.

Rebecca raised her eyebrows. "You remembered. I'm touched."

Ray opened his arms. "May I?"

She leaned into him and put her arms around him. Yes, Ray was an acute pain in the flanks, but he looked out for her. She knew that. He removed his other limb from his pocket and swung his arms around her. Not council to employee, or handler to agent, but as the friends they once were.

Ray released her and stepped back. Rebecca's breath caught in her throat. No matter how many times she saw his forearm ending in a stump, she couldn't get used to it. She looked away.

Ray strolled across the apartment as if he lived there. "I can think of worse libations I might've chosen than our favorite drink. How about the ones we consumed after that autumn night in Edmonton?"

Rebecca placed her hand over her face. "Please, don't remind me about Edmonton. That police officer almost threw us in jail."

Her handler placed the paper bag on the kitchen counter and removed the vodka. He rummaged in his pocket and produced a bottle of ginger beer and a plastic lime. While doing so, his left foot scuffed the carpet, his nervous tic. Something was up.

Ray reached for the cabinets with his single remaining hand. He opened one, then another. "That Edmonton cop was bluffing. What charge would he have brought against us?"

Rebecca entered the adjoining kitchen and picked up a spatula. "Drunk and disorderly."

Carefully scooping the diminutive dumplings onto a large plate, Rebecca added, "You were singing the national anthem of Elysium. Loudly."

Ray emitted a half-laugh, half-grunt, pulling out two tumblers. As Rebecca opened the silverware drawer, Ray uncorked the bottles. She knew he wouldn't talk about why he was here until they sat down and he made her drink. His reticence was a bad sign. For Ray to travel into the field to see her meant something was wrong. Rebecca was glad to see him after so much time had passed, but this wasn't a social call.

Nonetheless, I should take this opportunity to discuss the team.

She hadn't spoken to him about Joelle yet. Face-to-face might be an advantage. She had to figure out a way to slip that ticklish matter into the conversation.

Ray leaned over and sniffed the hot uszkas. "Smells great."

Rebecca waltzed to the table and set down the plate. She returned to the kitchenette to collect two smaller plates. Dumplings with alcohol weren't the best combination, but she had once eaten a fast-food cheeseburger with escargot on a stakeout—long story. This meal wasn't the most unusual dinner she'd ever had.

Ray was extremely adept at making the Moscow Mules and he carried each glass to the table separately. Rebecca almost helped him but refrained, knowing how much he liked to do for himself. When the dinner and drinks were on the table, they sat down.

Rebecca picked up a fork. No more stalling, she wanted his news before she told him about Joelle. "Let me have it."

"You're sure the room is secure." Ray spiked a dumpling and shoved the uszka into his mouth. "Delicious."

Rebecca locked eyes with Ray. "Do you doubt my abilities as an agent or as a cook? The room is secure. The uszkas are exquisite."

Ray snorted as he selected another dumpling. "I should've brought humble pie for dessert. You know I have to ask."

"Ray, quit stalling."

Ray chewed and swallowed his second uszka. "As you know, I authorized Sonya to tell you about our mole in the Venezuela compound. With our onsite agent's information, your plan was practically approved. But then we had a major setback."

Ray paused, and Rebecca leaned forward.

Ray set down his fork. "Our agent was discovered and killed, Rebecca. Though her notebook was encrypted and salted, we have reason to believe her notes were confiscated. Jorge Corto knows everything about us. And you."

"Sludge!" Rebecca slammed her fist on the table.

"The story only gets worse." Ray rested his stump next to his plate. "Corto pulled strings, and they now have soldiers from Venezuela's fourth army battalion on site. Our information is sketchy, but we think somewhere between fifty and eighty boots. They're led by a man named Roberto Alternez. He's known for his cruelty."

Jorge had only had criminals guarding the complex before. Trigger-happy thugs were what her plan depended on, not trained soldiers. Now, she'd have to accommodate both, and her small team couldn't take on so many.

Ray continued, "Corto's nasty, but he's not trained. Alternez is his friend. He's highly skilled."

Ray then took a drink while Rebecca mentally chewed on his news. He set down his tumbler next to his plate. "The council has rejected your plan."

Rebecca crossed her arms. "Of course, they have."

"Rebecca."

"DEED only sees the negative. They don't support their agents in the field when they have ideas."

She was being unreasonable, but she had to let him know her feelings. Now, he crossed his arms.

Rebecca brandished her fork like a knife. "Yes, I know this is bad, but why not ask me for a revision before outright rejecting the plan? I'm going to need at least three days to put together another proposal now instead of amending the one I had. Come on, Ray."

"On that point, I'll see what I can do." Ray unfolded his arms and grabbed his fork. "But even you would've stopped putting your plan in motion given this news."

"Not if we had acted quickly." Rebecca's eyes were ablaze.

"Once we had the information, we could've mounted the attack."

"Rebecca—"

"We still have the element of surprise."

"Rebecca."

"We infiltrate, recover only Aurora, and exit quietly."

This time, Ray didn't try to interrupt her. Rebecca wanted to yell at him, blaming him for being too slow. Curse her luck. If only she had thought of her plan a couple of days earlier. It would've worked.

Ray swallowed another dumpling. "We didn't act quickly. So, we must deal with it."

Rebecca threw back a large gulp of her Moscow Mule after her tirade and banged her drink on the table. "You mean *I* must deal with it. I must clean up after DEED, again and again. *How did Dimitra escape Elysium?* 'Rebecca, go get her.' *Why didn't we take Sigrid when we extracted her mother?* 'Rebecca, go obtain the package and break her heart that she'll never see her friends again.'"

Ray lowered his head and ate another uszka.

Rebecca finished her drink. She had better change the subject before she landed in trouble and was called back to Elysium. "Who was killed?"

Ray kept his eyes on his plate. "A brash, young agent who wanted to live up to our high expectations. Diana."

Oh, Chiron! Diana, her former partner! The energy sagged out of Rebecca's frame. "Why did you send her?"

"Perfect Spanish skills, a shape changer, attractive to distract. The question is why wouldn't we?"

Rebecca leaned forward. "And she had no partner?"

Ray caught her eye. He didn't have to ask her who her model was. Rebecca flinched. Instead, he cleared his throat. "She was deep undercover."

Rebecca stood and walked away from the table. She hated the lump in her throat. This was the job, and she couldn't feel too deeply about anyone. But Diana. "If we had been quicker about the assignment, and you had given me my team, then we could have extracted her with Aurora."

"That time's passed."

She ignored his response. "Instead, you sent me to check in on a yeti breaking the rules and an errant agent. You had me retrieving teenage girls."

"Joelle would've gotten Sigrid if you hadn't been assigned."

Joelle. She could have taken Diana's place. And maybe Lester could've taken Ofer's place. But she would've never thought of it if she hadn't visited Lester. Rebecca couldn't throw that back in Ray's face. And perhaps, if she hadn't rescued Sigrid and fought Joelle, her new human friend wouldn't have shown up in Jaipur.

Rebecca tilted her head. Riju. She had to tell Ray about Riju and Joelle. And now, what would Ray say? Rebecca revealing herself to Joelle wouldn't please DEED at all. And Riju had little leverage to stay in India.

Riju. Joelle. Lester.

Rebecca began pacing the room, her brow furrowed as something formed in her mind. Without looking at Ray, she held up her index finger. "Don't talk to me. I may have something."

CONVOCATION

April - Dublin, Ireland

Rebecca entered the Dublin International Airport with her list, hoping she was the last to arrive. Dublin had two terminals, and in the middle of the day, they were less busy than in the morning and evening. She dodged people dressed for business, for vacation, and for entertainment, the last strumming a guitar.

DEED's chartered plane was in the process of being prepped and would lift off in ninety minutes. An hour and a half wasn't a lot of time to accomplish everything she had to do. As she strolled across the tiled floor, she went over the speech she had prepared. She only hoped it would be good enough. Rebecca lacked confidence in giving speeches. She was a woman of action, not words.

With Rebecca's doctored clearance, she slipped past security and headed straight to the boarding areas. Crowds formed around a few of the entrances to the planes. Rebecca hoped her contacts were all at their designated gates.

The agent marched toward Terminal 2. The long hallway buzzed with life: men and women reading their tablets dressed in power business suits, families in more casual clothes chatting excitedly, a group of tourists demarcated by their carry-on luggage. Amazing how a terminal could bring such a disparate group together. Same with her people. They were as varied as the shapes and colors of rocks washed up on the shore of a lake.

Rebecca approached gate 412 first. A woman with a hat and an older teenage girl sat alone. No flight out of this terminal for two hours according to the sign. When the woman spotted her, she touched the girl's arm and they both sprang up and gathered their luggage.

Rebecca stopped in front of them and hugged the woman. "Sonya."

"Hey, Derby."

"That name better not stick."

"Oh, it's sticking." Sonya put a finger on her chin. "Breaking protocol. No tune?"

Rebecca smirked. "Not now. You must be you if you agreed to this mission." She folded her hands around Sonya's gloves. "Thank you."

Rebecca turned her attention to the teenage girl. "Sigrid. Sonya explained what was at stake?"

Sigrid lifted her chin, eyes defiant. "I'm ready."

"*Tusen takk*." Rebecca stepped back, regarding them both. "This means a lot to me. Sigrid, you haven't even been to Elysium, yet."

Sigrid shifted her luggage to her other hand. "I've talked to my mom. I'm excited to see what she's described to me. I hope I can help you free a little girl to go with me."

Another example of a crone breaking her stereotype.

Rebecca gestured to the main thoroughfare. "Let's gather the others."

They walked down the terminal when a medium-height Indian woman in Western clothes approached. She had a bindi on her forehead, drawing attention away from the rest of her features.

Rebecca let the woman approach. "Do I know you?"

The woman hummed the first few bars of "Gham Ki Andheri Raat Mein."

"Riju," Rebecca whispered.

The woman nodded and eyed Sigrid, her eyes questioning.

Rebecca put her hand on the Indian agent's arm. "I'll introduce everyone in the safe location I've reserved."

Riju whispered, his deep voice betraying his appearance. "Are you sure about this?"

"As I told you, no one is going to force you to Elysium, Riju. We have the council's promise on it."

The foursome proceeded down the terminal until they reached gate 417. At this boarding area, a seven-foot-tall man manipulated marionette strings in front of a group of four- and five-year-olds. Only a professional would spot his makeup job, and his clothes likewise hid every inch of his body. The puppeteer stooped, disguising his true size, but couldn't hide his bulk, and he'd attracted a small crowd.

Rebecca stood outside the area, crammed with people, and caught his eye. Frowning, the man said, "Oh, time to go, children. I hope you enjoyed the show."

He scooped up the marionettes in one motion and placed them in a carry-on bag. The children's disappointed groans followed him out of the boarding area.

Rebecca put her hands on her hips. "This is how you avoid attracting attention?"

"I made fifteen euros while waiting for you." Lester grinned, the putty on his face wrinkling.

"You're impossible."

Sigrid's jaw hung at Lester's height and width. Sonya patted Lester's muscular forearm with her gloved hand, and Riju nodded. Rebecca took him by the arm. "Come on."

They proceeded down the hallway, turning when they came to another terminal. A blonde-haired woman reading a book shut it when they came to the edge of the boarding area. She stood, gathered her things, and strolled toward them. Brushing the lint off her navy-blue blouse, she nodded at Rebecca. "How's our leader today?"

"Celisa."

"When DEED told me I had to take a leave of absence, this isn't what I pictured." Celisa straightened her shoulders. "I'm not a field agent."

"I need someone with your skills. You know why."

Celisa eyed Lester. "I thought I spotted you earlier."

"I'm hard to miss."

Celisa surveyed the others, her attention landing on Sonya. "Is your name Gail?"

"Sonya. My last name is Gale with an a-l-e." She stuck out her hand. "Verdurian."

Celisa grinned and shook her hand. "Sirin. Nice to meet you."

Rebecca turned down the aisle. "One more. I hope she agreed to come."

The group advanced to the end of the terminal to gate 426. There, in a mostly empty boarding area, a woman in a babushka sat next to her luggage. Dressed in a suit jacket with a pencil skirt, she tapped one toe of her high heels. When she saw the other six approaching, she stood and picked up her belongings. She made her way to them in the aisle.

The woman surveyed them. "Is this the team?"

"It is, Dimitra."

Even the short time Dimitra had spent in Athens had resulted in a Grecian accent. "No one is here to capture me?" Dimitra asked.

Riju turned sharply to Rebecca. "Why would we capture her? Who is she?"

Dimitra leaned back from the Indian woman. "And who is he?"

"All in good time," replied Rebecca. "Follow me."

The mythicals retraced their steps down the terminal in two lines of three. Rebecca walked in the front row, center, with a troubled expression. Was this the best team for the Venezuelan mission? But look at the layout, how could it not be? Doubts mixed with confidence and resoluteness much like the mixed drinks bartenders served in the lounges they passed. First, she needed to believe in herself if she was to convince them. Aurora sprang to mind. In Rebecca's thoughts, the faun was huddled in a cage, in darkness. She was bruised and battered. Crying. She was Rebecca's purpose. They couldn't fail her.

When they reached the main thoroughfare, Rebecca turned and headed for a lounge. She entered, and once inside, held the door for the rest. The room was rectangular with a window taking up one wall. Outside, they could see the tarmac. The lounge held a long coffee table in the center, a sidebar, and nine chairs. Most of the chairs were around the table but a few were against a wall. In one of the chairs near a wall sat a blonde Joelle, who had traded her green curls for a golden bob. Eyes alert, she smiled as they entered.

Sigrid immediately recoiled, pushing back into Sonya. "That woman tried to kill me."

Rebecca set her hand on Sigrid's shoulder. "She wouldn't have hurt you, Sigrid. It was an act to get me to back off. She was misinformed about you and is now on our side."

Sigrid still leaned into Sonya as she entered the room, and both mentor and student sat as far from Joelle as they could. The others stood, eyeing the snacks and beverages set out on the bar. The last to enter, Riju, scanned the room. He walked around, keeping his attention on walls and furniture. When he came to Joelle, he asked. "Who are you, anyway? You look familiar."

"An assassin," sneered Sigrid.

Joelle remained placid but raised an eyebrow.

"I need to secure the room." was Rebecca's curt reply.

After going through DEED protocol for ten minutes, Rebecca headed for the coffee table and set her tablet upright in a holder. Her device had a screen on both sides. When she called Ray, his image appeared to everyone in the room no matter where they were seated.

Everyone helped themselves to the beverages and packaged treats. Most of the assembly had taken a seat with only Riju and Rebecca standing. Rebecca would have preferred a cocktail but settled for a lemon-lime soda and positioned herself at the end of the room in front of the door.

"We're secure," she announced.

When everyone had settled in, they turned their attention to Ray, but he nodded back to Rebecca. After sipping the soda, Rebecca held it in her left hand. She transformed into a centaur. Sigrid grinned and Joelle's eyes widened. They hadn't often seen her shift into her natural state. Riju also returned to his normal form, and Dimitra edged away from him. Lester removed latex prosthetics and dabbed his face with a cleansing wipe. Then, the yeti leaned back in a chair whose legs buckled.

Rebecca cleared her throat. "I've called you and explained the general purpose of this mission. We must rescue an eight-year-old faun from a heavily guarded compound in Venezuela. Others may be imprisoned there, too. The mission is dangerous. For all of us. You've all agreed to come and hear me out and have expressed your willingness to participate."

The vines above Sonya's eyes furled. "Do you mean to put us in the field? I assumed the social agents and Sigrid would be in a safe house, monitoring the situation."

"We'll all be at the compound."

Sonya asked, "What the Hades?"

Riju leaned against a wall. "Begging your pardon, Rebecca, but this is not the team I expected. I thought you were handpicking enforcer agents like the two of us. Where's Ofer, Hans, or Fred? I recognize some people in this room, and they're not enforcer agents." He eyed Sonya. "No offense."

"None taken." Sonya grabbed Sigrid's hand. "And I'm not comfortable bringing a child on an assignment."

Sigrid released her hand. "I'm not a child."

Sonya's eyes flashed. "You're not an adult, either."

Rebecca spoke before Sigrid could respond. "Everyone here has unique talents that will help us penetrate the compound and perform the rescue. Yes, Riju, you and I have battle skills, but this is a stealth mission. And unlike humans who must learn skills, we all have natural capabilities."

Riju frowned. "Sonya's an educator. Lester's a guard. When was the last time they handled a weapon?"

Joelle folded her arms, smirking.

"You and I are the enforcers on this mission, Riju." Rebecca pointed her soda can at the rakshasa. "We've brought specialists in the field before. Our kind has many talents, some well-suited for this mission."

Riju raised an eyebrow.

"Sonya is a verdurian. Her tendril fingers make her an excellent lockpick. Dimitra is a gorgon. Her gaze is her weapon. And Celisa is a sirin whose song will stop enemies in their tracks."

"Dimitra Kotzidakis, the refugee?" Riju's attention swiveled from the gorgon to the sirin. "And I haven't worked with Celisa, but isn't she an admin? And what about the teen?"

"Sigrid is a crone. Though her abilities haven't matured, Sigrid's talents have developed enough to make a huge difference on this mission."

Rebecca didn't add how crones' bodies aged in their early twenties, making them unsuitable in the field. She wanted to be sensitive to Sigrid's feelings.

Lester put his hands behind his head. "I'm the muscle. Anything heavy gets in our way, I move it."

Riju's lips twitched. "You wouldn't hurt a fly."

Lester grinned in response.

"And who is this lady?" Riju turned to Joelle. "What is her talent?"

Rebecca could feel her heart beat faster. "Her name is Joelle. She's human."

Multiple protests, this time not only from Riju. Dimitra and Celisa both gazed on Joelle as if a cobra had slithered into the room. Lester laughed.

"She can speak fluent Venezuelan Spanish, and I'll vouch for her enforcer skills." Rebecca touched her neck. "Joelle will be our driver, and she will transport us safely to the compound."

Riju turned his attention to the monitor on the table. "Ray, are you saying the council is behind this plan?"

With an unwavering expression, Ray answered. "The council has approved proceeding."

Riju's eyes bugged out. He had expected a different answer, likely one that this was a rogue mission, allowing him to decline.

Ray swallowed. "The council hesitated with Rebecca's earlier plan, and it cost an agent her life. We're under pressure for a response."

Riju started. "But other enforcer agents—"

"Don't have the skills we need," interrupted Rebecca. "The people gathered here... Only we will be successful."

A hush fell over the assembly. Rebecca sipped her soda and gripped the can tightly. "You all want something, and DEED is prepared to give it to you."

Riju folded his arms. "Such as?"

"Permanent residence in India, a union in Greece, a side business, an enforcer role, and continued social media connections with your friends." Rebecca acknowledged each of them in the room when listing her reasons, ending with Sigrid.

Sonya picked up her coffee cup, positioning her tendril fingers over it to drink. "And what about me, Rebecca?"

"You and I want the same thing. We want Aurora back."

Sonya tilted her head. "Definitely. But I'm not as capable as an enforcer—"

"And you would also get a new safe house outside of Bangor near Canada," interrupted Rebecca.

Sonya's mouth dropped open as she returned the cup to the table without drinking.

Ray spoke next. "DEED is prepared to give all of you everything you want in exchange for accepting this mission. This is all about the package—em, Aurora Eidelweiss. You sneak in, obtain the target, and leave as if you were never there."

Riju stepped in front of the monitor. "Ray, DEED must be desperate to enlist a teenager and a *human*. This is completely against protocol. I can't help but feel I'm being set up."

The room grew quiet. Rebecca glanced around at the occupants. They were wondering if they were being asked to take a fall. Perhaps Ray had gone rogue, and Rebecca and her handler were lying about DEED's support. Or perhaps this was an information-gathering mission only, and DEED didn't expect them to return alive.

Rebecca took a deep breath. "Riju, I would've said the same thing a week ago about DEED. The department is a bureaucratic hierarchy with too much patriarchal thinking and not enough wisdom to do the right thing." She paused and licked her lips. "But someone reminded me of our true calling. DEED imperfectly strives for the ideal we all want—true freedom. None of the things DEED will give you will make you happy unless you continue to be what you were destined to be, what we're all destined to be."

For the first time, Joelle spoke. "And what is that?"

"Neighbors. Friends. Brothers and sisters. People have many words for it, but those really come down to one word. Lovers. DEED's missions aren't about rules. They're about love. In the past months, I've rescued a Canadian orphan and a Norwegian runaway. I've ensured a South Korean giant has a good home. I've even made sure someone in Oregon continues to watch over a newborn creature. But DEED is an imperfect construct in an imperfect world, and it can seem—at times—to be in opposition to what it stands for."

Rebecca had laid it all out on the table. She had said what she had come to say, but did the others believe her words? Rebecca did. Aurora's extraction was unlike any other mission for her. It had led her to this moment and these people. It had prompted a deep discussion with Freyarsha, a lecture in a field in France she would never forget. For this to work, she had to show them her vulnerability, possibly the hardest task Rebecca had ever undertaken.

Stuttering, she continued. "R...Right now, a scared, young faun is in the hands of people who don't know how to love. But that faun could just as well be a young crone, or a centaur, or a human. It doesn't matter. Aurora is a person who deserves love, and we're the people to restore it to her."

The expressions of the other seven let Rebecca know their decision. For the first time, Riju was smiling at her, his eyes alight. This wasn't the speech she had prepared; she wasn't even sure where the words and feelings had come from, but her heartfelt appeal had done the trick. She had a team.

As if to cement the idea, Lester's chair broke from under him, and he fell to the floor. The room erupted in laughter, most of it coming from Lester himself. He stood, squared his shoulders, and flashed her a toothy grin.

"When do we depart, O Sherpa?"

RESORT DE LOS MILAGROS

April - Resort de los Milagros (Resort of Miracles), *Venezuela*

J oelle turned the van into a semicircular alcove of trees, hidden from the main road. Here, the team would start and finish the mission. The road continued and dead-ended into Jorge Corto's Resort de los Milagros.

Huh! Some Resort of "Miracles." Corto, the greedy oedirex— *or scoundrel, if you want to soften it—was no better than a supposed miracle man selling potions.*

Corto was a barker at a fair, inviting people into his tent to see the so-called freaks. When would human culture end this type of exploitation?

Despite her momentary criticism of humans, Rebecca eyed Joelle with gratitude. The team's human member had promised she would navigate the culture and usher them to this spot. She had hit her mark better than a world-class ballerina. At the airport, she had spoken for the group at customs and adroitly bribed the guard.

Joelle's talents hadn't stopped there. She had fabricated a story of their being on a scientific study at the rental car agency. And then, she had whisked them through the checkpoint into this gated community. Joelle had bribed the sentry there as well, handing him a wad of cash while ignoring him and chatting to Rebecca as though she were paying a road toll. Her attitude of a carefree rich girl, her citizenship, and her colloquial language skills had transported them here without a hitch.

But the events that had shepherded them here were only the beginning.

Joelle, her pale complexion hidden under makeup, gritted her teeth. "And now it's your show."

Rebecca reached for the car door. "Jealous?"

"You betcha. Are you sure I can't come along? I have a uniform."

Rebecca opened the door. "To be used only in case someone comes snooping around. You've been a treasure to this point in the mission, and I'd love for you to join us. However, we need a getaway driver who knows her way around this country. And DEED said—"

"Do you always listen to DEED?"

Rebecca paused before exiting. Joelle wouldn't understand her answer, but she gave it anyway. "Listen? Yes. Agree with them? No. Follow their instructions?" Rebecca winked.

Joelle exited the van while Rebecca opened the rear of the Chevy Transit. When the door rolled back, the rest of the passengers eyed her with various reactions. Lester stretched his long arms. Riju sat like a statue, resolved and firm. Sigrid's hand found Sonya's and clutched it.

Reaching into his back pocket, Lester grabbed a military cap and put it on. "Why did you have to put me in a crate in the baggage area of the plane?"

"Oh, I don't know," replied Rebecca. "Maybe because a seven-foot yeti would blow our cover? Move it."

Lester grinned, bent over, and exited. Though dressed appropriately, he stood taller and more broad-shouldered than any soldier. Rebecca had told him he'd have to hunch over and hide in the back when they entered the site. His feet hit the soil with a thump. If Lester was too large, Sigrid was the opposite. The teenage girl was a head smaller than everyone else.

Hopefully, the darkness and the rest of them would cover her.

When everyone had exited the Chevy Transit, they gathered around Rebecca. For a moment, her head spun. Her team now stood in the green fatigues of the Venezuelan army. The humid April air warmed them, and flies buzzed around. Months of anticipation and weeks of planning had brought her to this minute in time. Her plan was in the execution phase. Her head and their lives were on the line.

Rebecca cleared her throat. "Our information is a week old, so expect surprises. Celisa, once we see the front gate, you head around the side to the soldiers' barracks. We need to keep them mesmerized there."

Celisa nodded.

"The rest of you, follow me. Riju and I are the leads in case you need direction. Dimitra, be careful spreading out your hood when you attack. Take care that only the enemy can see your snakes. And Sigrid, they'll think in Spanish. I need you to read their mind's sentiments, not their words. Sift for the image of a two, not the word *dos*. Understand?"

The teen nodded.

"Fantastic. Sigrid stays in the middle, and Lester, you're in the back."

"Scrunched down." He held up his hand. "Yeah, I know."

"Right."

Joelle touched Rebecca's shoulder. "Any inspiring words?"

Riju rubbed his left eyebrow. "We don't do that on our missions."

"Not normal ones," agreed Rebecca. "Among the captives, as you all know, is a little mythical the world has mistreated. This is about freeing her and showing her the world isn't all cruel or hostile. As hard as saying this is, the mission isn't about meting out justice. We won't kill anyone unless forced. This is intended to be a stealth assignment, so we abort if it goes sideways. I can't afford to lose my team. My friends."

The fear crawled up her throat, but Rebecca swallowed it down. "DEED is trusting us to see this through. Let's make them proud!"

"Here. Here!" agreed Lester. His shout scared off birds in the jungle, and he clamped a hand over his mouth.

Rebecca turned and found Joelle in front of her. The bounty hunter tapped her ear. "Call me if you need me."

"Keep the engine warm." Rebecca gave the "follow me" motion to the rest of the team and marched forward.

The jungle surrounded the compound like a hive enclosing wasps. The team followed alongside the road that led to the first checkpoint, a gate with a keypad. As they drew closer, Rebecca cursed. Corto had erected a new barrier around the guarded building.

The new outer gate was a chain-link fence with barbed wire, but the yellow sign on the outside displayed black lightning bolts. Soldiers walked within its perimeter, so even if the team could ground the electricity and cut through, they'd be spotted.

Riju crouched beside Rebecca. "Plagues," he cursed.

Rebecca's gaze swept over the fence, trying to spot weaknesses. "They read Diana's notes and constructed this."

Rebecca didn't want to admit defeat immediately, yet Sigrid was too far away to influence minds. Sonya could weave her tendrils through the gaps in the fence, but one wrong move and she'd sizzle like vegetables in a frying pan. Perhaps Riju could take the appearance of someone and convince them to turn it off. But after he convinced them, they would certainly spot the fact that the mythicals weren't soldiers.

Celisa stepped forward. "I can handle this."

Rebecca held out her arm. "No, the barracks are around the fence to the right. You must head that way."

Though her hands were shaking, Celisa sounded confident. "First, this."

She retreated and then emerged from the jungle behind them. She strode up to the front gate as if she worked there.

Riju glanced at Rebecca. "We're already off plan. Is this worth the risk?"

Rebecca reached for a pouch on her belt. "Earplugs, everyone."

After inserting her own earplugs, Rebecca watched as Celisa advanced toward the guards. Sensing something was wrong, they lifted their guns to aim at her, and Rebecca readied herself to transform. Instead, all the soldiers' faces slackened and then brightened as if they were witnessing a miracle. Rebecca counted five in the patrol, all of whom set down their weapons.

Celisa had succeeded. But the electricity?

Celisa set her attention to a woman near the gate on the chain-link fence. The woman's eyes were dreamy, and she swayed to whatever music Celisa was singing. The woman put on a pair of heavy electrician's gloves and then produced a remote from her pocket. She tapped the control a few times, then strolled up to the gate, setting her hand on the fence.

Rebecca drew in a deep breath. The female soldier was testing the fence. Hopefully, she had enough presence of mind to have taken the right action.

Satisfied, the woman removed her glove and grabbed the chain link. Celisa followed her maneuver and rattled the barrier. The sirin turned and waved over the others.

Rebecca exited the jungle and pointed to her ears. Celisa nodded, and their leader made a show of removing her earplugs to let the rest know it was safe.

Rebecca jogged up to Celisa. "Remarkable." She nodded to the guards. "How long will they be that way?"

"The effect will wear off in about three hours." Celisa faced the sentries. "Go about your business as if nothing has occurred."

Giggles and laughter met this command, but the soldiers obeyed. They picked up their guns and marched around, smiles planted on their faces.

Celisa jerked her thumb over her shoulder. "The barracks are this way?"

"Yes. Be careful."

Celisa grinned. "I'm not an enforcer agent, Rebecca. Being careful, double-checking, and ensuring everything is in order are the trademarks of a good admin. And I'm an excellent admin."

Riju observed the soldiers on the other side. "You're welcome to join the enforcer agents any day."

Celisa turned and sprinted away around the chain link fence. Rebecca grabbed the locked gate. "Can we get some help here?"

The soldiers, lost in their world without the sirin, ignored her.

Rebecca reached for her pouch. She'd have to pick the lock. As she opened it, a shoulder brushed against hers.

Sonya nudged her out of the way and wagged the tendril fingers on her hands. "This is why I'm here, isn't it?"

Sonya positioned her index, middle, and ring finger together and they entwined with each other to form one vine. Carefully, she inserted it into the lock.

"Are you sure you can pick a lock with a vine?" asked Dimitra.

Sonya's hand hardened into a bark-colored shade of brown, sturdy as the trunk of a tree.

Sigrid gasped. Dimitra nodded. "I didn't know verdurians could do that."

Click. Sonya stepped aside and held her arms up like a magician's assistant. "We verdurians have many skills."

Rebecca released the breath she had been holding. "One down, now for the two obstacles we planned for."

Rebecca's team weaved their way around the patrolling guards who were lost in their pleasant reveries. The next wall was made of brick with concertina wire on top. A single steel door without a lock or a knob barred their progress. A camera, mounted near the door, focused on the entryway. The person using the keypad had to be in view.

Riju straightened his posture. "I'm up."

He removed his hat and transformed into a medium-sized

man with a bowl haircut, a mustache, and a bushy beard. This was a close friend and advisor of Corto's, and Diana's notes said he had clearance to the entire compound. With a stiff walk that Riju had studied from a video obtained by DEED, he approached the door.

"Sigrid," whispered Rebecca.

"The thoughts these soldiers have out here are amazing. They're as happy as kids who have an amusement park to themselves."

Rebecca took the young crone's arm. "Focus. I need you to read the soldier's mind on the other side of the wall."

This task wouldn't be a problem for a crone in her twenties, but Sigrid was only just developing her abilities. The team stepped forward with Rebecca's hand on Sigrid's shoulder, making sure she stayed out of the lens's line of sight. Sigrid reached the wall and touched it.

"Oh, that's sad."

"What's sad?"

Sigrid retracted her hand. "The woman on the other side was supposed to get married, but the guy she was with dumped her."

"Sigrid!"

The teenage girl rattled off six numbers, loud enough for Riju to hear. He keyed them in and dropped his arms, eyes glued to the door.

"Lester. Dimitra. Up front," ordered Rebecca. "Sonya, take her back to the van."

Sonya grabbed Sigrid's arm, but the girl resisted. "No. I'm useful. I hear their voices, even inside the compound."

"That far?" Her range impressed Rebecca.

Sonya twirled Sigrid so they were face to face. "This is your only job, so we're going."

"I can help."

Rebecca brushed past them. "We can argue after we fight. Keep her here for now."

The door clicked and swung open a crack. Riju put his

hand on his gun and pushed the door. He entered with Lester and Dimitra on his heels. Someone had cut off a cry of alarm when Rebecca breached the door. She had her gun out, spotting a soldier trying to get a read on Dimitra. The gorgon separated the Velcro on the top of her hoodie. The special head covering spread out like a cobra's hood, allowing Dimitra a narrow line of sight to her targets. The skin of the two soldiers gradually turned gray. Surprised, they lowered their guns. Lester swatted them, knocking them unconscious.

Rebecca fired her stun gun and hit another soldier who was aiming at Dimitra. Out of the corner of her eye, Rebecca spied two other guards solidifying to stone to her left. On her right, Lester was wrestling guns out of the hands of two others. Nearby, Riju was locked in hand-to-hand combat with another guard.

Through the doorway, Sigrid called out her name. "Rebecca, someone's hiding behind the table."

To her left, Rebecca spied a wooden, overturned table. Eyes and a hand rested on its side. The gun was aimed at Lester, and a bullet fired. It nicked him in the arm.

Lester didn't even grunt but continued to wrestle with both of his adversaries. Rebecca retrieved a dart attached to her belt. She flung it to the underside of the table where its point embedded into the wood. Instantly, the missile hissed and released a thick vapor. She sprinted for the table as a man stood up, waving away the cloud. Leading with a judo kick, she connected with the man's chest, pushing him down and rolling away. An elbow to his cranium knocked him out.

When she stood, she surveyed her team. No one was hurt. The bullet that struck Lester hadn't pierced his thick hide, and Dimitra had her hoodie in place. They were unhurt, though the yeti guard and the gorgon nurse stared at her wide-eyed. They weren't used to close combat.

A gunshot and shouts likely had alerted others. Would they have to turn around before they even entered the compound? She lifted her arm with her fist in the air in a gesture to hold still for a minute.

Rebecca only took a second to decide on her option. "Sigrid, come here."

The teenager ran in with Sonya while Rebecca retrieved the earpiece and microphone from the guard she had knocked out. Sonya's eyes were flames of fire over their deviating from the plan to escort Sigrid back to the van—boy, would Rebecca catch an earful later. But she needed the crone's abilities. Rebecca inserted the earpiece, listening to the crackle of conversation in Spanish over the device. People demanded to know who had discharged their firearm.

Dimitra stroked the serpents under her hoodie. Was she reassuring them or herself? Rebecca wasn't sure. Lester nervously cracked his knuckles.

Rebecca put her hand on Sigrid's trembling shoulder. She was about to ask a lot of the young mythical. "Does any of the soldiers know an all-clear code? A catchphrase."

Sigrid's eyes were unfocused for two seconds. "Shot a birdie."

Rebecca hitched her breath. Trying to imitate Joelle's accent, she spoke into the microphone. "*No hay problema. Disparó un pajarito.*"

A moment of silence, then a nasal voice returned in Spanish, "Gamma, you couldn't shoot a birdie in miniature golf."

Rebecca put a hand to her head. She had thought the phrase was about killing fowl not playing golf. In English, the phrases were identical but not in Spanish. She had translated too literally. Rebecca had to be more careful. The adrenaline was causing her to make silly mistakes. Though she had recited the wrong phrase, the guards thought Rebecca had made a joke. She listened intently until the earpiece filled with nervous laughter and a command to go about their business.

After Rebecca had turned off the microphone and dropped it, Sonya stepped in front of her. "Sigrid returns with me to the van. I will make my way back to you if you need me."

Sigrid crossed her arms. "I just saved us. You can't send me back."

Sonya ignored her charge. "This is no place for a child."

"Child!" huffed Sigrid. She glared at her educator.

No doubt Sonya was right. But Sigrid's skills might be the difference between a successful mission with no loss of life and the alternative. Rebecca steadied herself for an onslaught. "Sorry, Sonya. As team lead, I'm allowed to change strategy in the field. She stays."

Sonya's expression turned as stony as if Dimitra had stared at her. "Fine. But I'm reporting I disagreed. And after this, *Rebecca Eidelweiss*, we will never work together again."

Yes, she had been expecting this reaction. Sonya may have been an educator, but she was also a fierce agent.

Waving them onward, Rebecca started toward the final gate around the compound. This one was less a security check and more a precaution by Cordo to record exactly who was coming and going into his abode. The door required a fingerprint scan.

Rebecca retrieved the glove from her pouch. As she was turning it inside out, she felt a tap on her shoulder. Riju stood next to her, hand out. "Leave this to me."

"We discussed this. You only duplicate at a visual, not a cellular, level. Your ability won't help you."

Riju moved his hand up and down. "And that is why I need the glove. You're the mission leader, and I'm the only other enforcer agent." He nodded to Sigrid. "If someone is on the other side of that door, I need to be the first one through."

Who was he kidding? Diana had specified that the front door to the compound was guarded. Riju was putting himself in danger again. But Rebecca realized he was right. She was too valuable to the mission to take the risk.

Rebecca handed Riju the glove, and he turned and stole across to the biometric keypad. He shoved the glove on his hand while the rest of the team took positions on either side of the door. Riju drew his gun and then slammed his hand down on the sensor.

The door clicked open, and the rakshasa charged forward. The thwip of his dart gun sounded twice before Rebecca could pass through the doorway. Three noises followed—a muffled cry, another thwip, and a body hitting the dirt.

When Rebecca crossed into the last area around the compound, she spied three unconscious guards on the ground. Riju was reaching for more darts to reload his gun. The DEED weapon held five rounds. Rebecca locked eyes with her efficient comrade. Forget the rest of the enforcer agents. Riju was a one-rakshasa army.

Approaching the door to the compound, Rebecca whispered, "Everyone gather around."

They made a semicircle around her. The looks—fear (Sonya), eagerness (Sigrid), respect (Riju), glee (Lester), and doubt (Dimitra)—met hers of resolve. "This is it. Diana said the compound has patrolling guards, but not as many as outside. We've all studied the floor plan. We proceed directly to the cells and back again, touching nothing and engaging with no one. We're a patrol like the others. Understood?"

Heads nodded, and Lester raised his thumb and grinned as if he wasn't taking her seriously. For a moment, Rebecca wondered if the person she should send back was Lester, not Sigrid. But Lester laughed at the impending peril.

Rebecca turned to the crone. "We should enter when guards aren't passing, so it's key that you read the thoughts and ensure the entry chamber is empty. Focus, Sigrid."

"Got it." Sigrid squared her shoulders and stared at the door. "No one. The nearest thought is someone wanting a cigarette about three rooms away."

"Good enough for me."

Rebecca put her hands on the large compound double doors. They were made of steel with iron rings, unlockable. She pulled, and the doors swung open. The immense entrance reflected a crepuscular level of darkness, making it hard to discern the furnishings inside.

The mission leader's attention was drawn to the right. The

floorplan indicated a hallway in that direction leading to the cells.

As Rebecca moved further inside, lights flickered on. They illuminated a decorated room with a table in the center, a divan to the side, and paintings of forests and lakes. Rebecca noticed doors leading in all compass positions with the entrance door on the south and another large, double door across from it. Her target was on the east wall.

The team walked in behind her, and Rebecca took a moment to review their location. The room was furnished as it had been in Diana's images but with four additions. Metal rectangular cabinets stood in each corner. The cabinets emitted a blue ray that spanned the side of the room where Rebecca's team stood. The lines bounced off the features of the mythicals.

Scanner!

Rebecca turned around. "We need to get out—"

An ear-piercing alarm drowned out the rest of her sentence.

THE PRISONERS

April - Resort of Miracles, Venezuela

Over the shrill alarm sounding through the room, Rebecca called for a retreat. As most of the team followed her order and moved toward the doorway, Sigrid dug in her heels and pulled back on Sonya's arm. She shouted something, but Rebecca lost it in the cacophony assaulting her eardrums.

The sound abruptly ended, and the after-effect sensation of cotton in one's ears made Rebecca talk louder than she needed to. "Let's go."

"We can't!" Sigrid wrenched her arm free of Sonya's grasp. "The soldiers are on their way. They're marching to the front gate."

Riju rushed to an ornate iron lampstand by the entrance door. "Sludge! Lester, will you find something to bar the other doors with?"

Riju quickly grabbed the lampstand and threaded the iron rings through the door handles while Lester headed for the divan. Rebecca assessed their next step. Celisa had failed! Did she have enough time before they tripped the alarm? Was she alive? Rebecca couldn't reflect on the sirin's fate now. She had to deal with the present. "Sigrid, how far is the nearest patrol in the house?"

Sigrid pointed to the north door. "Two rooms that way."

Lester had the six-foot divan in one hand, turned it lengthwise, and buttressed it against the north doors.

Rebecca pointed to the east door. "Anyone that way?"

Sigrid followed her line of sight. "No one right now, but there are hallways—"

Rebecca sprinted to the door. "Then this is our direction. The other imprisoned mythicals may be able to help."

"Maybe I should stay behind."

Rebecca stopped in her tracks and turned. Was that Lester who had spoken?

The yeti rubbed his hands. "I could be a distraction and head out the west door."

"No. We stay—"

"I'll stay with him," interrupted Dimitra. "If they see two of us, they'll think we're DEED enforcer agents. Agents come in pairs, right? Maybe, they'll believe we're the only ones here."

Riju grabbed Sonya and Sigrid. "Brilliant. We don't have time, Rebecca."

Rebecca shook her head but knew Lester's suggestion was their best chance. Riju ushered the verdurian and crone through the east door, brushing past Rebecca. She grimaced but reluctantly followed. As she exited, the north doors rattled but didn't open against the makeshift barricade. Rebecca shut the door on the grinning yeti and grim gorgon who had positioned themselves in the west doorway.

The three remaining team members were sprinting down the hallway ahead of her. She ran to catch up with them. Perhaps this was the time to change into a centaur and gallop past them into the lead? But they were still disguised as soldiers, weren't they? The other advantage splitting up gave them was with Lester's height and broad features and Dimitra's snakes, you couldn't mistake them for humans. Riju, Sonya, Sigrid, and she could bluff their way through. Maybe. If Sonya's makeup didn't wear off or the enemy didn't notice Sigrid's youthful features. Rebecca decided to stay in her human form for now.

Boots marched ahead, coming from an intersecting

hallway. Sludge! They were about to test her theory.

Rebecca stiffened with resolve, but Riju had a different idea and pulled the educator and crone into an office off the hallway. His plan, apparently to let them pass, seemed wiser. Rebecca followed him in and shut the door so that only a crack remained open.

Seconds later, soldiers marched along the hallway outside their door. They came to a halt, and the sound of weapons clicking made the DEED agent hold her breath. She peered through the crack. At least six guards stood outside.

The front man touched his ear. "What's that?"

A moment of silence followed, the man straightening up and facing the other guards. "We're to remain here in case they double back."

Baelz Bells. How could Rebecca convince them to move? No, she had no choice but to engage. If she and Riju were quick enough, they could take out the two in the back before the rest knew what was happening.

As she reached for her dart gun on her holster, Rebecca felt a tap on her arm. Riju's hand rested on her shoulder, and he leaned toward her ear. He spoke in Hindi to keep the conversation private. "I'll take care of this."

Rebecca shook her head, but Riju held up his hand. She had to let him follow his instincts. The hallway they had been in turned and hugged the outer wall of the compound. The cells were at the corridor's termination point. No more intersecting hallways lay ahead. They were close.

Riju transformed into the man with the bushy beard again and advanced through the door. A gasp of recognition rippled over the guards as he parted them. He spoke in Spanish. "What are you lazy idiots doing?"

Rebecca swallowed, hoping the ruse would work. The man in front cleared his throat. "Pablo told us—"

"Swine! Wait until I tell Corto how his guards reacted."

At Corto's name, the sentries in Rebecca's sight shifted uncomfortably. "We have our orders, *Senior Alternez.* If we break them, we will be punished. But if you led us, perhaps..." The man lifted an eyebrow.

Riju shoved his way past the soldiers and moved aside the man in charge. "Follow me into battle, cowards! Immediately!"

Heads nodding, the patrol resumed their march toward the entrance with Riju leading them away. Rebecca bit down the regret. Another team member lost! But perhaps Riju could lead them on a march away from Lester and Dimitra.

When the soldiers had left, Rebecca opened the door. "We are nearly out of time. Let's go."

Sonya and Sigrid were at Rebecca's heels. Sonya said, "Lester, Dimitra, and Riju are gone. Sigrid and I aren't fighters."

Rebecca rounded the corner of the hallway. "I know."

"Do you have a plan for retreat? It's our best option!"

Rebecca called over her shoulder. "Not without what we came for."

She pointed to a dogleg at the end of the corridor that she had memorized from the map. After the corridor turned, it ended with a door to the prison block.

Racing forward, Rebecca came up to the door and caught her breath. "Sigrid?"

"Six-four-nine-three-eight-six-two."

Rebecca tapped in the digits as Sigrid read them off. The teen was getting good at anticipating the next step of the process, having read the code from a guard somewhere in the compound. If they survived this, she'd recommend the crone for a medal.

The door lock clicked, and Rebecca grabbed the handle. Sonya mumbled behind her. "Now, at least we'll have help."

Diana had never been allowed in the cell area, but she had overheard it had room for eight prisoners. She had tried to gather intel on the types of mythicals imprisoned but only learned of two. Diana had reported on Aurora and a chupacabra. Rebecca could use the more ferocious cousin to Lester's yeti to help her extract them from this mess.

When she entered, Rebecca blinked at the bright light.

The cell block wasn't what she had expected. The chamber was built with steel and copper, which gave it a modern appearance. Four thick glass doors along either side of a central passage allowed the guards to see in each cubby. Keypads were placed next to each door, and the central corridor was a raised meshed walkway. This elevated the patrols over the prisoners. The walkway ended at another door at the far end of the room.

The two cells on Rebecca's immediate right and left were unoccupied. The ten-by-ten area of each consisted of a mattress and a latrine with a sink. The DEED agent surveyed the rest of the cells for any movement, seeing only one woman prisoner standing against the glass at the end of the guards' path.

Nyx's shadow! Where is everyone?

Rebecca raced up the corridor while ensuring the other cells were empty. She spied another figure huddled on a bed in the cell catty-corner to her destination. She couldn't determine the gender, but he was blue like in the Avatar movies. A huitzilopochtli! Perfect, she needed a warrior. But where was Aurora?

Rebecca bypassed the blue creature and proceeded to the woman. The brown-skinned female was lanky, with ebony hair, long lashes, and a small birthmark on the left side of her face. The mark enhanced, rather than detracted from her beauty. She wore a featureless green undershirt and a black mini-skirt—odd for a prisoner. She swayed on her feet, eyes unfocused. Through small slits in the glass, Rebecca heard her speak in slurred words. "We didn't cause the alarm."

"We did." Rebecca examined her. Perhaps she was human? Should she trust the woman? "Why are you in there?"

"Mother Earth!" Sonya swore behind her.

Rebecca rotated and spied what was in the last cell across from the woman's. Her breath hitched in her lungs.

In this cell, they had taken away the mattress and replaced it with a sealed tank of water, roughly coffin-shaped. A body floated inside. The navy-blue colored skin, gills, and Roman features of Diana lay preserved for all to see. Though she was a naiad and could easily survive underwater, her darkened skin tone betrayed the truth. She was dead.

Rebecca couldn't say that she was surprised. Ray had told her Diana's fate in Poland. Yet, Rebecca stared at the tank, mesmerized.

The thugs here had killed her, sure. But they had kept her body, likely to show it to interested parties. They were profiting from her corpse.

Sigrid, who had followed Sonya to Diana's cell, yelped and stepped away. She covered her mouth as tears formed in her eyes. Rebecca envied her. She, too, wanted to either cry or beat the man who did this. Corto wasn't human; he was a devil.

The woman knocked on the glass of her cell and steadied herself in the process. "Who are you?"

Right. Rebecca had to continue the mission for the living. "Sigrid. I need the combo." She turned and tapped the glass, pointing at the woman. "Better question. What are you?"

Sigrid was crying, and Sonya had her arm around her. What was Rebecca thinking by pulling a child into a combat zone? Yet, without her, she'd have to rely on DEED tech to open the cells. And DEED tech could be spotty.

"I don't belong here," the woman answered.

Rebecca locked eyes with the prisoner. No, she wouldn't leave her behind even if she was human, but she needed to know how much of an ally she could be. "Are you human or not? The truth now."

The woman's wandering eyes narrowed on the DEED agent. She bit her lip. Rebecca didn't have time for her stalling.

Rebecca tapped her breast. "Because I'm not human. We're called mythicals." She jerked her thumb over her shoulder, indicating Diana. "She was one of us. Are you?"

The woman's eyes focused, and her body stopped swaying. She had been faking her drugged state. "A mythical. Not a monster. Yeah, I'm one of you."

"Sigrid? Combo?" Rebecca turned her attention back to the woman. "Prove it."

"Prepare yourself."

Rebecca suppressed a laugh. Nothing amazed her about mythicals anymore. The woman's lower torso transformed into a segmented snake, the stretch band expanding to accommodate her wider girth. The silvery scales of her lower portion striated with an olive green. By mythical standards, she was lovely. Yet the woman lowered her head in embarrassment.

"A lamia," said Rebecca.

The woman nodded.

Ray must have suspected Corto had a lamia from local missing person reports he had studied. Why else would he have Rebecca's team pack nose plugs? "You're perfect. This is a rescue mission. We'll get you out of here."

Sigrid said, "The combination is the same as the door leading in. I'll recite it again."

As Rebecca followed the teen's instructions and typed in the numbers a second time, the woman transformed into human form. The glass swung outward with the last number, and the woman slipped out. "Oh, thank you." She held out her hands.

Rebecca took them. "What's your name?"

"Narline M'goub."

Rebecca dropped her hands. "Was there a little girl here? A faun."

Narline nodded. "The one with the goat legs. He took her once the alarm sounded."

Rebecca gritted her teeth. "Who took her?"

"Corto." Narline pointed to the door across from the one they had entered. "He went that way. Toward the stage."

Corto, the *scoundrel*. He knew Rebecca was coming for Aurora.

Sonya had used the same combination to open the door to the other prisoner's cell. She had called to him. "Hey, huitzilopochtli. Blue guy. Wake up."

The lamia wrangled her hands. "It's no use. They drug us. I've been lucky because they've underestimated my tolerance.

I've been pretending, though I'm still a bit foggy."

Rebecca turned and examined the drugged mythical. Huitzilopochtli were known to be courageous fighters, but this one was more of a liability. She'd have to carry him out. If she did, she would be encumbered.

Rebecca turned back to Narline. "Will you be able to walk on your own?"

"Yes."

Then Rebecca turned toward the door to the stage. "Good. Turn into your lamia form. You know by now it's the only way to use your powers."

Narline reared back. "But I'm hideous!"

Sonya, from inside the cell, was putting the huitzilopochtli's arm around her shoulder. "Human prejudice. In our world, you're beautiful. Humans made up all that 'eating babies' and seductress propaganda."

Narline's eyes widened and then resumed her snake form, growing taller by fifteen centimeters. Sigrid nodded. "You're both scary and awesome at the same time."

Rebecca ran to help Sonya. "Did you catch this guy's name?"

The lamia replied, "Tomás."

Rebecca grabbed Tomás' arm. "Tomás? Can you hear me?" She slapped his cheek. "Are you there?"

"They've drugged us heavily since that woman's death." Narline indicated the tank where Diana floated. "They killed Evan when he refused to transform. A chupacabra, Luis, defeated guards here and left the cell area. He was severely wounded when he said he would return for us, so I didn't hold out hope."

Rebecca's stomach churned at the news. Further dead mythicals. She was more resolved than ever to rescue Narline and Tomás from Corto.

The DEED agent observed the north door. To rescue these two mythicals, she'd have to leave Aurora behind. No choice. Going after Aurora would put them all in danger. Rebecca was out of options.

The agents carried Tomás out of the cell, his feet dragging along behind him. The only way they could successfully get out of here was to regroup with the others. Lester could carry the huitzilopochtli easily.

Rebecca glanced back at the door leading to Aurora and closed her eyes. If she could get Tomás to Lester, she could return.

No time, Rebecca. Retreat is the only option now.

But Aurora was the mission. No. Stop lying. Aurora was more than a mission.

Rebecca had to return to this cell block and through that door. DEED would never allow her a second chance, so she had to go after Aurora now. Even if they captured Rebecca, she'd be with Aurora. That was the play, wasn't it? Rebecca would give herself up, distracting Corto as the rest made it to safety.

Aurora couldn't be alone anymore. Even if they were separated in these cells, Rebecca would be able to talk to and comfort her. And at those disgusting shows, she might be able to put her arms around her. Allowing herself to be a prisoner was the only way.

Boots ran down the hallway outside the door the DEED team had entered. Because of the dogleg, they couldn't see the guard headed their way. Rebecca unburdened herself of the prisoner and grabbed her gun. Unfortunately, she had been distracted enough that she grabbed her revolver and not her dart gun. No time to switch it out. She had to kill whoever was at the door. She couldn't take stock of the situation since she had no clear line of sight.

Rebecca flicked off the safety and aimed her weapon.

THE BOREALIS DOOR

April - Resort of Miracles, Venezuela

Rebecca wrapped her finger around the trigger. This wouldn't be her first kill, but it would be her first premeditated one. If she made her way out of here alive, she'd have to face the council for her crime. And those who'd opposed the plan would do an about-face on allowing her to take a human or a child on the mission, claiming they never authorized any such thing. This was what came of a secretly sanctioned DEED assignment.

The footsteps were at the dogleg when Sigrid spoke. "Don't shoot!"

Rebecca had only moments to decide, yet she'd been hoping for any reason to relax the pressure on her trigger finger. Resolved, she slid left. She hoped to make it into a cell before the guard crossed the threshold. She didn't make it and stopped herself when the approaching stranger entered.

Joelle ran into the room, gun ready. She stopped on seeing Rebecca's revolver and put her hands up in the air, her firearm dangling from her finger. She surveyed the room—she'd make a good agent—and her eyes widened when seeing the lamia.

Rebecca lowered her gun and released a long sigh. Sigrid and Sonya emitted cries of joy while Narline edged backward. Joelle took them all in. "I disobeyed."

"Thank Mother Earth!" shouted Sonya.

Rebecca marched forward. "I knew I couldn't trust you." She placed her hand on Joelle's now lowered arms. "But thank you. We're in a bind."

Joelle examined the cell block. "You think? I left the van and followed you through the barriers. Alarms went off, no sign of Celisa, and infantry heading for the door. I slipped inside to hear a patrol chasing someone in the west hallway. Knowing the cells were this way, I assumed you split up. Where's the girl?"

"They moved Aurora. I must go after her." Rebecca nodded to the prone figure of Tomás. "Do you think you could carry this guy out?"

Joelle cracked her neck. "I don't work out every day for nothing. But what—"

Sigrid cried. "No!"

Rebecca's gun was raised again, and Joelle mimicked her action. Peering around the room, the agent found no immediate threat. What had Sigrid reacted to?

Tears dripped down Sigrid's face. "Lester's dead. I heard Dimitra's thoughts."

Years of experience and seeing people die didn't prepare Rebecca for the whirlpool of feelings she experienced with this revelation. Sadness, anger, and regret all threatened to drown her, pummeling her optimism. She wanted to drop to her knees and cry. Lester, with his goofy grin. Lester, who never took anything seriously. Lester, who only wanted to set up an online store. And she had dragged him into a warzone. The decision she had made earlier to stay with Aurora cemented in her brain. The rest had to retreat. Now!

Sonya was at Sigrid's side. The verdurian's sadness expressed itself in her wilting hair. Sigrid huddled against the educator. "I'm not going to listen to any more thoughts. Never again."

Rebecca swallowed down her emotions and laid her hand on Joelle's shoulder. "Take the blue man. Get everyone out of here to the safety of the van."

"What about you?" asked Joelle.

"I'm going after Aurora."

Sonya stared at Rebecca. "You can't. You know it's a trap."

Rebecca sucked in a breath. "I'm not coming back."

A moment of confusion crossed Sonya's features until she figured it out. "No! Rebecca!"

Ignoring Sonya, the agent nudged Narline. Rebecca tapped her nose as she addressed the lamia. "You have an awesome defense mechanism. Use it if you need to."

Narline nodded.

Sonya's voice cracked. "Rebecca! Don't do this."

Rebecca sensed Sonya's fear for her was from a place that swept aside taking an education agent into a battle zone or asking more of a young crone. Her concern was a moment of friendship that transcended DEED, missions, and protocols.

"If I can't get her out, I have to be with her." Rebecca took another long breath. "You've known for some time, haven't you? Aurora is not merely a mission to me."

Sonya's eyes watered. "Forget what I said before and listen to me now. They'll kill you."

Rebecca knew the risk, but to see Aurora again was worth it. "Maybe. Maybe not. I put my fate in DEED's hands." She winked. "They'll do me proud."

Rebecca turned on her heel and headed for the door at the other end of the block. Joelle grunted behind her, lifting Tomás and barking orders to the rest of them. The team leader had confidence the bounty hunter would get them out of there. Sonya's last protest died in her throat as Rebecca approached the door.

And then, Rebecca realized the direction this door faced. North, like Canada where she had first met the faun. North, where she had concocted this plan. And, especially, north toward the *aurora borealis*. She had told Kralston months ago that magic is how nature makes you feel. This was a magic door, a *borealis* door. She was going to cross over. Yet, no version of C. S. Lewis's Narnia existed on the other side. Aurora, her *Aurora*, was behind this *borealis* door, and she was determined to be with her at least one more time.

Rebecca opened the door into a compact hallway. It terminated at another door with a small glass pane. Peering through the glass, she discovered this door led...outside? This didn't make sense as the compound didn't have a back door. No, now she recalled the map. The compound had a small courtyard in the northeast corner, perhaps a break area in days past when real prisoners lived in the cell blocks. Narline had mentioned a stage. Yes, how fitting. They marched the mythicals out here to a platform for the viewing pleasure of their corrupt clients.

Anger boiled in Rebecca's veins as she raced for the door. She pushed it open and found herself at the southern end of a rectangular courtyard. Approximately fifty meters of grass separated her from a stage where three people stood: a short man, another man seated behind a laptop, and...

Aurora!

The faun stood before the short man, head lowered, the man's hand resting on her shoulder. Her eyes were half closed, her face blank, and her body as still as a statue. Was she drugged? Perhaps. Aurora hadn't reacted to Rebecca's entrance.

The short man did, however. Rebecca recognized him from the hundreds of images she had studied. Jorge Corto, in the flesh with hair slicked back, a thin mustache, and a mouthful of dazzling teeth.

Rebecca surveyed the field. Corto wouldn't give her an unguarded path to the stage. Sure enough, eight red target dots in four rows and two columns lined the center of the field. Four handguns on each side attached to a machine on spindly, iron supports projected the tiny, glowing circles.

Rebecca reviewed options in her head. Jorge Corto was too close to Aurora for Rebecca to charge him. This man threatened children, and all who did so were cowards. She was ready to surrender, but Corto spoke first. "Before you take a step, *senorita*, you should understand the peril."

"I understand."

Corto nodded to the other man. "Oh, but I don't think you

do. In case you're thinking of attacking me, the weapons are managed not by sensors but by artificial intelligence. A sensor is defeated by throwing a rock in a corner of the courtyard. AI, however, is not so stupid. It learns your movements in microseconds, anticipates your next move, and targets you. Those machines are better than eight of my best marksmen."

The man at the laptop wasn't armed that Rebecca could see, but she spotted the bulletproof glass barrier he sat behind.

Corto chuckled and spoke in English. "Quite a deathtrap, eh? Perhaps you gallop toward me, not caring if I kill the little one. Catch the big fish, you think? If so, I came prepared."

"I would never sacrifice her," announced Rebecca. "That's the difference between you and me."

"But not the only one. You're an agent who makes a living taking creatures from the world to an old home. I am a god who creates a new home for you beasts. You are a commoner, a cog in your DEED machine. I am a leader of a zoo, determined to reveal your degenerate kind to the world."

Rebecca gritted her teeth, letting him speak while she considered strategies.

Corto continued, "But what interests me most about you is that you are a centaur."

The compound's leader had read Diana's notes. Rebecca had expected it, mostly ignoring him. She was trying to send a mental message to Aurora that she was here now, and that she wouldn't leave her. Yet, the child was withdrawn, staring blankly at the ground. If Rebecca surrendered, if she and Aurora lived in the cells back in the block, would Aurora acknowledge her? Had the abduction done Aurora irreparable damage?

Corto pounded his chest. "I have trapped you here. Before I let the world know of your presence, I will ensure I profit from my discovery."

Rebecca shivered. She had to abandon the thought of surrender. Could she trade herself for Aurora? If she trusted this man, perhaps. But she trusted Corto as much as she trusted a scorpion in her shoe not to sting her. No trade.

Rebecca had to rescue Aurora before this monster did more harm. She had to succeed.

With his free hand, Corto indicated the guns. "Once you surrender, I'll have my technician turn off my protection."

DEED had discovered and regulated AI decades ago. Corto knew only what the secrets he had stolen from Nystar, the AI algorithm, would do for him. Rebecca understood something far more important—how it worked. She would never have caught Riju in Jaipur otherwise.

Corto continued, "And in case you want to know, armed forces are surrounding this compound right now. I've been in communication—"

Corto was stalling! A patrol was on its way. She couldn't hesitate any longer.

In one swift motion, Rebecca transformed into a centaur. Her pants, fastened along the sides, split open to become a blanket on her hindquarters. Not just any cloth covering, however, but one with heightened Kevlar. She used her powerful back muscles to leap onto the field, far into the air, like a horse in a steeplechase tournament. The guns' sighting dots lifted into the air where a five-foot-eight woman would be if she was running across the field, but not where an equine creature was leaping through the air, six and a half feet above the ground. Bullets whizzed under her.

As she landed, Rebecca reached inside her pouch for her next trick. Corto had mentioned throwing rocks to set off the sensors. Rocks, indeed! She had something far better than stones. As her hooves touched the ground, she braced herself to run and leap again. Bullets struck the Kevlar. She had to protect her legs; they were her most vulnerable body part besides her head.

Her hand grabbed one of her bolas inside her pouch. Bullets hit the ground near her feet. Time to spring into the air again. If her theory was wrong, the second row of guns would shoot her down, adapting to her movements. She leapt.

Again, metal projectiles cut through the air fifteen

centimeters below Rebecca. She twirled the bola in her hand while speeding toward the stage. For a moment, she wondered if she could take out Corto or the technician. But they weren't the immediate danger. She aimed for the legs of the mechanism holding up the gun in the last row. When she threw the weapon, it whizzed through the air and entangled the stilts, pulling them together.

She landed a second time, the bullets closer to her feet, uprooting the turf. She hit the ground awkwardly and required a moment to gain her bearings. Corto yelled at the technician, who stared at the scene in disbelief. Corto's expression said it all. The technician would suffer from the failure of the machines.

Rebecca trotted sideways. Not as a woman shuffling, but as a horse walks, hoof over hoof. The machines expected no gaps between her legs. And four legs? They whirred, trying to make sense of what they were learning, first aiming at the front legs, then aiming at her back, without firing a bullet.

Her strategy was working. As they said in her AI training, a machine can only learn what it knows about. It cannot make the leap to inspiration. The human technicians had trained the guns to shoot humans. The large memory models held trillions of bits of how humans track other humans when firing a weapon. In the algorithm's circuitry, centaurs didn't exist. The machines couldn't learn the way Joelle had when she witnessed Rebecca turn into a centaur. For Joelle, seeing was believing. An AI machine could never learn to believe. It had no imagination.

Rebecca still had to be careful. A stray bullet or acting too human would ruin her advantage. But Rebecca was first and foremost a centaur, and centaurs were more than half human and half horse. Centaurs were their own beings. They thought and acted differently than humans.

A bullet clipped the top of her hoof and ricocheted off. The missile proved the danger of a lucky shot. She had to leap again, and Rebecca tensed her back legs and was airborne once more.

Corto was reaching for his gun, and the technician banged away on his keyboard. Aurora stood still, eyes glued to the scene, but impassive. Rebecca had to mount that stage. She only had one more bola. She retrieved it from her pouch before coming down. The third set of bullets targeted her. She crouched, allowing the missiles to hit the Kevlar. They rocked her but didn't pierce her body armor.

Swinging the bola again, Rebecca pressed a button on the handle of her weapon. She saved the best for last so that the AI wouldn't compensate for it. Time to put into use the upgrades she had received in Greece.

The ball separated from the cord and flew directly at the fourth-row mechanism's legs and toppled it. The orb then flew across the field, drawing the attention of its twin. Bullets fired at Rebecca's bola ball but missed it. When the sphere came within centimeters of the target, the ball exploded. Punctured by shrapnel, the final AI weapon was destroyed.

The path was clear.

Rebecca thrust her head forward and raced to the stage. Her thoughts were all centaur now. She was the daughter of those who fought in Thessaly, in Plataea, in Leuctra. More recently, centaur DEED agents had undermined Mussolini in World War II. Many had warned her about the nature of centaurs —the conflict between savagery and domesticity. These qualities made strange bedfellows in Rebecca when the situation came to Aurora, yet were in perfect alignment as she leaped onto the platform.

Hand shaking, Corto aimed at her, but Rebecca reared up on her hind legs. The bullet smacked against the underskirt of her Kevlar blanket and fell without doing her any harm. Her front legs in action, Rebecca kicked, landing a hoof squarely on Corto's breastbone. A gasp of air escaped from his lungs. Then Corto flew across the stage, hitting a side wall, and slumping to the floor. His gun clattered to the ground.

Despite all her DEED training to ensure her surroundings were secure and that her opponent was, indeed, unconscious, Rebecca turned to Aurora instead. She swooped the girl in her arms and held her close. The faun succumbed to the embrace as a rag doll with no will of her own. Rebecca rubbed her back. "I've got you."

A whimper. Then a word. "Home?"

Tears pooled in Rebecca's eyes, but she blinked them away. She set the girl down and stared into her eyes. "Soon."

As they talked, the still-active machines powered down. Then, someone ran across the stage. Not toward Rebecca or Aurora but the field. Rebecca whirled around to spot the technician about to jump onto the grass below. Rebecca spoke in Spanish. "Stop. Turn off the guns."

The technician stiffened and halted. Rebecca laid a hoof on Corto's gun and kicked it away from the technician. Her eyes burned into him as the weapon skidded near the edge of the stage. "I have my orders and cannot kill him. But when he awakens, he will blame everything on you even if you shoot me now. You won't survive his wrath."

The man trembled at her words.

"You don't move while the child and I exit. Once we're clear, you do what you know must be done." Rebecca's eyes flicked between Corto's weapon and his unconscious form. "You may tell them I did it. Understand?"

The man nodded. Rebecca turned back to Aurora. She switched to English. "Time to go. Climb up."

She lowered her front legs, giving the child access, and nudged Aurora to straddle her goat legs around her centaur body. Aurora did as she was instructed, and now Rebecca rose to her full height. She took a moment to stretch her neck, then leapt from the stage onto the courtyard. At full gallop, the rescuer and abductee crossed the field, through the doorway, and into the compound's small hallway.

They sped through the cell block, turned around the dogleg, and down the compound's corridor. Rebecca's hooves clip-clopped in the passage, and the fierce blood of her ancestors flowed freely through her veins releasing an unsatiated desire for speed and to tromp on the ground beneath her hooves. No barrier could stop her. Wild, yet sensible; noble, yet common,

Rebecca raced ahead.

When Rebecca rounded the last corner, she spied the door to the entry chamber, still open wide. She burst through the doorway with Aurora on her back.

"I have her."

Several guns pointed at her. A patrol of guards had the mythicals at gunpoint. Sonya, Sigrid, Narline, and Joelle stood in a line, hands raised. Tomás lay on the floor. Dimitra, bound and with a bag over her head, kneeled on the ground. Lester lay spreadeagle, blood drooling from his mouth.

Baelz Bells!

At first, she thought Riju had switched sides and betrayed her. He was pointing a gun at Sonya. And then, she spied Riju with the rest, arms raised. The man he impersonated approached her, revolver trained on her head. "And you would be Rebecca Eidelweiss."

"Roberto Alternez." Rebecca stared down at him imperiously yet lifted her arms. "Let us go, and no harm will come to you or your guards."

The man threw back his head and laughed. "We have you at gunpoint and the Venezuelan army has you surrounded. You think you will escape this?"

"Corto is dead," announced Rebecca in Spanish.

Roberto waved his hand. "He understood the risks."

"Some friend," Rebecca spoke evenly. "But I guess, to people like you, loyalty doesn't mean anything. How many of these guards will you execute for letting us get this far?"

Roberto showed her his teeth. "Don't try to turn them against me."

"Why not? You've just shown how much loyalty you have for your so-called friend. These guards were Corto's. You're going to bring your people in now. But first, you need Corto's men out of the way."

"Shut up."

The guards shifted nervously, glancing at each other.

Roberto straightened his arm, moving the gun closer to

Rebecca's head. "Any last words?"

Rebecca spoke in English. "Yes, nose plugs everyone."

Roberto scrunched his eyebrows. "What does that mean in *Espanol*? Is that some idiom used by you beasts?"

A guard behind Roberto coughed, and then another grabbed his nose. One of them swore in Spanish while a fourth gagged. Rebecca's team, except Sigrid and Riju, held their breath. Riju was whispering something to the teenage girl.

Roberto stepped back and gave a glance over his shoulder. "What are you up to?"

By now, the soldiers were all covering their noses and mouths with their free hands. Eyes watering, they lowered their guns. One of them was on his knees, preparing to vomit.

Gun still trained on Rebecca, Roberto glanced at them. "What are you doing, you pigs?"

Rebecca reached behind and grabbed Aurora's arms to steady her. Then, she reared up. She planted a hoof on Roberto's shoulder as he turned back, and she pushed him to the ground. Most of the mythicals were reaching for their bags, pulling out nose plugs.

Rebecca was going to stomp on Roberto's arm holding the gun, but he shifted out of the way at the last minute. He swung his arm around and aimed at her heart.

"Bob-Bob, don't."

A young woman with curly black hair and full lips screamed at the man. He turned toward the woman, jaw agape. "Angelina! What are you doing here?"

The woman, in fatigues, folded her hands. "I'm not here."

She transformed into Riju. Roberto's eyes widened in alarm, but Rebecca's hoof against his head knocked him senseless.

At this point, the guards were holding their stomachs and being sick all over the floor. Sonya had uncovered Dimitra's hood to only expose her face and handed her nose plugs. Rebecca's attention swung to Narline. A lamia's best defense mechanism was an odor she could direct at an enemy. Inhale too much of it, and the result was incapacitation. Fortunately, humans were far more susceptible to the stench than mythicals.

The guards were all retreating from the room while holding their stomachs. The effects wouldn't wear off for at least an hour. They had time.

"You did good," Rebecca called to Narline.

The centaur retrieved her nose plugs and the extra pair for Aurora. As she fitted them, someone across the room bellowed. "Ah, yuck! Who invited the lamia?"

Lester sat up, wiping the blood off his mouth. "Someone, get me my satchel, will ya?"

Sigrid ran over and threw her arms around the yeti. She emitted a short cry. Riju grabbed the nearby pouch and rummaged through it.

Lester patted Sigrid's back. "Not to worry, my fave crone. They just knocked me out."

Riju handed Lester his nose plugs. "But the blood from your mouth."

Lester smiled a mouthful of teeth as he inserted the nostril inserts. "Fake yeti blood. I store it inside my false tooth. Big seller on the site." He rolled his eyes. "Before *someone* made me shut it down."

Rebecca ground her teeth. "You... Well, I won't say it in front of the children, but you scared the Hades out of us."

Lester winked. "The point was the blood made the guards think I was dead. When I came to, I planned to conk some heads. Boy, glad I'm wearing these." He tapped his nose. "The vomit smells worse than the lamia stench."

Narline crossed her arms. "Not sure I like this one."

The yeti stood up and extended his hand in a fist. "Lester. Great to meet you. Don't worry about my jokes. They're very lame-ia."

Rebecca trotted to the window and peeked out. "Roberto wasn't wrong about the army. I'm surprised they haven't breached the door."

Sigrid said, "They're waiting for orders from Corto. They

know we're wearing uniforms, and some of us can look like others. They're not sure who is who."

"Makes sense." Joelle adjusted Tomás over her shoulder. "The guards would know each other. The soldiers have newly arrived. They can't recognize friend from foe."

Rebecca estimated the number of soldiers outside. "Dozens" was her best guess. How would her team escape? The line of soldiers was a gauntlet—a death trap. They had to use their abilities.

But then the answer presented itself. Rebecca turned around and reached for her pouch. "Ear plugs!"

"Ear plugs and nose plugs?" Lester shrugged.

"Now!"

Rebecca turned back to the window while inserting her ear plugs. The soldiers weren't looking up at the soaring female figure gliding above, but a few seconds later, they lowered their weapons.

Celisa!

Reaching into her pouch for her extra ear plugs for Aurora, Rebecca retrieved them. She fitted the plugs into the young faun's ears and watched from the window as the infantry lay down on the grass. They reclined as if they were on furlough, putting their hands behind their heads or propped up on their elbows, watching the stars. Celisa made one more pass, ensuring any hostile presence had fallen under her influence. Then, she landed.

Rebecca opened the door and pulled her inside, removing her own ear plugs. She embraced the sirin. "Thank you."

Celisa shook her feathers. "Of all things, a deaf sentry. We had a tussle, but I won."

Sonya walked up. "I thought you were an admin."

Celisa smirked. "Everyone knows you don't mess with the admin."

SAFE PERSON

April - Somewhere over the Atlantic Ocean

Rebecca peered out of the transport's circular window over the vast aquamarine of the Atlantic Ocean. Awestruck, she stared at the breadth of the water below. She had spent too much time in human airplanes reading files and not observing all the natural beauty this world had to offer.

The passengers of the DEED aircraft were noticeably subdued without Lester. He and Riju had boarded other mythical transports to their respective homes. When they had left, Rebecca's smile faltered. She had tried to convince them to come to Elysium with the rest, but Lester was still looking after the unicorn. Riju had nodded and said he had to return to his first love, India. He'd eventually travel to Elysium to pick up his authorization to stay permanently in Jaipur.

Lester had clamped a hand on Rebecca's shoulder. "Eidelweiss, the next time you show up at my house? Please, don't. Every time you appear, you cause nothing but trouble for me."

Rebecca then quoted one of her favorite movie lines. "I'll miss you most of all, Scarecrow."

She had shaken hands with Riju. The esteem in his eyes was unmistakable. The respect in her final words to him was clear and direct. If Rebecca ever put together another team, Riju's name would top the list.

Strangely, Rebecca had only known them as fellow employees before Corto kidnapped Aurora, and now she missed them. Missing them as she missed Diana. Diana's tank was safely in storage in the shuttle thanks to the yeti who went back and carried her out of the compound. They'd had enough time to retrieve her, so Rebecca made sure she would come home, too.

Now, Rebecca stood and stretched in the aisle. In the two seats behind her sat Tomás and Narline. They passed each other papers and photographs.

Rebecca leaned on her seat. "How are you two settling in?"

Tomás touched his head. "Massive headache, but can I thank you again?"

Narline held up the papers. "Is this a dream? Tell me again I'm not going to wake up back in Venezuela in my cell."

"You're not dreaming."

"This says we're headed for some hidden land." Narline consulted the documents in her hands. "This Elysium. And other lamias live there?"

"You're here, and the other lamias live there."

Rebecca could add that the Sisterhood of Lamias had found Narline a place to stay while she acclimated, and they would be waiting for her with a large banner. She remained silent, not wanting to spoil the surprise. Tomás was adapting faster, having previously heard of Elysium and others like him. Yet, he still seemed on the precipice of being overwhelmed.

Rebecca advanced down the aisle to Joelle, sitting alone and staring out the window. "Hey."

Joelle turned her way. "Hey. Sonya said something about not allowing humans into Elysium. Only a few have been there, and human travelers are a rare exception."

Rebecca shrugged. "Yes. Elysium is our safe place and a hard secret to keep if we let outsiders visit."

"I'm not going to get you in trouble, am I?"

Rebecca scoffed. "Joelle, I'm breaking every DEED rule to have you here with us. I'm in for all sorts of trouble." She smiled, anyway.

Joelle wrapped a string from her hoodie's cowl around her index finger. "Ever since I found out about DEED, I've wanted to learn more. I don't want you to dump me somewhere and break all contact. I could be, you know, your human go-to or something."

"Or something. We'll talk."

"I don't want to ruin my chances. I can stay on the shuttle when we land, and the pilot can fly me anywhere you'd like. I'm worried some DEED dude is going to pull out one of those pens from *Men in Black* and erase my memory."

Rebecca set a hand on Joelle's shoulder. "We don't have that type of technology. You're getting off the shuttle with all of us. You were a part of the rescue, remember? You got us into Venezuela and then out into Brazil. And you disobeyed orders exactly when I wanted you to. I'm going to do the same."

Worry lines deepened on Joelle's forehead.

"You're going to be fine. I already requested quarters for you at DEED's main office." Rebecca's eyes widened. "It's a mini-suite for the bigwigs."

"Thank you, Rebecca."

Rebecca moved on to the next row of mythicals. Dimitra and Celisa sat together. Dimitra had her sunglasses and hat on, and Celisa had her human body uniform in place. The two were talking and Rebecca paused to listen.

"Poland isn't that far from Greece," said Celisa. "I could come down for a long weekend."

"Tito would love visitors." Dimitra adjusted her glasses. "We have very few friends because I have to be so careful around humans."

Noticing Rebecca, Dimitra roped her into the conversation. "You'll come too, I hope? I know you're busy with DEED assignments, but we'd love to have you."

"I'll find time," Rebecca promised.

Rebecca nodded at the two then proceeded to the last row on the transport where Sonya was busy typing on an electronic pad she had on her lap. She was likely writing up her report detailing how Rebecca had put a minor's life in danger. The best outcome Rebecca could hope for was a reprimand and demotion. The worst? She would lose her job at DEED and not be allowed around minors. Her destiny all depended on Sonya.

Because of Aurora and the others, Rebecca and Sonya hadn't had a chance to talk. First, the high-speed car race to Brazil, the bribe at the border, and then the dash to the airport. Rebecca had spent her time with Aurora, and Sonya focused on Sigrid. The few brief discussions they'd had, Sonya hadn't seemed angry. Maybe they were reconciled, maybe not.

In either case, Rebecca expected Sonya to provide full details in her report to DEED, as was standard protocol. The verdurian's report had to match that of the other agents. Rebecca expected a reprimand, but the sting of losing her job was nothing compared to the pain of losing Sonya's friendship.

Sonya looked up when Rebecca stood next to her. Rebecca wanted that talk. They wouldn't have a chance once the shuttle landed. But she'd let the verdurian decide when to discuss it. Instead, she asked, "Are the kids in the back observation booth?"

Sonya nodded.

Rebecca turned and went to walk through the curtain to the rear end of the shuttle when viny fingers wrapped around her wrist. She circled back to Sonya.

Sonya cleared her throat. "I said some hurtful things back in the compound."

Later was now apparently. "They were all true."

"No, they weren't," Sonya replied. "You had permission to take Sigrid to the first barrier, and you made a difficult call in the heat of battle. You made a decision some may use against you."

"I marched her into the compound and endangered her life."

Rebecca had raised her voice a little too loudly, and Dimitra's and Celisa's heads popped over the seats. Sonya's fingers tightened on her wrist. "No, you didn't."

"Sonya, what are you talking about? You said we were done working together." Rebecca's voice broke. "And being friends."

Sonya eyed the two mythicals in front of her. "What I remember is Sigrid getting the combination of the second barrier and then returning to the van. She waited there throughout the entire mission. We used DEED tech to get through the other combinations."

Dimitra nodded. "Yes, that tech took so long. DEED needs a better way of cracking locks."

Celisa brushed back a tangle of hair that fell in front of her face. "I recall seeing Sigrid in the car as I flew over the soldiers. She was putting in her earplugs. I'll detail it in my report."

Sonya released Rebecca's wrist and interlocked their fingers together. "Mine, too."

"Sonya—"

Sonya interrupted, "Any story about you taking Sigrid into the compound may inspire certain council members to decide to keep you away from children the rest of your life."

Rebecca flashed a helpless look at the verdurian.

Sonya blinked. "I know that Rebecca Eidelweiss, who was about to sacrifice herself for a young faun, would lay down her life to protect those she loves. Certainly, she'd sacrifice herself for a teenaged crone or an educator who still wants to be her friend."

Rebecca hated to make Sonya a liar, but her friend had that determined look in her eye. She wouldn't talk her out of it. "You're going to make me look too good."

"What? Like a hero, or something?" Sonya made a pshawing sound with her mouth. "Rebeca Eidelweiss is no hero. Never was."

Celisa snorted. "Didn't storm a warehouse and rescue anyone."

"Didn't chase a gorgon and then have the courage to lie to make her world better," added Dimitra.

"I'll finish the report before we land," Sonya said, recapturing Rebecca's attention. "After all, what are friends for?"

"Sonya—"

Sonya squeezed her fingers and let her go. "Now, Derby. Go see that little girl you saved. What hero does that?"

The four laughed, and Rebecca pictured them in a pub for a girls' night. Soon, she promised herself.

Rebecca strode through two sets of curtains to the back cabin. Encircled by glass walls and a ceiling with metal supports, the room provided spectacular views of the ocean. One-meter benches with cushions lined the three walls, allowing passengers to sit and watch the scenery zip past. Sigrid and Aurora sat on the benches facing each other. Sigrid, the teenager, had her legs crossed on the bench. Aurora, her faun legs draped off the side, leaned a shoulder against the glass.

Sonya had bought an orange children's ruffle-sleeved blouse, black leggings, and shorts for Aurora at the airport. Aurora had chosen the leggings. The verdurian had washed the child's hair in the sink, sprucing her up a bit. None of this had improved her mood.

The girls stared at each other for a long moment, then turned and regarded Rebecca. Sigrid laughed but Aurora's blank expression remained. Oh, they were communicating via Sigrid's telepathy, of course. For once, Rebecca envied the teen. Being a crone wasn't easy, but her being able to read Aurora's mind gave Sigrid an advantage. On the other hand, telepathy would be too intrusive. Rebecca had to use a lighter touch.

Before Rebecca could speak, Sigrid jumped off the bench. "I'm going."

See? Reading minds didn't respect proper boundaries. Rebecca would have to talk to Sigrid about it later.

Sigrid winked at Rebecca as she passed her. The DEED agent stepped forward and sat down in front of Aurora who had turned to look at the ocean.

Rebecca kept her eyes on the young faun. "Pretty, isn't it?"

Aurora nodded.

Aurora had said six things to Rebecca since Rebecca had rescued her, mostly one-word sentences. The agent wasn't surprised. Aurora needed to process her trauma. And Rebecca, who had seemed trustworthy at first, had let her down.

"I brought you something." Rebecca reached into her pocket and held out Aurora's passport.

Aurora accepted the gift. She opened it, eyes shifting between Rebecca and the small blue book. "May I keep it?"

"Of course."

Rebecca took a deep breath. She'd navigate this conversation slowly, at Aurora's pace. "Everything is going to change for you."

"Again," replied the girl.

"Yes, again. But this time, in a better way."

Aurora bit her lip. "Sigrid's never been to Elysium. She's excited. She's going to see her mother."

The talk with Sigrid had opened up Aurora a fraction. "Yes."

"She says... She says I'm going to see my mother, too. I just don't know it, yet."

Rebecca gulped. Baelz Bells, this conversation was harder than storming the compound. "A woman I know, Elisabeth Carter, will be there when we touch down. She works with people like you. People the world has mistreated. She's called a psychologist, but what's more important is that she's a very kind person."

Aurora pulled in her shoulders. "The snake lady scares me. This kind woman isn't like the snake lady, is she?"

Rebecca wasn't sure if Aurora referred to Dimitra or Narline, but the answer didn't matter. "Elisabeth's a faun, Aurora."

Aurora's eyes widened. "Like me? Will she be my mother?"

"Sorry, no. She has a family of her own."

Aurora broke eye contact and looked at her hands, appearing embarrassed. "Oh."

Rebecca bit the inside of her mouth. "You only want to be adopted by faun parents? Many different species exist in Elysium."

Aurora shrugged but didn't speak.

"Well, I'll make sure to say no snake ladies. No scorpion ladies, either."

Alarmed, Aurora looked at Rebecca again. "Scorpion ladies!"

"My hairdresser is an aqrabuamelu. That's the name for a scorpion lady. And she's a friend, also. Looks can be deceiving, Aurora. Some fauns are friendlier than others. But we'll get you in a loving family. I'll see to it."

"Why? You're just someone who rescues people. Won't you fly off after we land?"

Her words cut like a knife to the stomach, and Rebecca knew how that felt. "No, I won't fly off. I'm going to request an office job. I'll be sticking around a long time."

Aurora didn't react. Sonya's advice rang in her head. *The time has come for you to rescue yourself.*

"I have a house in Elysium," said Rebecca. "I'm all by myself. It's lonely."

Aurora regarded her shoes.

Rebecca swallowed down her insecurities and hesitancy, a bitter combination. "Aurora, I want to be your safe person. You may come live with me...if you choose."

"Really?"

Did Rebecca detect a note of hope in that question? She breathed in deeply. "I let you down before but never again. Never."

Aurora gulped and her lower lip trembled.

"If you don't want to live with me, I'll make sure DEED assigns you a family you want," said Rebecca. "Your family will be the one you choose. I'll be your guardian." She left off the "until then."

Aurora met her eyes. Did Rebecca see that vigorous faun of February briefly in her irises?

"Can a guardian become a...a...?" Aurora faltered.

Rebecca stared into the faun's eyes. "This one can."

Rebecca braced herself for a negative answer but asked the question anyway. "What do you say? Would you like to stay with me for a while?"

There. She had said it. She had no idea how Aurora would respond.

Aurora looked down, and tears formed in her eyes. "Are you sure you want a nothing like me to be with you?"

"Aurora! We Eidelweiss ladies aren't nothings! Never describe yourself in such a way." Rebecca put a finger under the faun's chin and tipped her head up. "I've traveled all over the globe and have seen much of great value, but you are more precious to me than anything in this world."

The tears came then, and Aurora rested her head on Rebecca's lap. Rebecca stroked the girl's head, her fingers running over the faun's shiny hair. Never, in all her life, had Rebecca felt so hopeful.

THE HIDDEN LAND

April - Elysium, Atlantic Ocean

"I don't see land."

Rebecca sat next to Aurora who stared out the window. The agent looked over the faun's shoulder at the ocean below. "Elysium has technology that hides its surface from all planes and boats. Until we pass through the barrier, it seems as though we're in the middle of the ocean."

Aurora put her hand on the glass. "But a boat would bump into it."

"They lift off into the air and sail above it." Rebecca made a wave motion with her hand. "They think they're riding on the swell of a giant wave. Little do they know they're over Elysium. Or what they call Atlantis."

"Atlantis!"

Sigrid, across the aisle, exclaimed from her window seat. Sonya sat next to her. The verdurian laughed. "Oh, here we go again."

"It *is* Atlantis, Sonya."

The educator lifted one tendril. "Elysium never sank." And then another. "It never had a human population. It never led the other worlds."

Rebecca countered. "Advanced technology, off the coast of Spain, a place with ancient architecture."

Sonya sighed. "We'll continue this debate some other

time."

Sigrid asked, "Is it Atlantis?"

Sonya laid a hand on the teen's shoulder. "If you want to think so, Sigrid, then you may."

Rebecca nudged Aurora. "We're approaching. Buckle up, please."

The pilot made a smooth landing. As they broke the illusion barrier, many passengers—first timers and former occupants—cried out in delight. The stone buildings and deep green grass of their island sanctuary were spread out below them. The babble of excitement from the lamia and crone sounded as if they were coming down in the middle of an amusement park.

The transport landed and taxied over the stone runway. Rebecca's window faced the wooded side of the landing strip, not the field. When the plane came to a stop, Sigrid put her hands on the portal-shaped window. "My mom! I see her!"

Many of the passengers rushed to windows on the field side. In the distance, three- or four-story pink buildings and glass walkways connecting floors, a spire with a pyramid, and figures jetpacking from one location to another caught their attention. Expressions of awe sounded from the first-time visitors.

Once everyone disembarked, the pilot would taxi the shuttle back to a small airport. Rebecca had pre-arranged the shuttle to release the mythicals, and one human, to a waiting crowd at the end of the strip.

Rebecca unbuckled and stepped out of the way. Aurora moved to the other side of the shuttle to peek out. The enforcer agent approached the door to open it. The exclamations of her team and the rescued mythicals made her smile.

"I've never seen another lamia in my life. And is that *my* name on the banner?"

"Mom. I'm right here. She sees me!"

"Tito! How is he here? Rebecca, did you bring him here?"

"The entire council of DEED is outside. What are they

doing here?"

Celisa asked the last question, and she directed it at Rebecca. Rebecca grinned. "Oh, I don't know. Perhaps they want to extend their gratitude."

Dimitra put her hands under her hat through the snakes on her head, rearranging them. "Bedhead, again! Good thing I must keep my hair covered."

Rebecca opened the door. "Come on, everyone. Let's do our victory lap."

The mythicals rushed to the door with only two passengers hanging back, Joelle and Aurora. Rebecca gestured for Joelle to approach. "Nervous?"

"As I said before, if DEED would rather I stayed on the shuttle, I will. I don't want to get in trouble, being a human and all."

Rebecca appreciated the irony of a human feeling out of place in the world, exactly how she felt in the field. "They won't be mad at you. I have clearance from DEED. They even flew Tito in for Dimitra."

"The blind guy? I'm a bit different."

Rebecca put her hand on Joelle's arm. "Yes, you're a hero. You recognized Ray, right? He was on the tablet in Dublin."

Joelle nodded.

"Good. Go to him and check in. Then wander around. Everyone knows your part in this mission. I'm sure they'll want to talk to you."

Biting her lip, Joelle descended the steps into the brilliant sunshine of the day.

Rebecca turned to Aurora, who was standing by herself in the aisle. The agent pointed at her shorts. "Thank you for changing. It's about time you showed off those legs."

Aurora removed her passport from her pocket. "I saw some out there like me. They have *antlers!*"

"Yes, I asked a few of my faun friends to come out and see you. Elisabeth is out there, too. I'll introduce you to her."

Fidgeting with her passport, Aurora nodded.

Rebecca tipped her chin, so their eyes met. "She's standing with my grandfather and my niece, Liliana. Liliana is about your age. Would you like her to stay the night with us?"

"Oh, I can stay somewhere else. I don't want to be an intruder."

Rebecca furrowed her eyebrows. "Intruder?"

The girl lowered her gaze and rubbed her passport between her forefinger and thumb. "Other-Parent always called me that."

Rebecca held out her hand. "Aurora, my home is your home for as long as you want it to be. Liliana will be our guest tonight, but only if you're comfortable."

Aurora stared at Rebecca's hand. "What if she doesn't like me?"

Rebecca edged her hand a little closer to the faun. "Liliana is the tiniest centaur in my family, but she's the biggest goofball. And she's everyone's friend. Immediately! She has this trick where she gets butterflies to land on her nose. She'll teach you. And my grandfather is the largest pushover. I'll bet he has a gallon of honeybee vanilla swirl to eat when we get home. He's friends with a yeti beekeeper who makes it." Rebecca rolled her eyes skyward. "It's the best you'll ever eat."

Trembling, Aurora put her hand in Rebecca's. Brave girl. Aurora didn't want to believe her life was going to work out after being disappointed so many times, but she was willing to try. And that was tremendous progress from when Rebecca had hugged her in the compound the previous night.

Hand-in-hand, they exited the shuttle. A cheer went up as they descended the stairs, and Rebecca blushed. She could've skipped this part; she was never one for the spotlight. Waving to everyone, Rebecca headed for her family and introduced Aurora to her grandfather, Liliana, and Elisabeth. Aurora seemed interested in Elisabeth after the woman told the faun about her antlers and explained the jewelry that hung from them. Who wouldn't love Elisabeth? The psychologist was naturally warm. And Liliana, not understanding Aurora's trauma, talked to her as if she had known her all her life and Aurora had only recently returned from vacation. Aurora's defenses were up, but Liliana blithely shoved past them. As Rebecca had predicted, Aurora and she were friends within five minutes.

Rebecca stood at the edge of the group. Aurora tensed her shoulders until Liliana told her she'd show her "how to dance with cloven hooves." When Rebecca's grandfather pointed out that Liliana didn't have cloven hooves, she grinned and said that was why she wanted to see if Aurora could do it. Though a bit concerned, Rebecca nonetheless turned around and walked toward Ray.

Ray broke away from the DEED council and started toward her. Rebecca had to dodge people who congratulated and thanked her. They wanted a selfie with her, the famous four crystal obelisks of Elysium in the background. Reunions and unions in small groups happened all around her. After one last selfie, she turned to find Ray asking for some privacy.

As the crowd dispersed, Ray stuck out his only hand. A handshake? She thought she knew him better than that. When she took it, he pulled her into a bear-like embrace. "Thank Olympus for you, Rebecca."

When they parted, she grinned. "I never knew you were so sentimental."

He snorted. "Eidelweiss. You're a major pain in my tail. You act so smart and sure of yourself. Of course, that's because you are so smart and sure of yourself. No one but you could've pulled this off."

"I had a handler who had my back. Even when he shouldn't have." She gazed at his stump.

Ray put his hand on her shoulder. "I had a partner who saved my life instead of my hand."

Rebecca never knew he viewed what had happened this way. She tried to think of a response but only "thank you" escaped her lips.

Ray dropped his hand. "And perhaps, I'll have my old partner back."

What was he talking about? Ray was going back to the field? Rebecca lifted her shoulders in a "what do you mean" gesture.

"I'm here to offer you a seat on the council, Rebecca. Janx will be retiring in a year. Her seat is yours."

The council! Rebecca loved the field, but this was an opportunity to make changes for people like her. "Are they sure? I'm not someone who will roll over. I'm going to bust up the boy's club and make some real changes for female mythicals."

"Yes, and you'll make enemies." Ray smirked. "I can't wait to see it."

"I have ideas." Rebecca found she couldn't stop talking. "The council needs to listen to its enforcer agents more. And let them live where they want to live. Sonya deserves a home in Maine, for example. And visitation rights. I almost was turned to stone after the council separated Dimitra and Tito. We must do better than that."

Ray put up his hand. "Will you save this spitfire for the council?"

"I'm going to tell you now, Ray. A few of the men on the council aren't going to like me. I'm going to hire women in my cabinet who might unnerve them."

"Rebecca. I offered you a seat on the council, not to start a revolution."

Rebecca pressed her lips together. Yes, she couldn't right every wrong, but a whole lot needed to be done. "I'll miss the field."

Ray straightened up. "We'll expect you to take an agent or two under your wing, Rebecca. Show them some of your techniques. We know you won't partner with anyone, but we were thinking of a series of meetups. Fred or Riju, perhaps?"

"Riju doesn't need me." Memories of Riju leading the troops away from them in the compound came into focus. "Fred would be excellent. But I have a different idea."

"Oh?" Ray quirked an eyebrow.

"I'd like to spend time here, on Elysium, and train

someone to take my place."

Rebecca looked across the field at Joelle who was chatting with a group of huitzilopochtli next to Tomás.

Ray followed her gaze and then snapped his attention back to her. "No way, Rebecca. They'll never go for a human enforcer agent."

"She's got the talent to be a great agent." Rebecca raised her index finger. "Not just good, mind you. *Great* agent. Think about it. A skilled human in the world who respects—no, loves, our kind."

"Eidelweiss—"

"It's almost as crazy as storming a compound with a group of untrained mythicals." Rebecca had planned that sentence, and Ray knew it.

Ray groaned and scraped his foot against the ground. "I'll take it to the council."

"And you had better not fail. I have high expectations for my partners, former and new."

Ray chuckled and tilted his head to indicate someone was behind Rebecca. Rebecca turned and spotted Aurora standing two meters behind her, waiting and wringing her hands. Ray mumbled, "She hurried over to you, then stopped."

Rebecca held out her hand to Aurora. "Aurora, come here. I want you to meet my friend."

Aurora stepped forward on her spindly legs. She took Rebecca's hand, and they faced Ray. "This is Ray Phist. He wasn't at the compound the night I rescued you, but he was part of our team that night." She wrinkled her nose. "I've known him since I was your age."

Aurora lifted a hand and then dropped it. "Hi."

Ray bowed to her. "I am so glad to see you here, Aurora. You're the reason Rebecca saved all the people around us."

Aurora's mouth dropped a little. She gazed at Rebecca who squeezed her hand.

Rebecca returned her attention to Ray. "I'm heading home. My grandfather will want to hear about the mission, so you can yell at me tomorrow about divulging classified information. And the rest of my family will descend on us. Will you stop by later?"

"I wouldn't miss it."

Aurora turned around but still held Rebecca's hand. Someone had shouted at the young faun to return, and she called. "Be right there, Liliana."

Ray's eyes shifted from Rebecca to Aurora. He whispered, "We have to get her in the system soon. How long do you think she'll stay with you?"

Rebecca tilted her head. After all this time, didn't Ray understand? She supposed this was an example of how she could teach the lunkheads on the council. Sometimes the answer was right before them.

Rebecca smiled while Aurora started pulling her away. What a silly question. So silly that she wasn't going to answer it. Not directly. Rebecca cleared her throat and hummed the first notes of Irving Berlin's "Always."

BOOKS BY THIS AUTHOR

Kingdom Come: Kingdom Fantasy Novel #1

A portal traveler from Earth lands in a fairytale world named Kingdom where he must unite five sisters to become queens. An epic story of boy meets pixie.

On Earth, As It Is: A Kingdom Fantasy Novel #2

A human couple help fairytale queens stuck on Earth return home. An epic story of changing identities.

Deliver Us: A Kingdom Fantasy Novel #3

A human couple travel to distant land to stop a trio of witches destroy a fairytale land. An epic story of remaining pure at heart.

Will Be Done: A Kingdom Fantasy Novel #4

A human couple reunite fairytale queens with their lost husbands. An epic story of lost memories.

Kingdom's Advent

The first collection of Kingdom short stories.

Kingdom's Ascension

The second collection of Kingdom short stories.

GLOSSARY OF EXTRAORDINARY EMIGRANTS (OR GEE)

Amabie: Sea creature with bird-like beak and three legs or fins (Japanese).

Aquabuamelu: A person whose top half is human and bottom half is scorpion (Middle Eastern).

Barghest: A person with canine features and senses.

Crone: A person who ages rapidly but has powers that seem like magic.

Dryad: A person of the woods with bark skin and twigs for hair.

Centaur: Half-person, half-horse.

Faun: A person with goat legs and antlers.

Giant: A person who is taller, bulkier and has exaggerated human features. Not a tall human.

Gnome: A person who is smaller than a human with rounded features and large noses. Not a short human.

Golem: A person who has few internal organs and a small brain.

Gorgon: A person with snakes on their head. May turn others to stone (temporarily).

Harpy: A winged person, more often a woman, with talons for feet.

Higpins (JD): A short pink creature about three-quarters of a human with snouts. They have hands, feet, but are stocky (think pigs).

Huitziloppchtli: A blue person with feathers (South American).

Kitsune: A person with a fox tail (Japanese).

Munglute: Talking horse - Bayard, Freyarsha.

Lamia: A person with the upper half human and lower half like a snake who emits a foul scent.

Naiad: A sea person who can breathe water.

Rakshasa: A person with cat-like features in birth state, but can transform into looking like any other creature.

Satyr: A person with horns and goat-like legs.

Siren: A person who sings to hypnotize people, often commanding them to take actions against their will.

Sirin: A person who can uplift another's spirits through song. They have wings and a bird-like body.

Sphinx: Part lion, part human.

Sphrax (JD): Part-tiger, part human. Like a sphinx.

Verudian (JD): A person who has many plant-like internal organs and tendencies.

Vuleryn (JD): A human sized, hairy creature with elongated noses (dog-like) and pointed ears. Think wolves.

Yeti: Tall person, covered in hair with exaggerated facial features.

All (JD) entries were created by the author.

GROUP STUDY QUESTIONS

Mythicals are beings that live undetected alongside humans. If these supernatural creatures actually existed, do you think it possible for them to remain hidden from the rest of the world?

If mythicals truly existed, what creature would you like to meet the most?

Often, the DEED novel honors and satirizes secret agent tropes. What espionage element of the book did you find the most interesting?

Rebecca assumed the Aurora case would be a standard mission. Instead, the assignment changes her. Have there been any experiences you've had when something mundane turned into an event that transformed your life (e.g. meeting a significant other or friend, attending a group for the first time, etc.)?

Rebecca calls Jorge Corto a "person who doesn't know how to love." Do you believe people are separated into such neat categories as "people who love" and "people who don't know how to love?" Why or why not?

ACKNOWLEDGEMENT

From: The Department of Extraordinary Emigration and Delivery
To: All employees
Subject: People to Monitor

It has come to our attention that a novel has been written about our department. We are still determining how such a leak has occurred. We have intercepted the publisher in time to change the novel's category from historical non-fiction to urban fantasy to dissuade people from believing mythicals actually exist.

Our operatives have infiltrated the author's domicile and retrieved notes on the "novel" along with a list of possible suspects who may have helped bring this book about. As such, surveillance of these individuals is of paramount importance to our secrecy.

First, an organization named Havok (an online site that publishes flash fiction) is where the first of these tales surfaced. An excellent site, the author praises the entire staff there for publishing stories about our top agent, Rebecca Eidelweiss. We'll put monitors on gohavok.com.

Second, three people gave the author feedback on an early draft, any of who may be passing along information in the form of code phrases. They are T. M. Doran, Michelle Tang, and Christina D'Arc. They all claim to be authors. We should perhaps read their works for any clues. As a side note, I hear their novels are quite good.

Third, editor G. Miki Hayden has worked with the author multiple times in the past. Did her excellent work make the book easier and better to read, or was she in on the conspiracy? This will require further investigation.

Fourth are so-called "family and friends" of the author, any of who may be the mole. Please record the following names: Ken Graham, John Doran, Daniel Johnson, Desiree Johnson, Ed Hosmer, Maria

Spada, Suresh Karri, Catherine Dovey, Ellen Doran.

Fifth are names, living and deceased, of people who provided inspiration for this book, and in particular Rebecca: Beatrice Doran, Cecilia Brukner, Virginia Doran, and Judy Malecke.

Sixth the author left a note with just a name and a code on it. We are running it through multiple code breakers to interpret it. It reads "Hope Doran" with a heart-shaped symbol next to it.

Last is a small slip of paper that simply reads: "The author gives thanks to God for providing illumination." We have nothing to add to this except for "Amen."

AFTERWORD

This novel was constructed from writing short stories for Havok, an online magazine (gohavok.com). They challenged their readers to write stories set around the world. I decided to write four stories, all starring Rebecca Eidelweiss. They chose three of them. "The Concrete City" and "Lester's Business Venture" are largely unchanged from their online counterparts.

Regarding this novel, I wrote "Nobody in the Attic" for their world travels theme, but it didn't quite fit Havok's needs. The story with little Aurora was my favorite adventure. While walking one day, I wondered if I could stretch this short story into a novel. The result is in your hands.

Thank you for taking this reading journey with me. I hope you enjoyed it.

FORMER COPYRIGHTS

Portions of this book have previously appeared as follows.

"The Cement City" first published in *Havok*, March 2023. All rights reverted to author September 2023.

"Lester's Business Venture" first published in *Havok*, July 2023, reprinted May 2024. All rights reverted to author November 2024.

"The Hidden Land" first published in *Havok*, June 2023 in a slightly different form. All rights reverted to author December 2023.

ABOUT THE AUTHOR

Jim Doran

Jim Doran is a genre writer who enjoys transporting his readers into worlds of wonder, mystery, and danger. Whether it's the fairytale hijinks in the six books of his Kingdom Fantasy series or his multi-genre short stories, Jim aims to entertain his audience with every word. Jim's YA horror novel, entitled Forlorn Harbor, will be published by Rowan Prose Publishing in May, 2026. He has had over twenty works published in various online zines and anthologies including Havok, Every Day Fiction, and Ye Olde Dragon's Monster and Fairy Tale series. When he's not writing, he's enjoying the seasons in Michigan, U.S.A.